Spotted Pony Casino Mysteries

Poker Face
House Edge
Double Down

Double Down

Spotted Pony Casino Mystery
Book 3

Paty Jager
Windtree Press

DOUBLE DOWN

Contact Information: info@windtreepress.com

Windtree Press
Hillsboro, Oregon
http://windtreepress.com

Cover Art by Covers by Karen

PUBLISHING HISTORY
Published in the United States of America
ISBN 978-1-957638-04-1

About this series

This series is set in and around a fictional casino on The Confederated Tribes of the Umatilla Reservation in NE Oregon. The reservation is real. I have researched, and while I've made up people and where they live, I will try to stay true to the life people live on the reservation.

The casino is modeled a little bit after the real Wildhorse Casino at the reservation. But I changed some things around. The operations of the casino in my series are all my own common sense, not a complete knowledge of how any casino is run.

A Special Thank you to:

Marcus Luke, Fred Hill, and Raina Moore for visiting with me about the people and area of the Umatilla Reservation.

Chapter One

Standing at the kitchen counter on one foot and her crutches, Dela Alvaro, spread peanut butter on her toast as Mugshot licked his lips.

"You can have one bite as long as you don't drool all over the floor," Dela said, smiling at her roommate, a 140-pound, three-legged, German Shepard Malamute cross dog. She'd saved him when a reckless teenage driver hit the animal. The dog's owner didn't want to pay for saving Mugshot, Dela stepped in and became, then Eats-a-lot's, new owner. They made a good pair, both being amputees.

Her phone buzzed on the counter beside the peanut butter jar. A glance at the number and her hand stilled, the knife resting on the toast. "Who do you think this could be?" she said to Mugshot, staring at a number she didn't know.

"Only one way to find out." She slid her finger across the screen and poked the speaker icon. "Hello?"

"Dela Alvaro?" a woman's voice asked.

"Yes. And you are?"

"Ina Winter. You saved my life three months ago."

Dela remembered the woman and the way her body had been flung out the door of her home. "How are you doing?" She'd heard the woman had been taken to another reservation and reunited with her son. The reason her husband had nearly killed his wife, was his trying to find out where she'd hid their son.

"I am doing good. My son is with me and we are starting over. Soon I will be free of my husband." The woman's words grew stronger as she talked.

"That's good news. Who has been taking care of your donkey?" Dela and Mugshot liked stopping by on their jogs to pet the woman's donkey. That was what they'd been doing the day she'd witnessed the woman fly out the door.

"Poor Jethro isn't doing well. A neighbor says my husband hasn't been home for two weeks. She has given Jethro all the hay I had there, but he is not getting enough. She can't take him. He was given to my son as a gift from my uncle who is no longer with us. Would you be able to take him? Care for him?" The pleading in the woman's voice reminded Dela of the night three months ago when the woman had pleaded to let her die.

"Sure. I have enough room, and Mugshot, my dog, likes Jethro." She thought about how she didn't really have a need for a donkey but it would give Mugshot company while she was at work.

"Thank you! Thank you so much. I didn't want him to go to someone who would treat him bad."

"Just make sure your husband knows you asked me to take the donkey." She didn't want to get caught up in their marital dispute.

"He won't care. He has never liked Jethro. And as

my neighbor says, he hasn't even been home." Ina ended the connection.

Dela glanced down at Mugshot. "It looks like you're getting a buddy."

♠ ♣ ♥ ♦

Two hours later, Dela was dressed in her work uniform and wearing a jacket to block the cold March air as she walked down the road to Ina's house. She jogged through the area most days with Mugshot on a leash beside her. It was their exercise.

She heard the donkey before she spotted him. He stood with his head pointed at the house across the street, braying. That must be the neighbor who had been feeding him. Walking closer, she called out to the donkey.

"Hey, Jethro. How would you like to come hang out with Mugshot?" She walked up to the fence and petted the animal. His ears had always fascinated her. They were so fuzzy and long. He rubbed his nose on her arm. "I need to find a rope to lead you with."

A quick scan of the yard didn't reveal a vehicle. She hoped Mr. Winter was still gone. She didn't need an altercation with him. He could charge her with trespassing even though she had his wife's consent to get the donkey.

She walked onto the property and opened the door to the small building beside the donkey's pen. The weak sunlight from the open door gave her just enough light to see a halter and rope. She grabbed that and turned around.

The man that had thrown his wife out of the house after beating her to near death, charged across the yard toward Dela.

Her mind switched to combat mode. She'd been in

the army seventeen years. Ten of those years had been with the military police. She knew how to deal with an enraged person wielding a knife.

Dela flung the lead rope at her attacker, looping the rope around the man's arm holding the knife. She jerked the lead, and her attacker lost his grip on the weapon. The knife flew through the air.

The man didn't stop. He lashed out with his other hand, catching her alongside the head as he'd done on their first encounter. She punched him in the face and tried to wipe his feet out from under him. Only too late she remembered her prosthesis didn't work the same as a real leg. She ended up on the ground. Before she could clamber to her feet, Mr. Winter grabbed the knife and dropped down on her, straddling her body on his bent knees.

"You took my wife and my son from me." He raised the knife up with both hands.

She slammed her hands into his balls and rolled out from under him. The knife dropped from his hands, he grasped at his crotch, moaning, and fell to his side. Dela picked up the knife and shoved to her feet. She carried the weapon into the small building and stuck it in a crack in the wall.

Walking out of the shed, she cast a glance at the man lying on his side, puking. Dela knew she should feel sympathetic, but after him attacking her twice, he could choke on his vomit.

She picked up the halter and rope, caught Jethro, and headed for home. On the way, she called Heath Seaver, her high school boyfriend, and now Tribal Police Officer. She wanted to make sure she gave her statement before Mr. Winter ran to the tribal police.

"Hey, Dela. I'm headed to the casino. A guest had

their car broken into," Heath answered.

"Can you send someone else?" she asked, looking back over her shoulder toward the Winter property.

"What's wrong?" His teasing tone was all business now.

She told him about the call from Ina and being attacked by Winter. "I left him rolling on the ground holding his nuts. I just wanted to say he attacked me and I had permission to take the donkey." Her hands shook remembering the way the man had charged her and how the sunlight had glinted off the long blade of the knife.

"Do you think he's going to say you stole the animal?" Heath asked.

"That and possibly that I assaulted him. But he came at me. I was minding my own business, doing a favor for his wife." She turned into her driveway and walked to the backyard. She needed to call Travis to come over and check the fence before she let the donkey loose in her large lot. She'd known the acre and a half was more than she needed, but the privacy it gave her had appealed.

"I'll go around and check on him when I finish up at the casino." Heath's calm voice eased the tension knotting her shoulders.

"Thanks. I'll head to work as soon as I get Jethro water and make sure he and Mugshot aren't going to destroy anything in the backyard." She ended the call, feeling relieved that Heath would be checking on Ina's husband.

She opened the gate to the backyard. Mugshot stood in the door of his doghouse. "Come on over and meet your new roommate."

Since the donkey hadn't had a halter on in the

pasture, she removed it from the animal and watched him slowly walk toward Mugshot. The two touched noses and the donkey went to mowing her grass.

"This might work out well," she said, watching the donkey eat and Mugshot laying back down in the dog house with his head out the door, his gaze on the animal in his domain.

"I'm going to get ready for work. You two get acquainted." She entered the house, tossed her muddy clothing to the side in the bathroom, took a shower, and braided her long dark hair before putting on the same shirt and new khaki pants. A study of her face in the mirror showed slight bruising on the side of her face where Winter had landed the first blow. She patted some concealer over it and picked up a clean jacket. She was ready for her job as head of security at the Spotted Pony Casino on the Confederated Tribe of the Umatilla Reservation.

Chapter Two

Dela arrived at the casino and entered through the back entrance into the security office.

"Good afternoon," the security guard on duty at the entrance greeted her.

"Hi, Margie. Anything new besides the car that was broken into?" Dela stashed her purse in the cabinet next to the desk she shared with her second in command. She hung her jacket over the desk chair and picked up her radio, clipped it to her belt, attached the mic just below the collar of her polo shirt, and shoved an earbud into her left ear.

"Nothing. It was a quiet night, even for a Monday."

"Good. I should be able to get the scheduling done for the upcoming conference then." Dela walked to the door leading out to the casino floor. "But first I'll check in with everyone."

Since becoming head of security at the casino, she never came in to or left work on a schedule. It kept all of the security personnel, and others who worked at the casino, on their toes. She always made the rounds of the floor and checked in with surveillance when she first arrived. Stepping out onto the casino floor, she took in the colorful carpet, slot machines, and Indigenous-influenced décor. The piped flute music could be heard over the few slot machines making noise. Her first stop was beside the water feature that could be seen from the entrance as well as the casino floor. The warrior on a spotted horse stood in the flow of water from a waterfall behind him.

Walking out among the slot machines and gaming tables she found her staff interspersed among all of the flamboyant colors. Each member either stood or roamed among the gaming tables and slot machines in their khaki slacks and blue polo shirts. They all had radios, earbuds, and mics like Dela wore.

She smiled at each one as she walked up, asked how things were going, and discussed little bits of their personal lives. After catching up with each security member, she walked over to the beautiful mural on a wall close to the event center and tapped her keycard on the lockbox. A door opened and she walked into the surveillance room. Four people sitting in chairs watched a dozen monitors each.

While she could surprise her staff, the surveillance crew knew when she entered the casino. And while she wasn't the head of surveillance, that was her friend Marty Casper, they all sat up straighter in their chairs.

Dela noticed Jacee Bing, Ina Winter's cousin. She walked over to the Umatilla woman in her thirties. "If you have contact with Ina, let her know I have Jethro in my backyard and he'll be well taken care of."

Jacee swung her gaze from the monitors to Dela.

"Why do you have the donkey?"

"Ina called and asked me if I would keep him for her. She said the neighbor had been feeding him and had run out of hay." Dela wasn't going to mention her run-in with the husband.

"Oh, if Ina called you and asked then it's good you have the donkey. I know an uncle gave the animal to Micah when he was two or three." Jacee glanced back at her screens.

Dela tucked away the name of the child and moved on to Marty's office. She knocked on the door and walked through.

"Hey, saw you came in. It has been slow after all that commotion on Saturday night." Marty leaned back in his chair in front of three large monitors.

"Anyone ever come back and tell us who that drunk was and why he thought he could walk in here and shove people out of chairs and order drinks?" Dela had been off Sunday and Monday, though she was always on call if something came up that needed the head of security.

"Not a word. Jacob hauled him off. You could call him to see what he knows." Marty spun back to the table under his monitors and began writing.

"Thanks. I'll be here until I leave." She grinned. It felt good to make her own hours of work. On a day like today that was usually slow and boring, she stayed only a few hours, working on paperwork and checking on things. On the busy nights, she'd put in well over eight hours and hang around until things settled down.

She crossed through the surveillance room and back out to the casino floor. As she walked to the security offices, she pulled out her phone and dialed Jacob Red Bear. He was a tribal police officer and the brother of her high school best friend, Robin. The two, she and Jacob, had bonded when Robin was missing and later found raped and murdered. It was a time in Dela's life she would never forget. The incident, which she still blamed herself for, had caused the break-up between her and Heath and sent her off to the army to punish herself for not forcing her friend to go home with her that day.

Jacob's voicemail.

"Hey, Jacob. I was wondering what you learned about that drunk that was at the casino on Saturday night. Give me a call." She ended the connection and walked into the security office. Her least favorite part of the job lay on the desk. Scheduling. She sat down, pulled out the calendar, and began juggling regular days off with asked for days off and vacations as she made up the schedule for the following week and the week after when they had a conference booked from Wednesday to Sunday.

♠ ♣ ♥ ♦

Dela shoved the calendar away from her and glanced up as the door to the security office opened. She smiled as Jacob Red Bear entered. "You didn't have to come down here to answer my question."

He didn't return the smile. That's when she noticed Detective Dick walk through the door.

"Dela Alvaro, we need you to come to the station with us for questioning in the murder of Paul Winter," Detective Dick said.

Dela stood, facing the detective she loathed and who had similar feelings about her. "All I can tell you is he was alive and clutching his balls when I left with Jethro." After the words came out and Jacob's eyebrows raised, she had a feeling Heath hadn't told them about her phone call to him after the altercation. Was he the one who had found the body when he went to check on the man?

"Fine. There isn't much to tell." She took off her radio, mic, and earbuds, and turned to Margie. "Let Kenny know what's going on. I'll come back when they finish talking to me."

Margie's face didn't look like she thought it would be okay. Her gaze darted from Dela to Detective Dick and back to Dela.

Opening the cabinet, Dela pulled out her purse and walked to the back entrance. "I'll meet you at the tribal station," she said, walking out the back door before Detective Dick could say anything.

What had happened? Who had killed Paul Winter and why did they think it was her? Sure, she'd had the altercation with him earlier in the day, but he'd been alive when she'd left him. She stopped as her hand with the car key reached toward the door handle. "Unless my jab to his testicles caused him to die…"

"Your what?"

She swung around and caught her balance as Jacob took three strides toward her.

"What were you talking about?" he asked, taking the keys from her and opening her car door.

Dela quickly scanned the back parking lot for Detective Dick. "Where's your buddy?"

"He told me to ride with you over to the station so you get there." Jacob held the door open for her.

She grunted and settled into the driver's seat, tossing her purse into the back seat. "Get in and tell me how Winter died."

Jacob hurried around to the passenger side and settled in the seat. "I can't tell you how he died or anything about the scene until after you've been questioned."

"Who called it in?" She could at least find out if it was Heath or someone else.

"The neighbor across the street said she saw you and the victim fighting. When she didn't see the victim get up after you left with the donkey she went over and found him with—" He stopped. "Found him dead."

"And you answered the call?" she asked, wondering what had happened to Heath checking it out.

"Yes. I arrived and found Sadie Swan standing by the side of the road, waiting for me."

Dela turned onto Timine Way and pulled into the parking area on the south side of the Public Safety building.

Her mind raced with who could have been hiding in the house because that had to have been where the killer came from. It had to have been someone who'd watched the man attack her and then killed him.

She automatically parked and shifted in her seat, staring at Jacob. "Someone, besides the neighbor, must have seen Winter attack me and then killed him after I'd left."

"You're admitting to being there is good, but you know Detective Jones is going to work hard at proving you killed him." Jacob peered into her eyes. "If you say you didn't kill him that's all I need to know."

She held his gaze. "I didn't kill him. He was rolling around on the ground clutching his crotch when I left there with the donkey."

Jacob's brows touched above his nose. "Why were you taking the donkey?"

"Ina, Mrs. Winter, called me this morning." She went on to tell him about the conversation.

Double Down

"She said her husband wouldn't be there?" Skepticism crackled in Jacob's voice.

"Mugshot and I jog by that house nearly every day. I hadn't seen a car in over a week and it was always dark. When she said her husband wouldn't be there, I assumed she knew he wasn't living there. The neighbor had been feeding the donkey."

Detective Dick, well, she better quit calling him that if she wanted to get on his good side. Detective Richard Jones stood at the back door of the tribal police station staring at her car.

"All I have to do is tell what happened and even he," she bobbed her head toward the detective, "will see I didn't do it." Dela exited her car and walked up to the door with Jacob beside her. She wondered where Heath was. He'd help her get out of this mess. He knew the truth. She'd called him as soon as she'd started walking down the road with Jethro.

"Take her into the interview room," Dick said.

Dela walked by the detective, following Jacob down a short hall to a door.

The room they entered was a small conference-type room. She sat at the table, facing the door. She wanted to see everyone who came through the door to question her before they opened their mouths. One of her specialties was sizing up people. Dela wanted to know if they were out to get her, like the detective, or on her side when they came through the door.

Jacob had taken her purse somewhere and now stood inside the room to the side of the door. His face was blank. He did believe her, didn't he?

Her stomach started gurgling with dread. She sat for nearly thirty minutes, either staring at her hands on the table in front of her or at Jacob. She finally cleared her throat. "If no one else is going to come in and talk to me, at least you could visit with me."

Her friend gave a slight, nearly imperceptible flick of his head.

Dela's gaze traveled around the room and that's when she spotted the light flickering on the camera up in the corner of the room. She was being videoed. Jacob didn't want to get in trouble by talking to her or possibly spilling something he wasn't supposed to tell her.

She leaned back in the chair, propping her prosthesis on the chair across from her. "I do have a job to do. It would be nice if I could get back to it today."

Another ten minutes and the door opened. She forced a smile on her face as Detective D-Jones dropped a folder on the table in front of the chair she had her prosthesis propped on. She pulled her leg back and sat up straighter.

"Detective Jones, could you tell me when and how the man I'm suspected of killing died?" She wasn't going to be treated like a suspect.

"How do you know you are a suspect?" The man's bushy graying eyebrows lowered down over his eyes as he stared at her.

"If I wasn't a suspect, I wouldn't have been escorted to the station. You would have asked me any questions you had at work." She crossed her arms and leaned back in the chair.

"Mrs. Swan called in that she found Paul Winter dead after seeing you and he in a fight and you walked off leading a donkey." The detective tapped a finger on the file. "Do you deny any of what Mrs. Swan said?"

"I will agree, I did go to the Winter's property to collect the donkey. Mrs. Winter called me this morning and asked if I would take in the donkey. It was out of food and her neighbor had been feeding it. She told me her husband wouldn't be at home. I hadn't planned on any confrontation with the man." She uncrossed her arms and leaned on the table. "I walked over and found a halter and lead rope in the building next to the donkey's pasture. When I stepped out of the building, Mr. Winter was running at me with a knife in one hand. I used the rope to tangle up his hand and fling the knife away." She left out how her prosthesis landed her on the ground. "I tripped and he jumped on top of me, the knife held in the air above me. I slammed my fists into his crotch and he rolled off, dropping the knife. While he moaned and rolled around on the ground, I picked up the knife, stuck it in a crack in the wall inside the building, and caught the donkey. Mr. Winter was still alive and moaning when Jethro and I walked back to my house."

Detective Jones stared at her. "Do you expect me to believe you put that knife in a crack in the wall? That knife is the murder weapon."

Chapter Three

Dela's gaze shot to Jacob. Had he known about the knife when he'd rode with her to the police station? "But I didn't stab him. I put the knife in the crack in the wall. If my fingerprints are on the knife, it's because I took it away from him. Not by using it on the man."

"You sure it wasn't self-defense?" Detective Dick accused, his eyes lighting up.

He was trying to get her to say something he could use against her. "No. I didn't stab him in self-defense. My self-defense move was crushing his balls. I put that knife in the building and never used it on him."

"We'll see. I have people at your place looking for proof you stabbed the man." Detective Dick stood. "You'll be detained here until your residence has been thoroughly searched."

Blood whooshed from her head and she felt faint. She didn't want the police to go through her house. To see the handicapped bars, the crutches, her running prosthesis. To the outside world she wanted to appear whole. Normal. There were few people she allowed into her disabled bubble. There was no way she wanted this jack-hole of a detective knowing her weakness.

The door closed and her gaze flew to Jacob, still standing by the door. He didn't say a word. She glanced at the light on the video camera. It remained on. *Double frickin' shit*! Rage shoved fear out of her head. Action was what settled her nerves and anger better than anything. But in this small room, any action she took would be recorded and Dickhead would take it as her fear of being found the killer.

She breathed in slow and let it out even slower. Oxygen flowed again and her thoughts collected. Once her anger was under control, she began to think clearly. Who would want to set her up for the murder of Paul Winter?

Her first thought was Ina. After all, she had asked Dela to go to her house and said her husband wouldn't be there. Dela would have never gone after the donkey alone if she had thought Winter was living there. And where the hell was Heath? She hadn't brought up the fact she'd called him after her confrontation with the victim. She wanted him in on the investigation. He wouldn't believe she'd kill someone.

Questions. She had so many questions to ask of Heath, the neighbor, Ina. Someone had to have been in the Winter house watching the man attack her and used that as a means to frame her for his murder. But who? And why?

♠ ♣ ♥ ♦

Dela glanced at the video camera every five to ten minutes. After an hour, the light finally disappeared. Jacob had been replaced with a female officer. Dela didn't know the woman. She appeared to be in her mid-thirties, a little younger than Dela herself.

"Can I get a glass of water?" Dela asked.

The woman stepped out of the room and returned within seconds. She didn't have a glass or anything. Reading her name tag, *Harper*, Dela tried to remember if that was the name of a Umatilla family. The woman had a deep bronze complexion, dark hair in a braid down her back, and brown eyes.

The door opened and a hand appeared with a bottle of water.

Officer Harper grasped the bottle, walked across to the table, and set the water in reach of Dela.

"Thank you." Dela unscrewed the top and drank half the bottle before taking it away from her lips. The room was stifling. She glanced at her watch. She'd now been in this room for over three hours. Raising a stink would only give Detective Dick more reason to think she did it.

She sighed, leaned back in the chair, and studied the officer. "Are you new to the tribal force?"

The woman glanced at the video camera and relaxed her stance. "Yeah. I've only been here about a month."

"On the force or on the reservation?" Dela asked. She didn't want to make friends with the officer but she was bored and needed something to occupy her mind.

"Both. I'd just received my degree in criminal justice when my husband filled an open teaching position at the Pendleton High School." Officer Harper leaned against the wall. "I saw there was an opening on the tribal police force and applied. I was shocked when they requested an interview."

"You must have had something they wanted on the

force," Dela said, keeping an eye on the video camera in case it came on. She didn't want to say anything, even if it had nothing to do with why she was here. Detective Dick would find a way to mix up her words.

The officer grinned. "It seemed they needed a woman on the force to help with domestic disputes."

"I'm sure you are good at your job, too."

The door opened. Jacob stepped into the room. "Detective Jones says you may go, but he'll be keeping an eye on you."

"I wouldn't have it any other way," Dela said, standing, taking a moment to move her leg back and forth before walking out into the hallway where she was pretty sure the detective would be hovering to get one more jab in.

A glance at her watch said she'd missed dinner. Popping in on her mom and grabbing something to eat there sounded better than going home, knowing the tribal police had rifled through her belongings. Tomorrow would be soon enough to let everyone at work know she hadn't killed anyone.

Halfway down the hall, Detective Dick stepped out of an office. "Just because nothing was found at your house, doesn't mean you didn't kill the victim."

She hid the giddiness his words unfurled. She'd known they wouldn't find anything but many a person had been put in jail over evidence that had been planted. "I will say it again. I did not kill Paul Winter. He was alive when I walked Jethro to my house."

At the end of the hall, the officer at the desk held out her purse. Dela took it, dug inside for the keys to her car, and walked out the front doors of the building.

♠ ♣ ♥ ♦

On the drive to her mom's, Dela tried to call Heath.

He either wasn't answering or was busy. Her evening brightened when she walked into her mom's house and found Grandfather Thunder sitting at the table eating a piece of apple pie.

"Dela, you didn't tell me you were coming over." Her mom placed a plate with pie and ice cream on the table and motioned for her to sit.

"It was a spur-of-the-moment idea." Dela dug into the treat, savoring the sweet apple and cinnamon flavor. Eating one of her mom's pies was a bonus. Her phone buzzed.

She glanced at the name. Heath.

Where are you?

Mom's.

See you in a few.

She had hoped to break the news she was a suspect in a murder to her mom easily. Now she needed to do it before Heath arrived. "Heath is headed over here."

"Oh, good. He'll get a piece of warm pie, too." Her mom rose from her seat at the table to get another plate with a slice of pie.

When her mom had sat back down, Dela set her fork down. She glanced at her mom, over to Grandfather Thunder, and back to her mom. "I've been at the police station for five hours while they questioned me and searched my house."

Mom's fork clattered on her plate. "Why would they do that?"

"Remember last fall when I stopped a man from killing his wife?" She glanced at Grandfather Thunder. He nodded.

"What does that have to do with the police searching your house?" Mom asked.

"The woman called me this morning and asked if I

could take in the donkey that was left behind when she and her son left. Mugshot and I always stop and visit with the donkey on our jog. Anyway, she told me her husband wasn't at their home and asked if I would get the donkey and keep him." She picked up the cup of coffee her mom had placed in front of Dela's plate and swallowed. Two sets of eyes watched her, with the same worry and caring they had her whole life.

"There wasn't a car in the driveway." She went on to relay what had happened just as she had to Detective Dick several hours before. "When I left with the donkey, Paul Winter was alive and clutching his crotch. The knife was stuck in a crack in the wall."

"Someone used your trip to get the donkey to get away with murder," Grandfather Thunder said.

Dela settled her gaze on the older man who had been the only grandfather she'd known. And he wasn't blood-related.

A knock on the door sent her mom out of the kitchen.

"Who would want Paul Winter dead?" Dela asked the elderly Umatilla man raising a fork of pie and melting ice cream to his mouth.

"There are many. He not only beat his wife, but he also made his money from illegal activities."

Heath entered the room, walking straight to Dela and crouching beside her chair. "Are you okay?"

She stared into his familiar brown eyes. Instead of the merriment they usually held, there was concern. Dela nodded. "I know I didn't kill him. He was alive when I left."

Heath nodded. "I went over there as soon as you called me instead of going to the casino. All I did was drive by and see he was sitting up when a call came and

I headed off to check on it."

Dela sat up straighter. "Did you tell Detective Dick you were there and saw the man was alive?"

Heath ducked his head, dropping eye contact. "The call I received was bogus. I got there and nothing had happened. That's when I received the call about a possible body at the Winter residence. As soon as I saw the body with a knife in his chest, I knew the only way I could stay on the case and help prove your innocence was to keep quiet about your call to me."

Dela started to protest.

"Think about it. If Detective Jones knew you had called me and I vouched that the man was alive, he would say we did that to give you an alibi."

Remembering how hard Dickhead had wanted to catch her up in anything that would make her the killer, she slowly nodded her head. "Do you know who searched my house?" Her gaze held his. He knew she was private about her disability.

He grinned. "A newbie and me. I made the new guy stand outside while I checked the house for clothing with blood."

She studied him. "You really searched the house?"

Heath shrugged. "I had to take as much time as it would take to search, so I just walked from room to room opening drawers and moving things to take up time." He peered into her eyes. "Even though I know the truth, I had to do my job."

"Thank you for being the one to do the search." She sighed. "I didn't want Detective Dick to see how I live."

Heath rose and sat at the table where Mom had placed the other plate of pie and a cup of coffee.

"So, what happens now?" Mom asked.

"We'll start digging into Paul Winter's life and see if we can come up with anyone who had a grudge." Heath dug into his pie. "Mmmm, this is good. Thanks, Mrs. Belden."

Her mom's cheeks flushed. "You're welcome, Heath. This brings back memories of when you two were in school."

Dela had been getting a lot of this kind of talk ever since Heath moved back. Her mom was excited that he was back in Dela's life. However, Dela was still trying to figure out her feelings for the man her high school sweetheart had become.

Grandfather Thunder cleared his throat. "You might look into the people Paul was making meth for."

Chapter Four

Dela turned her head at the same time as Heath and they both stared at the older man.

Heath found his voice first. "Paul Winter cooked meth?"

"That's why Ina sent their boy away. He started making it in their home and she didn't want the child around the fumes." The old man raised his cup of coffee to his mouth.

"Not to mention it can blow up." Heath leaned back in his chair. "Why doesn't the tribal police know about this?"

Grandfather Thunder shrugged.

Dela now understood Ina's need to keep her boy safe from his father and anyone who wanted to take revenge on the man. "Someone had to have been in the house watching when Winter attacked me and when Heath rolled up in his tribal vehicle." Dela spun her head to look at Heath. "How long was it between you driving up to the residence and the call that came in to take you away from there?"

"Only a couple of minutes. But if they were watching the road for traffic to sneak out and kill Winter, they would have seen the tribal car turn onto the road and could have called it in as soon as they saw me." Heath finished off his pie and sipped his coffee. "Which means they would have had to know I would get the call and leave."

"You think it was someone who knows police procedures?" Dela asked.

Heath shrugged. "That or someone who just knows how the tribal police operate. That could be anyone who has had dealings with us."

Dela stood. "I'm going home. I'm glad you searched my house. I didn't want to go back knowing it had been a stranger going through my things."

Heath stood. "I'll walk you out." He put a hand on Grandfather Thunder's shoulder. "It was good seeing you. I see Mrs. Belden keeps you well-fed."

The elder grinned and said, "She does a fine job of making me want to eat."

"Mrs. Belden, thank you for the pie," Heath said, his gaze on her mother, but his hand on Dela's elbow.

Dela leaned down, hugged Grandfather Thunder around the shoulders, and then gave her mom a hug. "Thanks for the company and the pie."

"You're both welcome here any time," Mom said.

The innuendo in her mom's voice wasn't lost on Dela. The woman would like to see the two of them together all the time. Dela walked to the front door and out to her car.

Heath followed close behind. "I'll do all I can to keep you out of jail."

She stopped at the driver's door and looked up into Heath's face. He stood a couple of inches taller than her. His slender body was bulky from the body armor under his uniform. There was a time when she would lean against him and he'd wrap his arms around her, making her believe she was safe.

Now she lingered, staring into his eyes and keeping her body away from his. "Thank you, I'm glad you saw I didn't kill Winter. No one else seems to believe me."

Heath put a hand on her shoulder. "Even if I had driven up and found the man with a knife stuck in him, I wouldn't have believed you did it. Not over a donkey."

She eyed him. "What about self-defense?" Detective Dick's words echoed through her head.

He studied her for only a few seconds. "If you had stabbed him in self-defense, you would have still been there trying to keep him alive when I arrived. You didn't stab the man."

Her arms wrapped around Heath and she leaned her head on this hard shoulder, whispering, "Thank you for believing in me."

His hand came up and cupped her head, holding her against him. "I have always believed in you. No matter what dumb thing you did."

She pushed away from him. "Dumb? What dumb thing?"

"You know how I felt about you going into the military." He rested his hands on his duty belt.

"Yes, even after we'd broken up, you made it perfectly clear you thought my joining the army was wrong." She'd never told anyone, not her mom or her friend Molly, how it had saddened her that Heath had thought her joining any military branch was the wrong thing for her to do. The year after her best friend was ripped from their lives, Dela had trouble studying, even just doing day-to-day things. The thought of someone telling her what to do had seemed like the right decision. And it had been. The military had shown her she was stronger than she thought and taught her how to deal with grief and anger.

"But you were wrong. It was the only thing that could have pulled me out of the downward spiral I'd gone into after Robin's death." She peered up at Heath in the growing darkness.

"I have to admit, you were strong and opinionated before but you seem to have become stronger and—"

"You better not say more opinionated." She frowned.

Heath laughed and said, "I was going to say more open to criticism."

"That's a good note to end on. Good night. We'll talk tomorrow. I'll see if anyone at the casino knew anything about the victim's pastime of cooking up meth." Her mind went straight to Ina's cousin who worked in surveillance.

"I don't mind your digging, but keep me in the loop of everything you learn and don't go talking to anyone by yourself. We don't know who could have killed Winter and if they tried to put it on you, they will try to make you look guilty." He held up his hands. "I can't control Detective Jones, he's my superior."

"I know. I'll be sure to keep you in the loop." Dela slid into her car and headed home. She was looking forward to a long soak in her deep tub and hugging Mugshot.

♠ ♣ ♥ ♦

Dela drove slowly by the Winter residence. There

was a tribal car and a government SUV sitting in the driveway. Lights were on in the house. She wondered if Detective Dick had brought in FBI Special Agent Quinn Pierce or if he had heard about the murder and showed up uninvited. She was sure Dick would tell Quinn all about how she'd killed the victim.

She drove to her house and smiled as Jethro's braying and Mugshot's happy barks greeted her. She parked and smiled at the small stack of hay Travis had left for her at the gate to the backyard. Molly and her son, Travis, had been the best part of returning to *Nixyáawii,* the Umatilla tribe's homeland, after being discharged from the army.

Travis had remodeled this house, making sure everything was fitted for her disability. And he'd insisted on a state-of-the-art dog house for Mugshot for the long, cold nights Dela worked at the casino. She'd called her friend Molly, a veterinarian who'd saved Mugshot's life, that morning after bringing Jethro here. She'd asked if Travis could bring some hay and figure out the cost of fencing the rest of her land off into two or three pastures with fencing that would keep the donkey and Mugshot in.

At the stack of hay, she pulled a pocketknife out of her purse and cut the strings. Then she took two flakes and opened the gate. To her surprise, as she entered, Mugshot put himself between her and the donkey. Not allowing the larger animal to get close enough to bump her.

Dropping the hay on the ground for the donkey, she patted the dog on the head. "Thank you, Mugshot."

Then she and the dog entered the house through the French doors into the dining room and kitchen. Dela hung her purse and jacket on the coat rack by the front door and heard the sound of a car door slam. A peek out the front blind and a disappointed sigh escaped. Quinn and his partner, Special Agent Milo Shaffer, were walking toward her front door.

She opened the door and asked, "What are you two doing here?"

Quinn studied her in the glow of the porch light that came on at the two men's approach. "We've been called in to help with the homicide that happened down the street today." Quinn motioned for her to open the door and let them in.

"Who called you in?" She studied his impassive face. "Oh, let me guess. Detective Dick. He wants to make sure I go down for this even though I didn't do it." She swung the door open and headed to the kitchen. "I just got home and was hoping to settle in for the night. Can we make this quick?" She grabbed a glass from the cupboard and turned on the faucet filling the cup to avoid Quinn's judgmental stare.

"Milo, search the premises," Quinn said.

Dela spun around and dropped her glass of water as she grasped the counter to keep from falling when her prosthetic foot didn't pivot as well as her real foot. "Why are you searching my house? It was already searched."

"By someone who is biased where you are concerned," Quinn said.

She glared up at him. He was a couple of inches taller than Heath. Where Heath had long dark hair, Quinn's was light brown and cropped short. Heath's dark brown eyes shone with life and humor. Quinn's gray eyes held censure and suspicion. "Heath would never let his feelings come into play when working a homicide."

Quinn snorted. "That's not what Detective *Jones* thinks." He made a big deal of saying Jones.

Dela heard Agent Shaffer moving about in the living room. He stopped at the start of the hallway.

"While you're in my bathroom, could you start the water running in the bathtub?" she asked, a smile pasted on her face.

Shaffer shook his head, and Quinn grabbed her by the elbow.

"This isn't a joke. You are under suspicion of killing a man." He led her over to a dining room chair and made her sit. Quinn took the seat across from her. "I heard this was the same guy who was beating up his wife a while back and you got in the middle of it. Why did you kill him over a donkey?"

Dela stared at the man she'd met in Iraq. She'd had the hots for him until he'd set a rapist free. Then she loathed him. When they'd run into each other here and worked a couple of murders that occurred at the casino, she'd been leery of the man and still a bit drawn to him. But this…his believing she would kill someone. He'd nailed the lid on any romantic feelings she might have had for him.

"I didn't kill him." She continued to stare into his eyes.

"The neighbor saw you and the victim fighting. You holding the murder weapon." Quinn stared back.

"Did you read my interview?" she asked, still keeping eye contact with the man. There had been times when she would have given anything to have him take her in his arms and kiss her. But there had been just as many times she couldn't believe the bull that came out of his mouth and the callous way he believed it was his way or no way.

"I did. You claim he came at you." His gaze drifted over her face, lingering on the cheek where Winter had hit her, and came back to her eyes. "You could say it was self-defense and get off with a lighter sentence."

She smacked the table with her hand and Mugshot sat up, growling, his gaze on Quinn. "I did not kill that man in anger or self-defense. He was alive when I walked away. If my prints are on the knife, it's because when he fell to the ground clutching his crotch, I picked up the knife and stuck it in a crack inside the shed. That accounts for the murder weapon and the man when I led Jethro down the road." She was getting sick and tired of telling the story over and over. But she knew the more times she told it and it came out the same, the more likely they were to believe her.

Shaffer returned. "I didn't find any clothes or shoes with blood on them."

Quinn returned his gaze to Dela. "Where are the clothes you were wearing when you had the altercation?"

Chapter Five

Dela stared at Quinn. Why was he being such an ass? She stood up. "In the hamper in my bathroom, except for this shirt and these shoes," and pointed to the security uniform shirt she wore. "Do I need to strip here in the kitchen?"

His eyes flashed, and she wished she hadn't let her anger and frustration get to her. She walked to the hall and over her shoulder said, "Agent Shaffer, you'll find a garbage sack under the sink that you can put the clothes in." Continuing down the hall to her bedroom, she locked the door and stripped out of the top layer of clothing and the sock and shoe on her foot. Dela pulled on sweat pants and a sweatshirt, before sliding her foot into a slipper and leaving the shoe as she always did on her prosthesis.

Opening the door, Quinn stood beside the door with the open garbage bag.

"You know, Detective Dick didn't even ask for my

clothes or even take any samples when he had me in for questioning." She dropped the muddy clothing from the hamper, her shirt, and shoe in the bag.

"Both shoes," Quinn said, staring at the shoe on her prosthesis.

She backed to the bed and sat down. "You really know how to hurt a person," she mumbled, untying the shoe and pulling it off the fake foot. With tears of anger and humiliation burning her eyes, she said, without looking up, "Do you want the sock, too?"

"Yes." His voice was softer this time.

She pulled the sock off her titanium foot and held it up without looking at him. "If it makes you happy, I gave you my underwear and the jacket I was wearing this morning."

He didn't move, she could see the toes of his leather shoes.

"Get out." She raised her voice and her head, looking at him with all the hurt and anger she felt over his believing she could kill someone.

He started to open his mouth, then clamped it shut, pivoted, and left the room.

Dela sat on the end of the bed, listening as the FBI Agents walked to the door and it shut behind them.

Mugshot walk/hopped into the room and lay his head on her lap. She stroked his soft fur and hugged his neck. "I never really liked him anyway," she said, sniffling.

♠ ♣ ♥ ♦

After a soak in the tub, Dela called Kenny, her second in command at the casino.

"Hey, Boss, what's going on? Margie said Detective Jones hauled you out of here this afternoon," Kenny answered.

"He thinks I killed someone. But I didn't and Heath is going to help me prove it." She had thought about how Heath had believed her. If someone had accused Heath of murder, she wasn't sure she would have been able to say to him, "I know you didn't do it." What made him so sure she hadn't? Or had he just said that to try and get her guard down? They had been apart a lot of years. In those years, they'd both grown and become different people. They'd both done things she was pretty sure the other would have never guessed when they'd dated in high school.

"We know you didn't. But you know Bernie, when he gets word of this you may be in trouble." Kenny was her upbeat sidekick. But he also knew Bernie Moon a lot better than she did. Bernie was his uncle.

"Yeah, I plan to talk to him tomorrow. In the meantime, can you see how many people at the casino knew about Paul Winter making meth and if they know who he sold it to?"

Kenny whistled. "Paul was cooking? That explains a lot. I'll see what I can find out. Good luck with Bernie."

"Thanks." She ended the call and sat in the recliner, thinking.

Knocking, and Heath's voice, invaded Dela's dream. She rubbed a hand over her face and opened her eyes. The amber glow of the living room light reminded her she was in the recliner. When she'd first moved in during the remodel, she'd slept in the recliner until she'd bought a bed.

Mugshot stood by the front door whining.

"Dela, it's me, Heath. Come on, I see the light on."

A glance at her watch showed it was a quarter to midnight.

"Just a minute," she said, fumbling for her crutches and rising up out of the recliner. Three steps and she unlocked the door and moved to the side.

Heath opened the door. He wasn't in his uniform, but his gaze scanned the room as thoroughly as if he were on duty.

"What are you doing here?" she asked, moving into the kitchen to get something to drink.

He followed her. "I couldn't quit thinking about what Grandfather Thunder said about the victim cooking meth. I came back out to have a look around. Then as I passed by, I saw the light still on and thought maybe you were having trouble sleeping." He sat in a chair at the table.

"No, I fell asleep in the chair after the Feds were here." She sat down, sliding a glass of iced tea in front of Heath.

"Quinn and buddy?" Heath asked.

"Yeah. He said Detective Dick asked him to help because you were biased." She raised the cup to sip and watched Heath.

He grinned. "I might be a bit biased, but I also know you wouldn't kill anyone."

She shook her head. Her shoulder-length dark hair brushed her neck. "You don't know that. I was an M.P. for the army in Iraq." She held his gaze. "I have killed someone. But it was in the duty of my job for the army. I have never killed anyone stateside."

Heath studied her. "You're telling me you have changed."

She nodded. "But not so much I would kill someone without thinking about the consequences. In Iraq, it was kill and protect, or be killed. Here, I don't plan on ever ending another person's life."

He grasped her hand and held it. "I know that about you. You take life, all life, seriously. That's why I know you didn't kill Winter." He released her hand and picked up his glass. "What did Quinn want?"

She stared into her drink. "He had Shaffer search the house and then he made me give him the clothes I had on." Tears burned her eyes. "Even the shoe from my prosthesis. It was embarrassing."

Heath was beside her, his arm around her shoulders. "Hey, you already told me he's a jerk and I've seen it myself. You didn't kill the victim and his blood won't be on your clothes. From what I saw on the reports, he bled internally so there was little blood that spilled."

"I've been thinking about how wild he looked when he attacked me. Do you think he was taking the stuff he cooked?" This thought had come to her when she was soaking in the tub.

"Toxicology on the body will tell us. The autopsy should show the usual effects. Sores or deteriorating teeth." Heath squeezed her shoulders. "Want me to hang out here tonight?"

She studied him. There wasn't heat or desire in his eyes. He was asking as a friend. Which was all she needed right now. Dela still wasn't sure she wanted to put the burden of her messed up life on anyone else.

"I'm not feeling the need for company. I just wish Ina had never called me or that she had better information when she told me that her husband wouldn't be at home."

Heath released her and sat back down across from her. "What made her think her husband wouldn't be living in their house?"

Dela studied him. "The neighbor said he hadn't

been around. I'll talk to her tomorrow." She grabbed her crutches and stood. "I really would like to go to bed. I have to go to work tomorrow and make sure no one there throws me under the bus with Detective Dick. Kenny said I'd probably hear from Bernie and he would ask around about Winter making and selling meth."

Heath rose and put both their glasses in the sink. "Sounds like you've been busy between your questioning and house being searched." He stepped up to her and again put his arms around her. "Remember, I'm only a phone call away." He glanced around the house. "I believe your remodel has been finished for a couple of weeks according to Grandfather Thunder. Am I still getting an invitation to move in as a roommate?"

She smiled as she peered up at his face. His long dark hair hung about his shoulders, framing strong cheekbones and a high forehead. It was a face she knew well. "I think when I am cleared of this mess, you may move in. If you do it before, they may not give you access to the case, which we'll need to find out who framed me."

He grinned. "I will work hard at getting you cleared so I can move in soon."

She pushed out of his embrace. "If I had said I'd changed my mind, would you have changed sides and helped Detective Dick railroad me?"

"I would never help Jones do anything to hurt you. I would have started looking for my own place. I'm tired of living with my mom and Grandfather Thunder."

Dela laughed. "I know that feeling. I enjoy my mom so much better with us living apart."

"Check in with me in the morning." Heath walked to the door.

"I will. Thanks for being such a good friend." She

swung over to the door with her crutches.

"I've never stopped being your friend. We just needed time and space." He opened the door and walked over to his car.

She waved, closed the door, and locked it, then headed down the hall to her bed. "Come on, Mugshot. We need sleep so we can prove I'm innocent."

Chapter Six

Dela sat up in bed. There it was again!

"Haw-eee-haw-uh-haw-eee!"

Light streamed through the slits in the blinds of her bedroom.

Mugshot walked into the bedroom, whining.

"I hear you and your friend. You both want breakfast. Hold on." Dela sat on the side of the bed, grabbed her crutches, and rose. At the French doors, she noticed the donkey was staring at the gate where the hay had come from the night before. She wore the shorts and tank top she'd slept in and wasn't ready to put her prosthesis on. There had to be a way to get to the hay by opening the gate and grabbing it without anyone seeing her.

Mugshot exited the door in front of Dela. "Keep your friend busy," she said to the dog and made her way over to the gate. The backyard fence was solid wood. She'd asked for a privacy fence so she could come out in the summer and enjoy the sunshine without putting her prosthesis on and not having to worry about anyone seeing her.

She opened the side gate and grabbed a flake of hay. The sound of the donkey walking toward the gate had her spinning around to toss the hay to the side of the opening in hopes it would keep him inside.

When she spun, her crutch caught on the handle on the gate and she went down. "Double frickin' shit!" she shouted and hastily struggled to get back on her foot. Mugshot came over to give her something to push off of. Jethro even walked over. He didn't step on her, he stood beside Mugshot giving her one more level to raise up to and right herself on her crutches.

She smiled. "You two make a good team for this one-legged woman."

Jethro raised his nose in the air and curled his lips back, showing off big yellow teeth. Dela laughed and patted his neck and Mugshot's head. "I'll be more careful getting the other flake of hay." She finished feeding the donkey and then fed Mugshot.

While the new friends ate, she made coffee and poured a bowl of cereal. Today was weight day. She'd set up one of the rooms with weights. That way she could work out at home and keep up the muscle in her arms and legs that she needed to function with a prosthesis and only one full leg. An hour later she finished her workout and was getting ready to take a quick shower when her phone rang.

A glance at the name and a moan slipped from her lips. Bernie Moon.

"Hello?" she answered.

"Dela, it's Bernie Moon. What's this I hear you are a suspect in a murder investigation?" He didn't even say hello.

"Good morning to you, too, Bernie," she said. "I am a suspect but I didn't kill the victim."

"But you and the man have a history?" It was a statement that sounded like a question.

"I kept him from killing his wife a few months ago. But I didn't kill him," she restated.

"I'm having a meeting with the board this morning. I think it would be best if you took some vacation days until this is cleared up."

"Bernie, I didn't kill anyone. I don't need to take a vacation." If she didn't go to work the people who worked under her would think she was guilty. If she kept on working and doing her job while the police did theirs, it would show she didn't have anything to hide. She voiced this to Bernie.

"We'll see what the other board members say." He ended the call.

Dela took her shower and dressed in her work uniform of khaki slacks and blue polo shirt. The blue polo shirt deepened the blue of her eyes. Growing up she'd worn her long dark hair like the girls she went to school with. As long as no one saw the blue eyes she'd inherited from her Swedish mother, she resembled a member of one of the tribes. Cayuse, Walla Walla, or Umatilla. Which pleased her as they were the only family she knew, even though they weren't blood-related.

Dressed and feeling she had to prove to the people around her she wasn't worried, Dela prepared for work. After putting her dishes in the sink, she checked on Mugshot and Jethro in the backyard and headed to the front door. She picked up her purse and stepped out the door.

Travis pulled up in his pickup. His friend, Melvin, was in the passenger seat. Travis exited his vehicle and said, "We're here to measure how much fencing we need."

"Just worry about fencing off a section closest to the house and backyard to start with. I'll probably need a shed to keep hay and feed in as well." Dela opened her car door.

"Do you want us to put a gate out your backyard fence into the pasture we make?" Travis walked over to her. "I'll also make one out here."

"That sounds good." She lowered into the car seat.

"Mom says to give her a call if you need to talk." The concern in the young man's eyes told her he and his mom had heard about her being a possible murderer.

"I'm fine. But she could come over and check out Jethro. I'm not sure if he needs anything. Shots or dewormed." She'd been around animals enough growing up to know they needed maintenance to be healthy.

"I'll let her know." Travis stepped away from the car.

Dela backed out of her driveway. There were two ways she could leave her house and get to the casino. She didn't have to go by the Winter residence and normally didn't when she drove to work, but she wanted to see what area the police had taped off as the murder scene.

As soon as she spotted Quinn's SUV, Dela wished she hadn't been curious. All she needed was him watching her drive past. Instead, she drove on by, her face forward, and at her normal speed. Out of the corner of her eye, she spotted the neighbor who had called in the murder. The one who had said Dela was in a fight and the man was dead when she left. Did anyone say the woman's name?

She continued on to work trying to remember if anyone had mentioned the name. As she turned into the parking lot it came to her. Jacob had said the neighbor who called the stabbing in was Sadie Swan. If she couldn't talk to the woman, she could ask Heath to talk to her or one of her relatives. Someone at the casino might be related to the woman. She'd like to know how well Sadie understood the concept of time.

Dela parked in her usual spot and walked up to the employee entrance at the back of the casino. She tapped her employee key card against the box by the door and it opened.

"Dela? I didn't expect you," Margie said.

"Why not?" Dela stood in front of the security member in charge of making sure all employees carried nothing in or out of the casino that wasn't allowed.

The woman ducked her head. "Bernie Moon told Kenny to find someone to take his shift as he would be working yours."

Dela cursed under her breath and stomped over to her desk. She opened the cabinet door and shoved her purse inside. "Where is Kenny?"

"He went home to get a few hours of sleep before coming back in." Margie's eyes widened as Dela picked up her radio and attached it to her belt.

"Then I guess I'm in charge until he gets back. I haven't been arrested because I didn't kill anyone. Make sure that goes around the casino and Nixyáawii gossip." Dela finished attaching her mic and slipped an earbud in her ear. "I'll be making my rounds."

Margie nodded.

Dela walked out of the security office and scanned

the casino. Tonight was Wednesday night Bingo. After lunch, the Bingo fanatics would be filling the Spotted Pony. She wasn't about to leave the casino short-staffed just because Bernie Moon didn't know her.

She glanced at the deli. Rosie, a cheerful woman a few years older than Dela who had a photographic memory, waved her over. Dela turned to her right and walked up to the deli counter. "Hi, Rosie. Did you want to talk to me?"

The woman reached out patting Dela's arm. "We know you didn't kill Paul. But what were you doing over there? You know he blamed you for losing Ina and Micah."

Dela nodded to a table. "Can we sit down?"

"Sure. You sit, I'll be right there." Rosie called to the back she was taking a break and then she filled a cup with coffee and a large cup with a soft drink and carried them over to the table. Her full colorful skirt swished around her athletic shoes as she walked over to the table. Rosie placed the coffee in front of Dela and settled her short, round body on the chair across the table.

"It seems Bernie has decided I killed Paul. He told Kenny to find someone to take over his job while he does mine." Dela stared into her friend's round face. "I'm being treated like a murderer before anyone has even found proof. Of which they won't find any, because I didn't kill him."

"It's Detective Jones. He's always had it out for you. Now he thinks he can bring you down." Rosie sipped her drink and continued. "My cousin who works in family services said that Paul sent threats to several people in her office trying to get them to tell him where Ina is."

"Why would he care about her and the child if all he did was abuse them?" Dela asked.

"Word is, Ina not only hid Micah from Paul but also money he was given by someone who expects something in return." Rosie nodded her head.

Dela stared at her. "Does this money have anything to do with the fact he was cooking meth?"

Rosie leaned back, looked around, and then leaned forward, whispering, "You didn't hear it from me. But yes. I heard Gus Sander, he lives in Pendleton, was the one paying Paul to make it."

Dela pulled out her phone. "He would have more motive to kill Paul Winter than I would. Because I didn't have any motive." She found Heath's number and dialed.

"Is your morning going better than yesterday?" he answered.

"Not much. Bernie believes I need to take a vacation. But that's not why I called." Dela went on to tell him what Rosie told her.

"I'll check out Sander. Maybe you should go home. That way you won't make matters worse with Bernie and no one can say you are tampering with the investigation."

"Are you saying I should keep my nose out of proving my innocence?" She couldn't believe Heath would suggest she sit idly by and think Detective Dick and Quinn would find the real murderer.

"I'm saying that maybe a vacation would give you time to *talk* to people." The innuendo in his voice clicked a lightbulb in her head.

"You don't think my bowing to Bernie's demands makes me look guilty?" She had never backed down from hard tasks in her life. Not when her best friend was murdered, not when she lost a leg. She was a fighter and giving into Bernie's request she take a vacation felt like weakness to her.

"No. It makes you look smart to step back and let law enforcement do their thing." His voice was muffled as he talked to someone on his side of the line then said, "Are you at work?"

"Yes."

"I'll be by and visit with you." The call ended.

Dela stared at her phone. Was he correct in thinking no one would think the worst of her if she took a vacation right now? It would give her lots of time to find out more about Gus Sander and the victim.

"You look upset," Rosie said.

Dela glanced across the table at her friend. "Heath thinks my taking a vacation is a good idea." She studied the woman who knew everyone who worked here. "What do you think the employees would think if I did?"

"That you need a vacation. You haven't really taken one since you started this job three years ago. A day here and there is not a vacation." Rosie picked up her soda and stuck the straw in her mouth.

"I happen to enjoy my job," Dela said.

Rosie set her cup down. "So do I, but I also like to take time to visit people and go on trips."

"The only people I have to visit are all right here. Where would I go?" Though in her mind she didn't plan on going anywhere. All the answers to who really killed Paul Winter were right here in Nixyáawii and Pendleton.

Chapter Seven

Dela was visiting with Jacee Bing in the deli when Heath walked into the casino. She texted him. *Deli.*

"Did you know that Paul was staying in the house?" Dela asked the woman whose face had gone from tired to scared when Dela took a seat across from her. Jacee was a cousin to Ina. One who had congratulated Dela when she'd saved Ina from near death at the hands of her husband last fall.

"I haven't spoken to him in years. When Ina showed up at my mom's house with bruises, I promised my mom I'd stay away from there. She said if he would hit the mother of his child, he'd hit any woman he thought wronged him." Jacee's hands were in her lap. Her lunch went untouched.

"Hey, surprised to find you hanging out in the deli," Heath said, grabbing a chair from another table and joining them.

"Tribal Officer Seaver, this is Jacee Bing, Ina Winter's cousin," Dela said by way of introductions.

Heath nodded his head at the woman. "Do you have any idea who would want Ina's husband dead?"

The woman glanced back and forth between Heath and Dela. "Why do you think I would know?"

"We're not accusing you. We're just trying to figure out who killed him," Dela said, to calm the woman who appeared about to bolt.

"Do you know who his friends were?" Heath asked, pulling out a small notepad.

Jacee shook her head and then stopped. "He was in here a couple of weeks ago talking to three people I've never seen before."

"You haven't seen them before? As in they don't frequent the casino or they weren't locals?" Dela asked.

"Both."

"Where were they having this discussion?" Heath asked.

"I was watching the gaming table monitors. I think they were huddled together over near the event center. I wouldn't have paid any attention except I saw it was Paul. He has always talked trash about the casino since he didn't get hired when he applied."

Dela pulled out her phone. "Can you think of anything that would give us a better time frame than a couple weeks ago?"

Jacee plucked at the crust on her sandwich. "It was around Valentine's Day. The decorations were red and pink hearts. I remember all the "Fall in Love" banners on the walls behind where they were standing."

"Thanks." Dela stood. "Let's go see Marty."

Heath caught up to her as they stepped onto the casino floor. "Have you thought about the vacation? If you weren't working you could look into things that I can't as a law enforcement officer."

She stopped and faced him. "Are you saying I can do illegal things to find the proof I didn't kill Paul Winter?"

He peered into her eyes. "I'm saying you don't have your hands tied by legalities."

"But who do I use for backup? I'm smart enough to know I can't go digging around by myself. I could end up on your homicide list."

Worry wrinkled his brow. "I know. That's something I haven't figured out yet. And you can't let Quinn know what you're doing."

She put a hand on his arm. "We'll figure it out. Right now, let's see who Paul was talking to at the casino." Tapping her security clearance card on the box on the large mural wall, a door opened and they walked through.

The four surveillance members seated in chairs in front of banks of monitors all swiveled and in a jumble of voices told Dela they knew she hadn't killed anyone.

"Thanks, everyone. It helps to know you believe in my innocence." She pointed to the door across the room. "Is Marty in?"

"No, he's taking some time off. You'll find Farley in there," Mick, a large man who ate the whole time he sat in front of the monitors, said.

Heath raised an eyebrow as they opened the door to the surveillance office.

"Hey, Dela. I heard the—" His words stopped as his gaze landed on Heath in his uniform.

"Farley, did you know Paul Winter?" Dela asked.

"The man who the cops think you killed?" He glared at Heath.

"Yeah, him," Heath said, taking a seat next to the young man sitting in front of a desk with three large monitors.

Dela took the chair on the opposite side where Marty kept a box for her to prop her prosthesis on. "Jacee said she saw him and three men talking over by the event center sometime around Valentine's Day. Any chance you can find that."

The man in his twenties wearing a t-shirt with four chiefs' faces on Mount Rushmore started clicking the keys on the keyboard in front of him. "I'll start on February fourteenth." He shoved his long dark hair out of his face.

"All the decorations didn't get taken down until around the sixteenth," Dela said. "Start on the sixteenth and work backward."

Farley nodded and the monitor in the middle showed the entrance to the event center. He had the video running in fast forward. "Did she say what time she saw them?"

Dela shook her head. "Isn't she usually on the night shift? Why is she in here today?"

The young man shrugged. "I'm not the boss. You'd have to ask Marty."

"Well, we'll say she was on the night shift. Start looking around ten." Dela pulled out her phone and texted Heath. *I can ask Marty to be my sidekick if he isn't out of town.*

Sitting on the other side of Farley, Heath pulled out his phone. Didn't even glance at her as he read the message and replied, *We'll talk later.*

She sighed and stared at the flashing video. The 16th didn't reveal four men gathered near the event center. Neither did the 15th or the 14th.

Farley set up the night of the 13th. It fast-forwarded, the image was blurry. At midnight men started converging near the center.

"Slow it down," Heath said, leaning toward the monitor as Dela leaned forward as well.

The video stopped and then proceeded with the characters moving naturally. Two men, one dressed in a western shirt, jeans, and western boots and the other in athletic shoes, jeans, t-shirt, and a denim jacket, stood beside the door to the event center. They were talking but the man in the jacket was definitely keeping an eye on everything around them.

Paul Winter and another man walked up to the other two. They didn't shake hands. It didn't appear to be a meeting of friends. The first two did most of the talking. Paul's face remained blank. The other man, about ten years younger than Paul with shoulder-length hair, a baseball cap, faded jeans and hoodie, and well-worn boots showed his anger. His face grew darker and his mouth pursed tighter with each comment the man in the western shirt said.

"Any idea who those men are?" Dela asked.

Farley shook his head. "I haven't lived in the area very long. And sitting up here, I don't learn people's names."

Dela nodded. She knew he had moved to Nixyáawii from Lapwai to help with his aging grandmother.

Heath sighed. "The guy in the western shirt and acting like he's in charge is Gus Sander."

Dela stared harder at the video to make sure she would know the man the next time she saw him. "Any idea who the man is with him or Paul?"

"No. But if Farley prints out a photo, I can ask around." Heath glanced at the younger man.

He glanced at Dela.

She nodded for Farley to go ahead and print the photo. It always warmed her insides when the employees at the casino took her instructions over the local law enforcement and the Feds. It meant they trusted her. She sure wished Bernie Moon trusted her as much as the employees at the casino did.

Farley clicked keys and the printer whirred to life.

"Can you make two copies?" Dela asked.

He clicked the keys some more and two sheets of paper slid out of the printer.

"Thanks. I'll let you know if we need anything else," Dela said.

"Do you want to know what they are saying?" Farley asked.

Heath and Dela both stared at the young man.

"How can you get that?" Heath asked.

"I can copy this and take it home. My grandma is deaf and reads lips." Farley shrugged.

"That would be great," Dela said. Knowing what the men were talking about would help them figure out if Sander had anything to do with Paul's death.

Dela and Heath walked out of the surveillance area each carrying a photocopy of the three men and the victim.

"Are you going to talk to Ina? Paul's wife?" Dela asked.

"Quinn is questioning the wife." The neutral tone of Heath's words told Dela he had wanted that job.

"She would have cooperated better with you than with a Fed," she offered.

"We both know that, but Quinn felt it was his duty since she is up at the Colville Reservation in Washington."

Dela led Heath into the coffee shop and they slid

into a booth. "What do you think of Marty helping me dig around?"

The waitress arrived, filled cups with coffee, and walked away.

Heath sipped his coffee, watching her over the rim of the cup.

She took that to mean he was weighing the pros and cons of her and Marty sleuthing. "He would be able to look things up on the computer and go with me when I talk to people. That is if he isn't off on one of his adventures."

Heath's brow wrinkled. "What kind of adventures does he do?"

"He's a rock climber. Marty has climbed every rock wall in Oregon and half of them in Idaho."

"Then he's strong. Could help out if things got rough." Heath watched her. "Does he have a concealed carry permit?"

"I've never asked him." She frowned. "There shouldn't be a need for firearms. I don't plan on busting up a drug deal or anything. I'm just going to talk to people."

"Which could make some people uncomfortable." Heath's concerned brown eyes peered into hers.

"I won't poke any bears. I know how to question suspects." She sipped her coffee.

Heath studied her for a few more seconds. "Call him and see if he's interested."

Dela pulled out her phone. Before she pressed Marty's name she asked, "Are you sure you won't get in trouble with Detective Dick for knowing I'm doing this?"

Heath shrugged. "He won't find out, and you'll keep me apprised of everything you learn as you learn it." His voice held authority as he said it.

"Why are you allowing me to do this? You could lose your job."

He reached across the table and grasped her hand. Holding it in his large warm hand, he said, "You could lose your life if Detective Jones and Special Agent Quinn decide to bring charges against you. We," he moved his free hand between them, "have to prove you're innocent. Because from what I've seen and heard, everyone in law enforcement, except Jacob and I, have you as good as behind bars."

"That's why Bernie is so persistent that I take a vacation. He's buddies with Chief Steele." Dela felt her gut twist. She knew she was innocent and had believed anyone who knew her would know that. But it sounded like Rosie was correct in saying Detective Dick had it out for her.

She pressed Marty's name and waited while it rang.

"Yo, Dela, I'm not at work," Marty's cheerful voice announced when he picked up.

"I know. What are you doing on your days off?" she asked, watching Heath study her.

"I thought about going skiing, what's up?"

"Have you been listening to the gossip?" She was going to see what he had to say before she asked him to help her.

"That you supposedly killed Paul Winter? Yeah." There was a pause. "Do you need me to come bail you out? I kind of figured your mom would take care of that."

She laughed. "No. While they are treating me as the prime suspect, they didn't have enough to keep me. But Bernie wants me to take a vacation."

"Come skiing with me," he said enthusiastically.

"Thank you, but I was wondering if you'd be willing to help me dig up other suspects. People who would have a motive to kill Paul Winter."

"I could do that, but what about Special Agent Pierce and Detective Jones? I heard they are working hard to find more evidence against you."

"That's why we have to look for the real killer." She noticed Heath's attention was on the door. He motioned for her to hurry the call. "I'm headed home in fifteen minutes. Can you come to my house and we'll come up with a plan?"

"Sure, see you in thirty."

The call ended as Quinn walked over and slid into the booth, shoving her over. She grimaced, trying to dig in with her fake foot to move her body away from the infuriating man.

Heath's face had gone blank. A trait of the culture that she'd found frustrating as a teenager, but had taken to using the same tactic when things became stressful or she had to deal with someone she didn't like in the army.

Quinn stared across the table at Heath. "What are you doing fraternizing with a suspect?"

"She's not a suspect. She's a friend." Heath glared at the Fed.

Dela slid her cup of coffee to the center of the table. "I need to go." She pushed on Quinn's shoulder with a hand, trying to pry him out of the bench seat.

Chapter Eight

"I'm not going anywhere until you tell me exactly what happened at the Winter residence yesterday." Quinn shifted in the seat, facing Dela.

She scooted with her back against the wall and glared at him. "All you have to do is listen to the interview Detective Dick recorded."

The FBI agent shook his head. "I read the transcript. You didn't tell everything."

"I was there. I know what I did. What the hell makes you think I didn't tell everything?" She flicked a glance at Heath. She hadn't mentioned her call to him.

"There was blood in the house. It's being checked but I'm pretty sure it will be the victim's. The blood was found on the meth-cooking apparatus torn apart as if someone had put it out of commission on purpose." Quinn's gaze drilled into her.

"I didn't go in the house and didn't know the man was cooking meth until late yesterday." She continued to peer into his eyes. There was no way they could pin this on her. "Did you find any of the victim's blood on the clothes you took from my house last night?"

Heath cleared his throat. "I searched her house, why did you go back?" The tone was clear he felt as if the Fed had overstepped.

"Detective Jones felt you wouldn't be impartial, given who the suspect is." Quinn twisted his head and stared at Heath.

"I did my job. Nothing in Dela's house had blood or looked like evidence she'd killed the man. I gave my report to Jones." Heath's face was darker than she'd ever seen it.

Not only was Detective Dick not believing he could be unbiased, but so was Quinn. Dela didn't care if he was biased. He believed her. "Who would want to kill the victim and ruin his meth-cooking operation?" Dela asked to take the heat off of Heath.

Quinn swung his face back in her direction. "You want me to believe you didn't know he was cooking?"

She nailed him with an angry pointed look and said through clenched teeth. "I've always known you were an asshole but now you are proving it. Get out of my way. Your insinuations aren't going to get any more help out of me. I'd rather deal with Detective Dick. I've known all along he hated me." She shoved Quinn in the chest and kept shoving until he slid out and stood.

Dela rose to her feet and faced Heath. "I'll be in touch." She walked out of the coffee shop without another glance at Quinn.

She seethed all the way to the security office where she encountered Bernie Moon sitting in her chair, waiting for her.

"Dela, I told you to take a vacation until this all goes away," Bernie said, standing as she walked over to get her purse out of the cabinet.

"Did everyone on the board think it was best for me to take a vacation until they find the killer?" She crossed her arms and stared at the man shorter than her.

He placed his hands behind his back, making his belly protrude even more under the untucked, loose-fitting shirt. "While most believe you are innocent, you did have an altercation with the man last year which appeared in the papers. We just feel it would be best if you stayed away from the casino and the reporters will stay away from here, too." He cleared his throat. "Bad publicity and all."

She wanted to cry. After all she'd done for the casino. Uncovering their head of security was working with a human trafficking ring and keeping the murder of an accountant and a conference speaker out of the news. She had hoped they would have more respect and confidence in her. "I won't cause a scene, but I want it in writing that my job will be here for me when the killer is caught because I can tell you it wasn't me. Though your lack of confidence in me has me wondering if during my vacation I need to look for another job. I'm not sure I want to work for someone who believes I would kill a human being." She had taken her mic, radio, and earbuds off as she talked. She placed them in the drawer and pulled her purse out of the cabinet.

"We are just concerned that," he coughed, "you did learn to take lives in the army and maybe you had an episode or…"

She faced him. Stared into his eyes, and said,

"When they tossed me out because I was no longer useful to them, I promised myself I wouldn't become a statistic that couldn't handle civilian life." Dela walked over to Margie. "I'll see you around. Let everyone know that I didn't want to go, to take a *vacation*. It was forced on me by the board of trustees."

Margie gave her a weak smile. "I'll let them know."

Dela walked out the back door and over to her car. She hated leaving, but Bernie Moon could have had her fired. She took a deep breath in and exhaled slowly. She, Heath, and Marty would uncover the real killer. It was plain that Quinn and Dick believed it was her.

On the drive home, she contemplated who would have smashed the meth-cooking apparatus. Not Sander if he was in business with Winter. It could have been someone else in the business. But why kill the victim and then smash the equipment? If he was dead, he couldn't make any more of the drug.

Due to Quinn's arrival at the casino, Marty had arrived at her house first. Travis and Marty sat on the tailgate of Travis' pickup. Dela parked and walked over to where the two sat sipping sodas and talking.

"Where's your help?" Dela asked Travis.

"Melvin had to run errands for his mom. We got the posts in before he had to leave. I've been wiring up the panels."

Dela glanced at the sturdy wire panels with squares. They would keep both the dog and the donkey in. "It looks secure. Thank you for doing all of this."

"Hey, you're family and you pay pretty good, too." He grinned.

She laughed. "True. You've been the recipient of most of my savings after I bought the house." Dela glanced at Marty. "Let's talk inside."

He slid off the tailgate, thanked Travis for the soda, and followed her into the house. "So for our vacations, we're going to find evidence to clear you of murder."

Dela faced him. "You do believe I didn't kill anyone?"

He grinned. "Yes. I wouldn't have come over if I thought you were just trying to cover up your crime."

She sighed. "I wish other people thought that way. I just had an intense conversation with Special Agent Pierce. I didn't like how he thinks I'm a suspect, but he gave us some information I didn't have." She told him about the blood in the house and the damaged property. Dela pulled the photocopy of the four men meeting at the casino out of her pocket and unfolded it. "Do you know any of these men?"

Marty stared at it for a while. "That's Paul Winter." He moved his finger. "That is Daniel Booth next to him. I think he's a cousin or something. That is Gus Sander. He likes to come into the casino and spend big when he has a pretty woman with him." Marty's finger moved to the fourth man. "I don't think I've ever seen him before."

"You gave me one more name, that's better than I had before." She went on to tell him that the victim had been making meth for Sander. Or at least that was what she'd found out. "Farley said his grandmother can read their lips. He is taking a copy of the conversation home to see if she can tell us what they were talking about."

"That's a good idea, as long as Farley can keep his mouth shut that he did that." Worry wrinkled Marty's brow.

"Do I need to tell him to keep it quiet?" Dela didn't want any harm to come to anyone helping her.

"I'll call him. Just in case someone is keeping track of who you call." He raised an eyebrow.

"What are you talking about?" Dela asked.

"The Feds can get a warrant to see who all you call and who called you. Which, since you said Ina Winter called you to tell you to get the donkey, I'm sure they checked up on that."

The mention of Ina reminded her she hadn't managed to ask Quinn what the woman had said to him. Then she snorted. He wouldn't have told her. She was a suspect in his eyes.

"While you call Farley, I'll call Ina. I'd like to know why she thought her husband wasn't staying at the house when it is pretty evident, he was." She pulled out her phone and scrolled through her recent calls. She found the call the morning before from Ina and hit call.

The phone rang and went to voicemail. "Hi, Ina, this is Dela. I wanted to let you know I have Jethro and see how you were doing. Could you call me back, please?" She ended the call and headed to the kitchen to make coffee and dig out a notebook and pen so she and Marty could start figuring out where to start.

Mugshot stood at the door watching her. She opened the door and he walked through, straight into the living room.

"Whoa, back off," Marty said.

Dela glanced at the sofa where Marty sat. Mugshot had his head in the man's lap. "He likes you."

"I wouldn't think dropping his head in my lap was a way to endear him to me." Marty shoved Mugshot back and stood.

"I've got coffee ready. Come in here and we'll figure out what we need to do." She plopped the second cup she'd made in the one-cup brewer on the table and sat in front of the first cup she'd made. Pulling the notebook in front of her, she opened it to a fresh page and wrote what they knew.

Marty sat across from her and pushed the coffee to the middle of the table.

"Do you want something else?" she asked.

"No. That soda Travis gave me is enough for a while. What are you doing?"

"Writing down what we know so far." When her list was done, she turned it for Marty to read.

"Tell me what happened," he said.

Dela told him everything she'd told the police and about her call to Heath.

"The timeline doesn't make sense," Marty said. "You had the fight with Paul and the neighbor saw it. You walked away leading the donkey, and Heath drove up and didn't see anything? Did he get out and look?"

"No, he got a call and headed to respond, only when he arrived at the address nothing had happened." They needed to find out who made the call. "I'll ask Jacob Red Bear if he can find out who made that call." She spun the notebook toward her and made a note under action.

"Did the neighbor go looking before or after Heath drove by?" Marty asked.

"I don't know. I'm not sure who talked to her. Maybe Heath can find out." She picked up her phone and texted Heath. *Can you find out who talked to the neighbor? Did she find the body before or after you drove up?*

I'll see what I can find. They are keeping me out of the loop on this one.

She had been afraid he'd soon lose the ability to help them due to Detective Dick's vendetta against her.

Double Down

Dela tapped the words *blood in the house and destroyed meth lab*. "The killer went into the house after they killed Paul because Quinn said the victim's blood was in the house." She glanced up at Marty. "I had assumed the killer had been in the house with Paul when I arrived to get Jethro. That would be how they saw the fight and would have known I'd touched the knife when I picked it up and put it in the shed. But if that is true, they would have destroyed the lab first and then came out and finished off Paul, wouldn't they?"

"Unless they wanted to strike while Paul was still incapacitated, they might have run out, finished him off, and then returned to the house."

She nodded. "That makes sense as well."

"I can ask around and see if Paul was Sander's only supplier. I can't see him making enough to be the only one Sander bought from. And someone had to get the supplies for Paul." He picked up the photo. "It could have been either his cousin or this other guy." Marty set the photocopy down. "I can put out some feelers about Daniel."

"Thanks. I'll wait to hear from someone about the neighbor's statement and I'm waiting for Ina to call me back." Dela sat back in her chair and sipped her coffee. "I'd like this better if I could have stayed at work." She studied her friend. "Do you think the employees will think I did kill Paul because I'm not at work?" The thought that the people whose respect she needed to do her job could think she was a killer, put a knot in her stomach.

"Don't worry, no one will think you are running or hiding. I'm sure word will get around that Bernie made you take the vacation." Marty smiled. "I'll make sure of it."

Dela grinned. "You are a good friend."

"You would do the same for me."

"Yes, I would!" Dela pushed to her feet. "I just don't know what I'm going to do sitting around here all day long."

Marty glanced at his watch. "We can go talk to the neighbor who saw you and then go to dinner at The Rowdy Spur."

Dela studied him. "Go to dinner? Why would you want to take me to dinner in Pendleton?"

"Because it happens to be where Daniel Booth hangs out at night." Marty grinned.

"I see! Good idea. Let me get out of my uniform and feed Mugshot and Jethro and we can go."

"While you do that, I'll call a couple of friends to join us at the Spur. That way we don't look like we are only there to question Daniel." Marty pulled out his phone.

Dela walked down the hall to her bedroom, Mugshot following behind. As she changed, she wondered who Marty would invite. She didn't know any of his friends outside of the casino. And actually, she didn't know any of his friends in the casino. They were friends who only talked about what they'd done, never mentioning any names.

Dressed, she walked into the kitchen and out the back door. Travis had already tossed some hay over the fence to the donkey. Which reminded her…she needed to let Molly know she could come by tomorrow and check out Jethro. It looked like Dela would be home a lot until the murderer was found.

She filled Mugshot's bowl and set it outside. Closing the French doors, she walked into the living room. "Okay, I'm ready."

Double Down

Marty stood up from the recliner and opened the front door. "Want to take separate cars?" he asked.

"Yeah. There's no sense you having to come back here to bring me home or to get your car." She locked the door and walked over to her car. "Follow me to Mrs. Swan's." Sliding in her car, she started it up and backed out of her driveway.

A mile down the road, she parked in the driveway across the street from the property with yellow crime scene tape fluttering in the cold March wind. It would be April in two weeks but the weather wouldn't warm up much. Not until the snow on the Blue Mountains had melted.

Dela stood by her car waiting for Marty to park behind her. She wondered if the body had been in the exact spot Paul had been holding his jewels or if he'd been stabbed as he started back to the house. In a macabre way, she wanted to see the crime scene photos. Maybe she would see something that might help find evidence against someone other than herself.

"Ready?" Marty asked, walking up beside her.

"Yeah." Dela walked up to the door and knocked. They waited. She knocked again.

"I don't think anyone is home," Marty said, peering into the window next to the porch. "Does she live alone?"

"I don't know anything about her, other than her name. I don't remember seeing anyone when Mugshot and I jogged by. But then, we were always looking at the donkey. We'd stop and pet him. I think that's why Ina asked me to take Jethro. She'd watched me petting him." Dela turned from the door. "Let's go to town. Maybe I can catch up to her tomorrow."

They returned to their cars and drove to town. Dela

wondered how much they could get out of Paul's cousin and who Marty had called to have dinner with them?

Chapter Nine

Marty walked over to a table in the corner of The Rowdy Spur. Dela had been in this bar a few times as a teenager during the Pendleton Roundup when there were so many people packed in here that no one bothered to check I.D. Tonight there was room to move with only half the tables filled and three people sitting at the bar.

After scanning the establishment, Dela returned her gaze to the table and was surprised to find her friend, veterinarian Molly Taylor, Travis's mom, and Marie James, a security guard. "What are you two doing here?" she asked, taking the chair between Marie and Molly.

"Marty and I come here about once a week," Molly said, her cheeks flushing. Dela watched her friend. Molly hadn't said a word about seeing anyone.

"I'm glad you're here. I don't have to call you now." Dela turned her attention to Marie. "And you?"

"Marty thought you'd like to hear the gossip running through the casino." Her eyes twinkled as she took a sip of the wine in front of her.

"I see." Dela settled her gaze on Marty. "You're going to be the talk of the town entertaining three women tonight."

He nodded toward the door. "I have backup."

She twisted in her seat and watched Heath, in civilian clothes, meander through the tables toward them. On his heels was a man she'd never met.

When Dela turned back to the table, Marie had moved, leaving a spot next to Dela.

Heath hooked the chair, pulled it back, and sat, scooting up to the table. He studied her for a couple of seconds. "This was a good idea. Getting out."

Dela motioned to Marty. "It was his idea. Since neither one of us has to go to work tomorrow, we might as well enjoy ourselves." She couldn't hide the sarcasm in her tone.

The man who had followed Heath now sat beside Marie.

"Dela, this is my husband, John. John, this is my boss at the casino."

Dela and John exchanged pleasantries and Marie said, "I wanted you to know that everyone at the casino knows Bernie made you take the vacation. And they all know you didn't kill anyone. I heard what you said about finding another job. Please don't. We will all petition the board of trustees to get you back if you do."

Tears burned in Dela's eyes. "You don't know what it means to me to know you are all behind me."

A waitress appeared at the table and everyone who had just arrived ordered drinks and asked for menus. When the woman left, Dela turned to Molly.

"Since I'll be home tomorrow, could you come over and give Jethro a physical? Make sure his health is okay and let me know what I need to do to keep him healthy."

"I can be there around nine if that works." Molly picked up her fruity-looking drink and sipped.

"That would work for me." Dela notice that Marty held Molly's other hand on his thigh. She was happy for her friend. She couldn't have found a better man than Marty. She now understood why he and Travis had been sitting on the tailgate acting like old friends. She'd figured Travis had never met Marty before and would have been skeptical of him waiting for Dela.

"I tried to get that information you asked about," Heath said, drawing her attention to him. "Detective Jones has locked me out of the case. I asked Jacob if he could look at the files and let me or you know what he finds. I hate putting him in Jones's crosshairs but I don't trust anyone else to not buckle to the detective."

Dela nodded. "I asked Jacob to get me some information, too. We're going to have to be careful and not get him fired."

The drinks arrived and everyone ordered dinner. The conversation turned to sports, animals, and some local issues.

Dinner arrived and halfway through, Marty said her name.

Dela looked over at her friend. His gaze was fixed on the bar. She would have to turn around to see what had his attention. Instead of twisting her body, she excused herself to walk to the restroom. She spotted Daniel Booth. But what surprised her was the woman seated beside him laughing. Jacee Bing.

She continued to the restroom and washed her

hands as she tried to decide whether or not to talk to Jacee.

Molly walked in. "You've been in here a while."

"Trying to decide if I should butt in on a casino employee's date. She's with the man Marty and I came here to talk with." Dela dried her hands.

"How about you and I bump into them? She doesn't know me so it won't look as if you planned to find her and her date here." Molly handed Dela paper towels.

Smiling at her friend, Dela dried her hands and walked out of the restroom with Molly in tow. She angled her way to the bar and stood beside Jacee, catching the bartender's eye.

"What can I get you?" the bartender asked, smiling, showing off large white teeth under his 1800s mustache.

"Two, what is that you're drinking?" Dela asked Molly.

"Cowgirl's Delight." Molly smiled.

"Two of those." Dela wondered if she'd be able to drive home after having one of the bar's specialty drinks. She shifted and stared into Jacee's eyes. "Oh! Hi!" She smiled at the woman whose eyes widened. "It must be the night for friends to connect." Dela drifted her gaze over to the man on the other side of Jacee.

"I guess so." Jacee finally found her voice. "I'm sorry you were told to take a vacation."

Dela shrugged. "It just gives me some time to catch up with old friends." She motioned to Molly. "We went to school together." Dela stared at Daniel. "Is this an old friend of yours?"

"N-no." Jacee stammered.

Daniel put his arm around the younger woman's

shoulders. "Jacee and I are dating if it's any business of yours." He stared at her as if she'd insulted them.

"I see." Dela glanced at Jacee. Her eyes were downcast. Had the man forced her to come with him? She didn't think so, the woman had been laughing earlier. Was she worried that Dela knew about his connection to a man the woman hated? She studied them. Had they conspired to kill the man beating on her cousin? And she had said she didn't know any of the people Paul was meeting that night around Valentines in the casino. It was clear by their body language she'd known this man longer than a month.

"How did you two meet?" Dela asked as the bartender put the drinks on the counter in front of her. Molly paid for the drinks and carried them over to their table.

Jacee's gaze drifted in that direction and she sat up. "We need to go."

"Why?" Dela asked, knowing it was because she saw the table of casino employees and possibly Heath, a tribal policeman.

"We have dinner reservations somewhere else." Jacee slid off the stool and pulled a confused Daniel behind her toward the door.

"That didn't work," Heath said, in her ear. She turned and bumped into him.

"Are you what scared her off?" Dela hadn't learned a thing except that Jacee was dating the man who worked with the victim.

"I'm not sure if it was me or Marty. He is her boss. Why did you want to talk to her?" Heath asked, leaning against the bar.

"She was with Daniel Booth, the man with Paul Winter when he visited with Sander at the casino." Dela stared at the entrance to the bar. "Jacee didn't like Paul. She was glad I'd stepped in when he was beating up Ina. Do you think she and her boyfriend killed Paul? She definitely didn't mention him when she told us about Paul meeting three men she didn't know."

Heath cupped her elbow and led her back to the table. "I think it is something to look into. Tomorrow."

They sat, rejoining the conversation and finishing their meal. By the time everyone was ready to leave, Dela's head was fuzzy. She didn't know how Molly could look unfazed after drinking two of the fruity drinks. Dela only had two-thirds of her drink and she knew she shouldn't be driving home.

"I'll catch up with you tomorrow morning. I'll get a line on where Booth works and we'll talk to him there," Marty said, his hand clasped with Molly's.

"Okay," Dela started to nod and thought better of it.

"I'll keep you updated on what is going on at the casino," Marie said, before turning to follow her husband.

Heath pulled her to her feet. "I'll drive you home."

"What about your car?" she asked, glad he'd offered.

"I rode over here with John. He and Marie live down the street from my mom." He grinned. "I'd hoped we could have some time alone."

She grinned back. "Oh, I see. Did you put Molly up to ordering that drink full of liquor to get me drunk?"

His gaze zeroed in on her eyes. "If I remember right all those years ago, we were both sober when we made the pact to always be there for each other."

Her mind and heart raced. They'd sealed that pact by making love in her bedroom while her mom was at a school board meeting. She gulped. "I'm not ready…"

He put an arm around her shoulders and led her out of the restaurant. "I'm going to be right here when you are."

Heath made light conversation as he drove her home. At the house, Mugshot and Jethro were making a lot of noise.

"Sit tight, I'll go check it out." Heath exited the car and went to the gate in the board fence.

Dela shoved up out of the passenger seat and walked to the front door, causing the front light to come on. Someone darted out from the shadow at the corner of the house. "Hey! Stop!" she shouted and caused pain to spark in her head.

Heath was beside her in seconds. "What did you see?"

"Someone ran from the corner of the house out to the street." She pointed to the left.

Heath ran out into the street and stared in that direction for several minutes before walking back. "I didn't see anyone. They could have ducked down in the bar pit. Come on." He took the keys from her hand and opened the door.

"What had the animals upset?" she asked, walking into the house, dropping her purse in the recliner, and walking over to open the back door to let Mugshot in.

"It might have been the person you saw." Heath patted Mugshot on the head. "Do you have a flashlight? I'm going to take a look around outside."

"The drawer closest to the door." Dela scratched Mugshot's ears. "I'm going to get comfortable." She walked down the hall and into her bedroom. Standing inside the door, she smiled staring at the mural Toby, one of Travis's friends, had painted above her bed.

Some nights when the moon was full, she'd leave her window shades open and lay with her head at the foot of the bed and stare at the mural to fall asleep. The dreamcatcher with five feathers on either side of it was painted in the shades of a summer sunset.

"Do you need help?" Heath's voice asked from behind her.

She startled and faced him. "No. I was just enjoying my mural."

"It is the best work I've seen in a while. And an image that I'm sure gives you peace." He put a hand on her shoulder. "I'll go make popcorn."

"Didn't you get enough to eat?" she teased.

"I plan on watching a movie. Your house is more peaceful than Mom's. She's always asking me if I'm okay or if I need anything. When I was a kid, she always told me to get things myself, now she's smothering me."

"That's because she missed you and maybe she felt like you wanted to stay with your dad's side of the family rather than come back to her. She's just trying to show you, you do matter to her." She studied Heath's face. He was a good man. But he was also his own man. He wouldn't hurt his mom, but he would do what made him happy. She liked that about him. He'd never cared what others felt. She, on the other hand, had always tried to be a good daughter, student, and friend. But there were many times she felt like she was lacking in all departments.

"Get changed." He closed the door and she heard his footsteps fade down the hall.

She undressed down to her underwear and a t-shirt and began the task of removing her prosthesis. Even in her slightly inebriated state, the task was automatic. Her leg stood, leaning against the wall as she took off the socks that covered the stump. She stared at the bright pink skin on the six inches of leg below her right knee. Did this make her any less of a woman?

A knock on the door and Heath said, "Are you sure you don't need help? You've been in there a while."

"I'm fine." What the hell. "You can come in." She watched as the door opened and he stepped in.

"Do you need help?" His gaze was on her face.

She glanced down at her stump. "What do you see?"

He walked over and sat on the floor beside her leg. "I see honor and bravery." His fingers gently glided over the pink skin. "If anyone cannot let this affect them, it's you. All your life you have been logical and level-headed. Just because you are missing part of a leg doesn't make you any less of a person." His gaze met hers. "Or a woman."

Her face flushed. There was a time she'd wanted to see that heated look on a man's face.

He stood and held out her crutches. "Let's go eat popcorn and snuggle on the couch watching a movie."

She pushed to her foot and glanced down. All she had on were her boycut underwear. Those weren't very sexy. She glanced up at Heath. Or maybe they were. His gaze roamed up her legs and met her eyes.

He cleared his throat. "You might want to put some shorts on."

"Hand me that pair on the end of the bed." She sat back down on the chair and pulled the shorts up to her thighs, then stood and pulled them the rest of the way up.

"Much better if you want me to behave myself." He motioned for her to walk ahead of him out of the room.

When they were seated on the couch, the bowl of popcorn between them and a romantic comedy playing on the television, she asked, "Did you find anything when you looked around outside?"

"Footprints alongside the house and where I think he was trying to go over the fence into the backyard. I'm pretty sure between the dog and donkey, and us showing up, he changed his mind."

"He was trying to break into my house? Why?" Her head had started to clear. "We should call the police."

Heath stared at her. "I am the police."

"Yeah, but is Detective Dick going to believe you that someone was breaking into my place?" She grabbed her crutches.

"What do you need?"

"My phone. I'm going to at least call Quinn. This could have something to do with what happened down the road." She shoved the crutches under her arms.

"I'll get it, but I don't think he'll be any more interested than Detective Jones." Heath dug her phone out of her purse and handed it to her.

She hesitated. What would he think with her and Heath cozily sitting here? Did she care what he thought? Anger pushed her to scroll and press the icon by his name. He believed she could kill someone she barely knew. He didn't know her, and she didn't care what he thought.

"Pierce," he answered in a sleepy voice.

"It's Dela. I was out with some friends tonight and when I came home Mugshot and Jethro were making a lot of noise. Heath went to check on them and a man ran out from the side of my house. Heath said there are footprints that show he was trying to get in.”

“Heath said that, did he?” Sarcasm dripped from his words.

“Pull your head out and listen. Someone was trying to get into my house. I have nothing to steal, why would they be trying to do that?” She was becoming clearer and clearer headed. The only reason she could think of was to plant evidence against her.

“Do you want me to come out there and take a look?” he asked, in a tone that stated he’d rather stay right where he was.

“I just want it to go on record that someone tried to break into my place.” She ended the call. “Asshole,” she said under her breath.

“That’s no way to talk about a federal agent,” Heath said, grinning.

She shifted to face him. “Why do you think someone was trying to get into my house?”

The grin disappeared. “Not knowing about the animals in the backyard, I would say he wasn’t a burglar. Otherwise, the place would have been checked out earlier, and he’d have known about them. I think the woman and man who left the bar, told someone you weren’t at home and that person came over here to leave behind something that would incriminate you more in the homicide of Paul Winter.”

She nodded. “That’s what I think, too.” She picked up the bowl of popcorn and set it in her lap as she scooted over next to Heath. “Any chance you can stay here all night?”

Chapter Ten

The following morning, Dela woke to the smell of coffee and bacon. She'd hobbled to bed about 1 a.m., leaving Heath to sleep on the couch. After using the bathroom and combing her hair, she swung down the hall and into the kitchen.

Heath was a welcome sight, flipping bacon in his bare feet and rumpled clothes.

"Good morning. What time do you have to be to work today?" she asked, picking up a cup and popping a coffee pod in her one-cup brewer.

"I don't have to go in. It's my day off. If you can take me home after we eat, I'll change clothes and come back over here for your meeting with Marty."

She studied him. "Are you sure you should know what we're doing? I mean we are civilians trying to solve a murder. Don't you have to report everything to Detective Dick or your Chief of Police?"

"I'm planning on telling the chief everything. As

for Jones… I won't tell him anything. Let him and Pierce discover they won't find anything else against you." Heath placed a plate of bacon and eggs in the middle of the table.

Dela glanced at the two eggs that had been flattened and cooked all the way through. Just the way she liked them. "You remembered."

Heath sat across the table from her. "I remember everything. The memories of our times together are what got me through the tough times looking for my dad. And dealing with the problems at Pine Ridge." He searched her eyes. "Are you ready for a roommate yet?"

She pulled the plate of food towards her. "I could get used to someone cooking for me."

"You never have liked to cook."

"You say that as if it's a bad thing." She smiled.

Heath laughed, and said, "I imagine that was one of the things you liked best about the military. You didn't have to cook your own food."

"It was one of the perks."

A knock on the door startled them both.

Mugshot began barking.

"I'll get it." Heath stood and walked into the living room.

The only person she could think of who would be here this early would be her mom. She probably heard about Dela taking a mandatory vacation and came over to keep her company. But it wasn't a female voice she heard.

Quinn strode into the kitchen. "Well, if this isn't homey." His face was blank but for the ticking of the muscle over his jaw.

"I didn't want to be alone last night after we chased that man away," Dela said, hoping Quinn stayed angry and didn't look under the table. The thought of this man seeing her footless leg bothered her. He'd belittled her so much in Iraq that she didn't want him to see a real flaw.

Heath walked into the kitchen with his shoes on. "Come on, I'll show you the tracks." He picked up a piece of toast and headed to the front door.

Quinn spun and followed Heath.

Dela let her breath out and sipped her coffee. She was no longer hungry. A huge knot had taken up residence in her stomach. Maybe he'd take a look at the prints and then leave. No sooner had the thought emerged than the two men walked back into the house.

Heath walked over and made a cup of coffee as Quinn took a seat at the table. "I need your statement about what happened."

Dela began as Heath placed the cup of coffee in front of Quinn and sat back down.

"Who were you with at the restaurant?" Quinn asked.

Dela listed the names of the people.

Quinn's right eyebrow rose. "I didn't know you hung out with the people you work with."

"There are a lot of things you don't know about me." She couldn't help the retort. There had always been something about the man that made her want to battle him.

Quinn raised an eyebrow, and Heath snickered.

"What time did you come home?" Quinn asked.

Dela wasn't sure. She glanced at Heath. He had only had one beer at the start of the evening.

"It was ten-thirty," Heath replied.

The FBI agent narrowed his eyes, studying Dela. "You didn't know what time you came home?"

"Molly bought me a drink. I didn't realize how strong it was until I'd had about half of it. That's why Heath drove me home. After we chased off the burglar, I didn't want to stay by myself because of still being fuzzy." She picked up her fork and played with the cut egg on her plate.

"Any idea who the person was that ran away from the house?" Quinn asked. "Or any description?"

"I didn't see him," Heath said.

"He was average build, had on a hoodie, dark-colored. He ran out from the side of the house when the porch light came on. Then onto the road and he headed south." Dela shifted her attention to Heath.

"I ran out to the road when she told me he went that direction but I didn't see anything." Heath picked up his cup of coffee.

"South? That's toward the crime scene." Quinn studied her. "If it weren't for the footprints, I'd say you were making this up to throw suspicion off of you."

Dela wanted to throw what coffee was left in her cup in the man's face.

Heath reached over, stopping her arm before she'd even flinched. He did know her well.

"I would never do that. My years as an M.P. trained me on how important evidence is to catch a suspect. I gave you my clothes and jacket. Did you find any of the victim's blood on them?" She would turn the tables and question him.

Quinn had a glint in his eyes. He'd known she had planned to retaliate at his statement. "You know there hasn't been enough time for the clothes to even get to a lab to be tested."

"Was the victim cooking meth to sell himself or for someone else?" Dela asked.

"I would think you would know that since you trashed the equipment." Quinn held her gaze.

"I didn't go in the house, and I didn't know he was making meth until you told me." She peered back at him, steadily.

Her phone rang. It was in her bedroom. Dela started to pull her crutches up when Heath stood.

"I'll get that for you." He jogged down the hall and came back, handing her the phone.

It was Marty. "Hey," she answered.

"I'm going to be late. Ummm… so will Molly. I never made it home last night," Marty said.

Dela grinned. "I see. Well, there's no hurry. I have company."

There was silence. "Why don't you text me when you're alone."

"Sounds like a plan." She ended the call.

"Who was that?" Quinn asked.

"Marty. He wanted to let me know Molly would be late coming over to check out my new pet. It appears the two of them spent the night together." She smiled, happy for her friend who had been in a bad first marriage. Dela met Marty when she went to work at the casino and had never seen or heard him deride or hurt anyone with words or fists.

Quinn studied her. "Why did Marty call you? I would have thought your friend would call."

"That half of a drink I had last night that made me fuzzy? Molly had two and the last half of mine. I'll be surprised if she even makes it out of bed before noon." Dela glanced at Heath.

"Yeah, she was pretty wasted when they left the bar last night," Heath added.

"Did you tell me the name of the place?" Quinn's

pen was poised over his notepad.

"The Rowdy Spur," Heath said.

"I heard they have good food." Quinn glanced up from his scribbling.

"It was a fun night out, given the mess my life has turned into," Dela said.

Heath rose and started brewing another cup of coffee.

"Don't you need to go to work?" Quinn asked.

Her friend faced the FBI agent. "Today is my day off. I know with a homicide you'd think I'd be needed but I was asked to take my two days off by Detective Jones. He seems to think he has this homicide all but closed." Heath studied Quinn. "Are you feeling the same way?"

Quinn stared defiantly back at Heath. "I'm following the evidence."

"The word of an old woman who may have lost track of the time she saw me fighting with Winter and when she walked over to check on him." Dela slid her unfinished breakfast to the middle of the table. She would have stood and left the room but she didn't want Quinn to see her stump sticking out below her shorts.

The Special Agent sat back in his chair. "She is a reliable witness. She stated what time she saw you fighting. It had been right as she had finished a television show she likes and was headed to the bathroom. She said you and the victim were struggling, you both went down, and she saw you standing with a knife in your hand."

"Then she should have seen me walk to the shed, put the knife in there, and go catch Jethro," Dela said. "If she didn't see me put the knife in the shed then she didn't stay by the window to see what happened."

"How much time had elapsed from the time she saw the fight until she checked on the victim?" Heath asked.

Quinn stood. "I'm not giving you our evidence. And don't go down there and harass the woman." He stared at Dela.

"What about Mrs. Winter? Did she vouch that she'd asked me to go get Jethro and she'd told me that her husband wouldn't be there?" Dela asked.

The muscle in Quinn's jaw twitched. "She wouldn't talk to me."

Dela rejoiced on the inside. "Oh. Well, I hope you find someone she will talk to. She is the reason I collected the donkey. I was asked."

Heath walked to the front door. "I hope when you and Detective Jones discover the real murderer, you'll both personally apologize to Dela." He held the door open, waiting.

Quinn glanced at Dela and walked to the door. Before stepping through he said, "For your sake, I hope you stay out of this investigation. If you stick your nose in, it will only muddy up the evidence."

Chapter Eleven

Dela texted Marty as soon as the door closed.

"I'm getting dressed. You can use my car to run home and get some clean clothes and come back," she said, pushing up onto her crutches. "We have work to do. I want to have a talk with Mrs. Swan."

"We'll have to be careful. After Quinn's comment, I wouldn't put it past him to have someone watching her house to see if you try to talk to her." Heath picked up the dishes on the table and placed them in the sink.

"Do we know who her family is? And maybe her habits? We could talk to her someplace other than her house." Dela had wanted to check on the woman's mental state from the beginning. The time frame didn't work. Winter had to have been killed a good twenty minutes to a half-hour after she'd left him for it to have happened after Heath had driven out to check on him and been called away.

"I do know who her daughter is. She works at the

travel center. After Marty gets here, we can go talk to her." Heath headed to the front door. "I'll be back in thirty minutes."

"I'll be dressed by then." Dela heard the front door close as she swung into her room.

♠ ♣ ♥ ♦

When Marty arrived, he was followed by Molly. Dela and Marty stood watching Molly check over Jethro.

"He seems to be in good condition. I'd say he's about ten. You'll have him for a good twenty more years if Mrs. Winter doesn't take him back." Molly released Jethro's lips after looking at his teeth.

"Twenty years? I hope she or her son does. I'm not sure I want to have an animal I can't take with me on trips." Dela patted Mugshot's head as they watched the donkey's check-up.

The sound of another vehicle arriving had to be Heath.

"We're in the backyard," Dela called out.

The gate opened and Detective Dick stepped through.

Mugshot growled and Jethro's ears went back.

Her home had become a magnet for law enforcement. "Can I help you?" she asked the detective who stared at the donkey and then Marty and Molly.

"I have some more questions. What is going on here?" Detective Dick asked.

"This is Jethro, the donkey Mrs. Winter asked me to get because he had run out of food and her husband wasn't there to take care of the animal."

"But her husband was there. Did he think you were stealing his donkey?" Dick pointed to Jethro.

"I don't know what he thought. He attacked me

before I could say anything. Once he was no longer a threat—"

"Dead." Dick peered at her.

"No, not dead, holding his crotch. I haltered Jethro and walked him back here. Molly is checking his medical condition." She decided to see if she could get anything out of the man. "Did you talk to the neighbor? Get times when things supposedly happened?" Dela watched Molly look at the donkey's hooves rather than look at the detective.

"Mrs. Swan has given her statement."

She glanced up. He was smiling. He wasn't going to give her more than that. "What questions did you have for me?"

"We can go inside." He motioned to the French doors leading into the dining area.

"I'd rather talk to you out here where I have witnesses." She smiled.

Detective Dick frowned. "I want to know why Officer Seaver didn't bring in the clothes you were wearing during the attack? FBI Special Agent Pierce had to make an extra trip to get the clothing from you."

"Because you sent Officer Seaver here to collect clothing with blood on them, which he didn't find in my house because I didn't kill Mr. Winter. And while he was searching my house, I was sitting in your interview room, wearing some of the clothes I had on during the attack, talking to you." She stared at him. He didn't flinch at her being sarcastic about the clothes being in front of his face the whole time.

"Did Special Agent Pierce tell you about the person who tried to break into my house last night?" She studied the man. His eyebrows rose and the sneer on his lips puckered. "I see by the surprise on your face he didn't. I called him last night and told him. Agent Pierce came by here first thing this morning for my statement. You might want to work more closely with the FBI."

"Tell me about this supposed break-in?" He pulled out a book.

"I'm not going through it again. You can look at Special Agent Pierce's notes." She heard another vehicle. She hoped Heath didn't come back here. It would only give this man more reason to keep him off the case.

It was several minutes before the gate opened and Travis walked through carrying some posts. "Hey! I didn't know you were having a party." He and Melvin carried the posts into the backyard and set them down.

"It's not a party. Your mom is checking out Jethro. Marty came with her. And Detective Jones was just leaving," Dela said.

The man glared at all of them and pointed at her. "Just because you have these people fooled into thinking you aren't a killer, doesn't mean I'll fall for your innocent act." He stomped over to the gate and disappeared.

She let out a deep sigh. "I wish that man would go away and let someone who is more open-minded take over the case."

"Like Heath?" Molly asked.

"I'm glad he believes in me, but they would never let him take on this case because of our past." Dela was happy for that past and his belief in her.

"What about Quinn?" Marty asked.

Dela humphed. "He has a more open mind than Dick, but he isn't happy that Heath and I are spending so much time together, which could taint his motivations. And he believes the eye witness." Focusing on the posts the young men had dropped in her yard, she asked, "What are you doing with those? I thought the fence was finished."

"It is. But we need to build the gate from the backyard to the pasture and the gate from the pasture to the driveway." Travis walked to the backyard fence. "I thought we'd put it here in the middle. We'll make it in what's called Dutch door fashion. You'll be able to open the top and let Jethro look over into the yard and see Mugshot, or Mugshot can look over and see Jethro. Or you can close both the top and bottom."

"Where do you come up with these great ideas?" Dela asked. The young man had impressed her with his insights into her remodel, the dog house, and now this gate.

Travis's face reddened. "I like reading online building blogs."

Dela faced Molly. "You should be very proud of this young man."

"I am." Molly's face glowed with pride.

Heath walked into the yard from the house.

"Dick was just here," Dela said.

"I know. I spotted the car and went around the corner. I waited for him to leave. I didn't expect all of you would be outside." He stood with his hands on his hips. "We need to get some backyard chairs and a barbeque."

"We?" Molly said, studying Dela.

These were her friends and they'd learn soon enough. "When I'm cleared of this murder, Heath is moving in as a roommate."

"Is that what you old people call it these days?" Travis asked while he was bent over measuring the back fence.

Molly and Marty burst out laughing. Heath grinned, and Dela was happy her friends didn't seem to think it was strange.

Molly finished with Jethro's check-up and left.

Dela, Heath, and Marty decided to all go in one car and see if they could learn more about Mrs. Swan from her daughter.

At the travel center, they stopped inside the door. Dela had been here on various occasions for one or two grocery items on her way home from work. It also had a gift shop of sorts for the interstate travelers who came in for snacks and drinks and everything a truck driver would need while traveling across the country.

Heath walked over to a woman stocking shelves. "Hi, Ruth."

The woman in her early fifties glanced up. "What do you want, Heath? I have work to do." She continued putting boxes of cereal on the shelf, ignoring him.

"I was wondering where I could find your mom. I have some questions for her."

Ruth straightened, shoving her hands on her hips. "You police have been harassing her enough. She did her duty by calling you when she found Paul. Leave her alone."

Dela stepped forward. "If you don't want your mom bothered, maybe you could answer our questions."

Ruth studied Dela. "Who are you?"

"A neighbor who is concerned about Ina." Dela didn't think the woman would answer questions if Ruth knew she was the woman her mother said killed her neighbor.

"Ina? She's living on another reservation. She

wasn't even home when Paul was killed." Ruth continued to study Dela.

"Had Paul been staying at the house?" Heath asked.

The woman shifted her gaze to him. "I don't know. I visit my mom once a week when I take her to her doctor appointments. My nephew, Levi, takes her shopping every other week and visits her in between. You could ask him."

"Where can I find Levi?" Heath asked.

"He works at Yellowhawk. He is in behavioral health. It is *Pyaxí*."

Dela shook her head. She didn't know what the word *pyaxí* meant.

Heath said. "Thank you for your help."

Dela and Marty followed Heath out of the travel center. "We'll find him in the green department at the health center. *Pyaxí* means bitterroot which is green,"

When they were all seated in Dela's car, Heath said, "Three of us walking in and asking Levi questions might make him nervous. Marty, why don't you walk around and visit with people in public health, and ask about Mrs. Swan's living conditions. It's *wíwnu*, it means huckleberry and reflects the purple department."

At the main entrance to the building, they split up. Marty followed the signs indicating public health and Dela and Heath followed the green signs to behavioral health.

A receptionist looked up from where she was typing on a keyboard. "May I help you?"

"We're looking for Levi?" Heath said.

Dela hoped there was only one Levi in this department because they hadn't asked his aunt for a last name.

"He is in a session at the moment. If you want to wait, he'll be finished in fifteen minutes." The woman indicated a row of padded chairs.

She had nowhere to be and it was Heath's day off. They sat.

They couldn't discuss what they would ask the man, since the receptionist was sitting only twelve feet away.

Dela leaned toward Heath. "You need to be careful," she whispered. "Detective Dick is out to get you."

"I've had a target on my back since I returned and took this job. Even though he's retiring, he's not happy to have me take over. And there were two other locals who had applied for the position of MDI. They weren't happy to not be picked." He'd said all of this as a whisper in her ear.

She leaned back and studied him. "I didn't even know there were that many Medicolegal Death Investigators in the area."

"Ever since the implementing of the 'Safe Trails Task Force' which brings all the local law enforcement together on a reservation when there is trouble, many of the tribal police officers have taken the MDI training." Heath leaned back. "I took the training when I was in South Dakota."

Dela was impressed with the man Heath had become. In high school he hadn't known what he wanted to do after he graduated. That and feeling it was her fault Robin had been killed, Dela had pushed him away and set off for the Army.

A dozen men of varying ages sauntered down the hallway toward the lobby where she and Heath waited. From the look of the men, they had been at a sobering meeting. They all stared down at the multi-colored carpet. They didn't talk. They kept their distance from one another. When the last man had walked out into the main hall, the receptionist picked up her phone.

"Levi, there is a couple out here waiting to talk to you." She replaced the phone. "He'll be out in a few minutes."

Dela glanced at Heath to see what he thought of the woman thinking they were a couple.

He just winked at her.

A man in his early thirties walked down the hall toward them. He wore his dark hair long, flowing over his shoulders. He was dressed in jeans, a t-shirt, and athletic shoes.

Dela wasn't sure what she'd expected, but it wasn't this man who looked like he'd just stepped out of a pickup game at a basketball court.

He walked up to Heath and held out his hand. "I'm Levi Murdoch. How can I help you?"

Heath stood, shook hands, and motioned to Dela. "We'd like to ask you some questions about your grandmother."

The man's gaze roamed over both their faces. "I thought you were here for a marital consultation." He glanced over at the receptionist.

She shrugged. "They just said they wanted to talk to you."

"Come back to my office. I'm not sure why you are worried about my grandmother. She still has all her faculties and gets around well." Levi led them down the hall to a small room without any windows.

He sat down on a chair and motioned for them to take what her mom called a love seat. It was like a couch but smaller. She and Heath sat touching shoulders.

"Now, what did you really want to come see me about?" Levi asked, his gaze bouncing back and forth between her and Heath.

"We aren't a couple and we don't need counseling." Dela had a brief glimpse of Levi Murdoch's Master's diploma for couples counseling hanging on the wall.

The man younger than both she and Heath studied them. "You are at ease with one another. Are you work partners?"

Heath shook his head. "I'm with the tribal police, and Ms. Alvaro is head of security at the casino."

Levi's eyebrows rose. "Why are you wanting to talk to me about my grandmother? She doesn't believe in gambling."

"We're here to ask you if she's talked to you about what happened Tuesday. Her finding Mr. Winter." Heath pulled out a notepad as if he were on duty.

The man's gaze flicked to Dela. "I don't understand. What does that have to do with the casino?"

"We have reason to believe Mr. Winter was conducting unlawful dealings at the casino," Dela said, not looking at Heath to see what he thought of her half-truth.

"I see. Well, she talked to me after finding the body. She was upset. I had Barbara cancel my appointments for the rest of the day and stayed with my grandmother until she calmed down and felt safe."

"Why didn't she feel safe?" Heath asked.

"She was afraid the woman who killed Mr. Winter would come after her. She saw them fighting and thought the woman might have seen her." Levi narrowed his eyes. "I heard the woman worked at the casino." He glared at Heath. "Why aren't you in uniform if you're really with the tribal police?"

Heath pulled his badge from a pocket and showed the man. "I am with the police. Can you tell me where I could catch up with your grandmother today? She wasn't at home when I went by."

Levi appeared skeptical even though Heath had shown his badge.

Dela hoped the man would cooperate.

"It's Thursday. She meets friends at the museum coffee shop in the morning and will be home later. But she has nothing more to tell you than what she already did." He stood. "I have an appointment in five minutes."

"Thank you for your time," Heath said, walking to the door.

Dela wanted to ask so many more questions but it was evident the man had shut that down as skillfully as he ushered them out of his office.

"Why do you think he's being so protective of his grandmother?" Dela asked. "I would think if she feared for her life, he would want to do everything he could to make her less fearful."

"Have you ever met Mrs. Swan?" Heath asked as they walked out of the building and spotted Marty leaning against her car.

"No. I've waved to her a time or two when I'd see her out in her yard as Mugshot and I jogged by." She sighed. "I'd like to talk to her and find out if she's the one who told Ina her husband wasn't at the house anymore."

Heath stopped at the car. He glanced at Marty. "I think you and Marty need to go to Colville and talk to Ina. Face to face. That way you can tell if she is telling you the truth."

Dela was up for the road trip. She glanced at Marty. "You want to go?"

He shrugged. "I don't have anything else to do since I'm on vacation."

Once they were all in the car, Marty told them what he'd learned. "Mrs. Swan and her "hunky" grandson. Not my words, that was from Lucy Farr. Spend Wednesday afternoons together. He takes her shopping. He also visits her a couple times a week in the evening. Since his sister died, he spends a lot of time with his grandmother."

"Doesn't he have other siblings or a mother or father?" Dela asked, driving back to her house.

"It seems his grandmother raised Levi and his younger sister. I don't know the whole story."

Dela glanced over at Heath. "I think we should ask Grandfather Thunder about Mrs. Swan and her grandchildren."

He nodded. "Drive by her house and let's see if she's home now."

Dela drove past the road she usually turned on. It was a straighter shot to her house. To go by Mrs. Swan's and the Winter house, she continued to the second right turn and then followed that road down to the corner that was the start of the Winter property. Mrs. Swan's house sat across the road from the pasture where Jethro had been.

"I don't see a car," Dela said, checking to make sure there weren't any law enforcement officers at the Winter residence before turning into Mrs. Swan's driveway.

"I'll go see if she's in." Heath slid out of the passenger seat of her car and walked up to the front door.

"Did Lucy ask you why you wanted to know about Mrs. Swan?" Dela asked Marty, peering at him in the rearview mirror.

"Not really. I just said I was asking for a friend who wanted to visit with Mrs. Swan." He shrugged. "She didn't seem to care about sharing information. It wasn't like I was asking anything confidential."

Heath returned. "She's not home."

Dela backed up and headed to her driveway. As soon as she turned off the engine, the barking and braying could be heard. "I think they are happy I've returned," she said, smiling. It was nice to come home to someone, even if it was animals that were happy to see her.

"It looks like Travis finished the gates," Marty said, staring at the one in the fence beside where she'd parked. "Want to give me a ride home? Or I can call Molly to come get me."

Dela glanced at the two men. They both needed rides home. "Let me feed Mugshot and Jethro and I'll take you both home."

"I'll toss the hay over if you want to take care of Mugshot," Heath said.

She unlocked the front door and crossed the living room to the dining room where she opened the door to the backyard. Mugshot shoved his head through the opening, waiting for his usual ear scratching. Dela scratched his ears and told him he was a good boy. Then she filled his dish with food and carried it to the yard.

"You have a lot of cleanup to do back here," Heath said, kicking at a pile of donkey droppings.

"Tomorrow, I can put them both out in the pasture

and pick up the piles." She noticed that Travis had left the top half of the gate open. "I wonder if Jethro has been looking out?"

"If so, he would probably rather have the fresh green grass peeking out of the dried last year's grass than this dry hay." Heath walked to the back door. "I can hang out here longer if you want?"

She shook her head. "I might as well drop you both off at the same time." After a short discussion in her head, with herself, she said. "If you want to grab a pizza and come back about seven, I'd be ready for dinner."

Heath's face lit up. "I can do that."

They walked through the house and out the front door. Heath made sure both doors were locked. On the drive to drop Heath off at his mom's and then Marty at his place in Pendleton, they had come up with the questions Dela and Marty needed to ask Ina the following day.

Driving back to Tutuilla, Dela hoped Ina would cooperate when she was questioned. It bothered her that the woman hadn't returned her call from yesterday.

Chapter Twelve

It was a four-hour drive from the Umatilla Reservation to Nespelem, Washington and the Colville Reservation. Heath had learned the address where Ina was staying from Jacob Red Bear. Her best friend's brother felt bad that he hadn't asked more questions of Mrs. Swan when he talked to her. After the FBI came into the case, he'd been sent back to his regular duties. Quinn knew he and Dela had history and wanted to make sure he was kept out of the loop.

"Have you been here before?" she asked Marty.

"No. I grew up in Portland. My mother and father put us through schools that were predominantly white. I've always been fascinated by other cultures." He sipped from the liter of cola he'd brought with him. "When I saw the job opening at the casino for a surveillance head, I thought it might be a good way to learn more about Native American life."

"And what have you learned?" Dela followed the

automated voice on her GPS to turn at the next corner.

"That the Umatilla People are open and willing to share their heritage. I think it's cool."

Dela pulled up to a small house. "This is the house Ina and her son were given to live in." She slid out of her car and walked up to the door.

Marty joined her and she knocked.

The door opened. The boy, Dela recognized from the photo she'd seen the night she'd helped Ina, stared up at them.

"Hi, Micah. We're friends of your mom's. We'd like to speak to her." Dela smiled.

The boy studied them and slammed the door. The sound of running feet faded behind the door.

"Do you think he is afraid of us?" Marty asked.

"It's hard to say." Dela raised her hand to knock again when the door opened.

Ina stood on the other side of the threshold.

"Hi, Ina. You didn't return my call." Dela motioned to the door. "Could we come in?"

The woman nodded. Her face was fuller, the color back in her cheeks, but her eyes were still wary. She opened the door wider, allowing them entrance.

Dela sat in one of the two chairs in the small living room. Marty sat on the stool by her chair, while Ina and her son sat on the love seat.

"How are you and Micah doing?" Dela started with.

The woman relaxed. "Good. My cousin watches Micah when I work." Her gaze drifted around the room. "This is nice. Small, easy to keep clean."

"You look good." Dela smiled. Then she started with why she was here. "Why did you think Paul wasn't at your house the day you called me?"

Her cheeks flushed. "When I'd talked to Sadie, she said he hadn't been there in over a week. That meant she was trying to take care of Jethro."

"Jethro!" the boy said excitedly.

Dela smiled at the boy. "He's at my place. He has a new friend, my dog, Mugshot. They hang out together during the day when I'm at work." She pulled out her phone and showed him a photo she'd taken of the donkey and the dog.

Micah laughed. "Funny friends."

"Yes, they are. But they do like one another."

"I'm glad I called you. Sadie said she didn't know when Jethro had been watered and she couldn't find any more hay to feed him. That's why I asked you to get him." She stopped and swallowed. "I didn't mean for you to…to…"

"Be accused of his death?" Dela filled in.

"Yes." Ina nodded her head.

"Would you mind if Marty took Micah outside to play?" Dela asked, motioning to the back of the house.

"Micah, go outside and play with this man, Marty," Ina said, helping her son off the couch.

The boy studied his mother, before running toward the back door. Marty followed at a slower pace.

"I didn't kill Paul," Dela started. "But I did get in a fight with him. When I went to get Jethro, Paul came at me with a knife."

"Oh, no!" Ina put a hand to her mouth, her eyes wide with fright.

"I managed to get the knife away and hurt him bad enough that he left me alone. But when I walked away from there leading Jethro, your husband was alive." Dela shook her head. "But Mrs. Swan, Sadie, told the police she saw the fight and I had the knife in my hand.

When she went over to check on Paul, he was dead with the knife stabbed in his chest."

Ina wailed.

Dela studied the woman. Could she possibly still love the man who had nearly killed her? She moved to the love seat and put an arm around the woman. "I'm sorry, I shouldn't have told you so bluntly what happened."

"No, it's good. You aren't telling me anything I don't know. The FBI man was here. He told me how Paul died. And he said you did it." Ina stared into her eyes. "I didn't believe it when the Fed told me, but I remembered how you had fought hard with Paul and beat him before."

"I'm trying to find out who bought the meth your husband cooked. I think it has something to do with his manufacturing the drug that got him killed." Dela straightened and sat studying the woman. "How long had he been cooking in your house? I didn't see it the night I saved you." She'd run that night over and over in her mind. She hadn't seen any signs of the drug cooking apparatus when she'd gone in for the washcloth or the blanket. She'd opened the door to every room when she'd thought there'd been a child hiding.

"I told him if he didn't quit doing it at our home, I would send Micah away. He didn't stop, I sent Micah away." She sniffed. "Then he cleaned up everything and ordered me to get Micah back. I told him, not until he proved he wasn't cooking anymore." She sucked in air. "He hit me good and hard that night, knocking me out. A week later after he asked every night for me to bring Micah back, I heard him talking on the phone. He was talking about needing more supplies. I knew he hadn't quit. That's when I vowed I would not bring my son back to that man."

Dela nodded. "What phone did he use to talk to the man about supplies?"

"He had a cell phone that he only used for talking to the man who bought from him."

Making a mental note to see if Jacob could find out about the phone, Dela asked, "What about Daniel Booth? We have a photo of him and your husband talking to a known drug dealer."

"I told Daniel not to get caught up in anything Paul did. But he likes money. Easy money. He knows all about the cooking and whom they did it for."

"Ina, I appreciate all this information you're giving me. But the tribals say you have money that Paul was supposed to use for supplies." Dela watched as the woman's face went from sad to worried.

"If the police think that, the man, the one who gave Paul the money, will be looking for me." She frantically looked around the room as if the person was hiding in the corners or behind the chair.

"Do you have the money? I could find a way to get it back to the man so he doesn't hurt you or Micah." Dela knew it was a risk, but it was one she was willing to take.

Ina stared at her. "I took the money to use to get away from Paul. I no longer need it. But I did use some."

"How much?" Dela hoped it wasn't enough to make Sander mad.

"Almost five hundred. I used it for food and clothes and toys for Micah." She stood. "If I give it to you, do you think you can get it back to Daniel? He will know who it belongs to."

"I'll make sure it gets back to the owner so you don't have to worry." Dela stood, watching the woman leave the room.

Ina returned with a small backpack. "I used this to carry the money." She held it out to Dela. "Please, take it away."

Dela grabbed the bag. She texted Marty to meet her at the car. "Thank you for talking to me. The FBI agent was angry you hadn't talked to him."

The woman shook her head. "I couldn't. He would have arrested me for having that money."

"But I do need you to call and tell him that you sent me to get the donkey. Right now, they are saying I was caught by your husband while stealing Jethro. And that in the altercation I killed Paul." Dela stared the woman in the eyes. "I didn't kill him. I did take the knife away from him and put it in the shed."

Ina swallowed, holding her gaze. "I have his card. I will tell him I had called you."

"Thank you." Dela walked out of the house with the bag of money.

Marty raised his eyebrows but lowered down onto the passenger seat.

She tossed the bag in his lap. "Count that on the way back. I want to know how much is there when we give it back to Sander."

♠ ♣ ♥ ♦

Dela called Heath on the drive back and asked him to find Daniel Booth. They needed to make sure the money was from Sander before she waltzed into his home and handed the money over.

"You're not handing that money back to him," Heath said.

"I promised Ina I'd make sure whoever the money

110

belonged to wouldn't come after her." Dela wasn't going to hand the money over to the tribal police or the FBI.

"I'll talk to Booth and he and I will take it to Sander or whoever it belongs to."

"You aren't going to turn it over to the police?" Dela asked.

He blew out a breath. "If I turned it over to them, they would ask me where I got it. I'd have to say the victim's wife gave it to you and you gave it to me. It would look like you and the wife were working together to get rid of her husband."

"We weren't!" Dela hadn't thought about her seeing the woman would make them both look guilty.

"I know you weren't. But the way Detective Jones likes to spin things, he could get the Chief thinking along those lines. Just take the money to your house and I'll go find Booth." Heath ended the call.

Dela glanced over at Marty. The phone had been on the speaker. "Can this get any more screwed up?"

Chapter Thirteen

After dropping Marty off, Dela drove straight home. She didn't want to be caught with the money. At her house, she carried the backpack in and hid it in the guest bath linen closet behind the towels. Not that anyone other than Ina, Heath, and Marty knew she had it, but she was paranoid. Too many people believed she'd killed someone. Who knew when they would decide to search her house again?

She froze. If they did, they'd find the money and think…that she'd been paid to kill Paul? She wished she had an outbuilding. Travis was planning to build one.

Opening the door to let Mugshot in, she spotted the dog house. "Let's go have a look inside your roomy house." She walked across the yard with the dog and donkey following her. On her hands and knees, she stuck her head in the house. It was quite roomy. She could put the bag in a small tote and hide it in the corner.

Dela backed out and sat on the grass. She scratched Mugshot's head. "You wouldn't mind guarding a box, would you?"

He licked her cheek and she laughed. "That's what I thought."

Jethro had walked over to see what they were doing. He nudged Mugshot to the side and put his head with long fuzzy ears in front of Dela.

"I can pet you, too." She scratched his forehead and stroked his ears before moving to prepare to stand. Both animals moved to either side of her. She used them to help push up to her feet. "Thank you, gentlemen."

In the house, she found a small tote with paperwork in it. She dumped it out on her bed and carried it to the guest bathroom.

A knock on the door stopped her hands from pulling the towels out. Her heart thudded in her chest.

"Dela, it's me, Heath!"

She let out the breath she'd been holding and walked out to the front door. Mugshot was whining and wagging his tail. Dela opened the door and stepped back.

"I found out that money came from Sander. Booth doesn't want to go with me when I return it." He shut the door as he talked.

"You shouldn't go alone." Dela led the way into the kitchen. She poured two glasses of iced tea and set them on the table.

Heath sat down and guzzled half a glass of tea before asking, "How'd your trip go, besides bringing a drug dealer's money back?"

Dela stopped the glass she'd been raising to her

mouth. "I was just getting ready to hide the money in Mugshot's dog house. I told Ina to call Quinn and tell him she had asked me to get Jethro. But I thought, what if she also tells him about the money? Then they'd think she paid me to kill Paul." She was talking fast as the scenario flashed through her mind again.

"Calm down. I'll take that with me now and give it back to Sander."

"She said she spent about five hundred of it. If he counts the money, he'll know it's missing." Dela had been trying to figure out how to make up for the discrepancy. But it was late and she didn't want to cash a check that large at the casino. It might cause attention.

"I'll let him know Winter's widow spent some of the money. I'm sure he'll let it go since he has most of it back." Heath finished off the glass of tea and stood. "I better go now and get this over with."

"Don't go by yourself. You're a cop and he might not like the idea of you knowing why he paid that to Paul." Dela stood. "I can go by and pick up Marty. We can return the money."

"I'm not having you two walk into that drug dealer's house alone." Heath took a step toward her.

"I won't be alone. I'll have Marty and you'll be outside." She pulled out her phone and dialed Marty.

"Yo, what's up?" Marty answered.

"Heath says the money does go to Sander. You want to go with me to return it?"

There was a pause. "Just you and me? When?"

"Tonight. Heath will be outside. I don't think it would be good for Heath to hand money over to a drug dealer. You don't know who might be watching." That thought had crossed her mind when Heath said he'd take the money. Especially if Booth knew about the money being returned.

"You want to pick me up at Molly's?"

"We can do that." Dela ended the call. "We're to pick him up at Molly's," she said, walking to the back door. "Out Mugshot. I'll be back soon."

The large dog walk/hopped out and turned around watching her through the plate glass window on the door.

"It's not a good idea, you taking money back to Sander," Heath said as she walked down the hall to her bedroom to grab the bag of money.

She returned with the child-sized pack. "We know no one at the tribal police will believe where I got it and at this point, I'm not sure Quinn wouldn't think I'd be lying as well. Maybe when we give this back, Sander will oblige us with whether or not he killed Paul." Dela walked to the coat rack and slipped on a coat. The wind had picked up and there had been a forecast of snow in the mountains.

They exited the house and she slid into the driver's side of her car. Heath surprised her by opening a back door.

"You can sit up front," she said, starting the vehicle.

"This way I don't have to swap with Marty. It would look funny for him to get out of the backseat and if you happen to be followed by anyone, they will just see you pick up Marty and won't know I'm back here."

She glanced in the rearview mirror as Heath slumped down in the back seat. It would make sense if a tribal or county cop saw her driving around, they may decide to follow and see what she was doing.

Leaving her house, she took the direct route to the highway, not passing the crime scene or Mrs. Swan's house. If a policeman happened to be at either place, they might become suspicious of her out driving around.

She crossed the highway and drove by the casino, her gaze lingering on all the vehicles in the parking lot. It was a busy night and she wasn't there to help out. In the back of her mind, she hoped they had an altercation that Kenny couldn't handle and needed her help. It would show Bernie Moon and the board of trustees they had been hasty in asking her to take a leave of absence. Just as quickly as that flashed through her mind, she was ashamed to wish Kenny couldn't handle a situation. She liked her second in command and knew he was capable.

At Mission Market, she headed west toward Pendleton. "Where does Sander live?" she asked.

"He's on the hill north of the Umatilla River off highway 30."

The glow of Heath's phone in the back seat had her asking, "Do you think just showing up at his house is a good idea?"

"I was thinking when we stop to pick up Marty you can call Sander from Molly's landline and ask for a meeting to give him back his property." Heath's tone didn't sound sure.

"Don't tell him what I have?" She wondered whether or not the man would even meet her not knowing what she had to give him.

"No. Just tell him you know he would like to have it back and ask where he'd like to meet you tonight."

"I'm using the landline so the call won't be found by someone looking through our cell phones?" she asked.

"Yes. Law enforcement would have to have access

to Sander's records to see where the call came from. I wrote the number on this slip of paper." He tapped her shoulder.

She pulled into Molly's veterinary practice parking lot, grabbed the piece of paper, and exited the car.

Marty was walking across the yard toward her.

"I need to use Molly's landline," she said. "Go ahead and get in the car and Heath will fill you in." Dela continued up to Molly's door and knocked.

"What did you forget—" Molly opened the door with a wide smile. The smile remained but the merriment in her eyes dulled. "Oh, I thought Marty was meeting you."

"He is. I just need to make a call from your landline." She walked over to the phone, read the number on the paper, and dialed.

"Hello?" a woman's voice answered.

"Hi, could I speak with Mr. Sander, please," Dela asked, trying to sound business-like so the woman didn't think her husband was fooling around.

"What is this about?" the woman asked in a tone as icy as the winter wind that gusted off the Blue Mountains.

At a loss for words without knowing if this woman, Dela suspected was Mrs. Sander, knew anything about her husband's meth business, she said, "I have something he lost and would like to return it."

"You can take it to his business office tomorrow," the woman said.

"No. I would prefer to give it back to him tonight. Please, if he's there would you put him on the phone." Dela never liked to beg, but this was an instance when she wanted this money as far from her as she could get it, as soon as she could.

"Gus! Gus, there's a phone call for you!" the woman yelled, showing her irritation at whoever had called. The phone clunked down and the sound of someone walking away faded.

Dela glanced at Molly. Her friend was watching with a hint of fear in her eyes.

The phone scraped. "Who is this?" a male voice bellowed.

"I have the money you gave Paul Winter. I'd like to give it back to you tonight. Where can we meet?" Dela clipped the words off in a no-nonsense manner.

"You have the money his wife stole?" the man said in a loud whisper.

"Yes. She wanted you to have it so you don't come after her or her son." Dela remained calm, waiting for the man to decide what he wanted worse—the money or revenge on the woman.

"I'll meet you in thirty minutes at Harry's Bar. I'll be in the back booth." He hung up.

Dela smiled. She knew the seedy bar that had been in Pendleton since before prohibition. Rumor was the underground tunnels that provided a tourist attraction in Pendleton these days had at one time ended or began at Harry's.

"Thanks, Molly. I'll try to get Marty back here in an hour."

"Just bring him back in one piece," Molly said, studying Dela.

"Heath is with us and I'm meeting this guy in a public place. We should be fine. I'm more worried about law enforcement seeing me than being hurt by the bad guys." Dela exited Molly's house and walked over to her car.

Marty was sitting in the driver's seat. Dela didn't

say anything, she opened the passenger side and slid in.

"We're meeting at Harry's Bar," she said.

"I know where that is," Marty replied and backed the car, turning and leaving the veterinary's parking lot.

"That's going to make it hard for me to keep an eye on you two," Heath said.

"Sander said he'd be in the booth in the back. Maybe you can come in the back door and be somewhere behind him…" Dela offered.

"At least it's in a public place," Heath said.

Dela shifted in her seat to look back at Heath. "I think he was hesitant to meet. He might think this is some kind of a set-up. I didn't give my name. I just said I had the money he gave to Paul Winter. That his wife gave it to me to return."

"And he fell for it?" Marty asked.

"Not completely. If that guy he was with in the casino is there, we'll know he doesn't trust us." Dela faced forward as they entered Pendleton city limits. She didn't want anyone watching to see her talking to someone in the back seat.

"Let me out a couple of blocks behind the bar. Then give me time to walk there and get inside before you park and enter." Heath's voice was calm. His directions were good because Dela's stomach had started twisting and her mind was wondering why she'd offered to hand the money back to the drug dealer.

Marty did as Heath asked, barely stopping long enough for the door to open and close before rolling away from the curb and down the block.

"How long do you think it will take Heath to get inside the bar?" Dela asked.

"We'll give him fifteen minutes." Marty pulled over a block before the bar and they sat in the car, staring at the front of the brick building with grungy windows that no longer let light in or out. There was a good crowd filing through the doors in both directions. After all, it was Friday night.

Just as Marty pulled away from the curb, a city cruiser parked in front of the bar with the lights blinking. Two policemen jumped out and ran into Harry's.

Chapter Fourteen

"Great! I hope Sander doesn't think I called the police." Dela sat in the passenger seat as Marty drove into the bar's small parking lot. Five bikers ran out the back of the building and hopped on motorcycles parked in a corner of the lot. They took off as a policeman appeared at the back of the building.

"Let's go in while the place is buzzing with the biker's escape," Dela said. She grabbed the small pack from the back seat and followed Marty into the dark, stagnant building. The voices of people talking were more like yelling to be heard over the blaring music. Even the clank of pool balls banging together seemed amplified.

Marty made a path, through the people standing around tall tables, toward the back of the room. There were three booths along the back wall. Sander and the man who'd accompanied him at the casino sat in a corner booth away from the tall tables.

Dela didn't like sliding to the inside of the booth, but Marty was more able to get up faster if trouble started. She'd held the small pack down by her side as she'd entered and crossed the establishment. Now she had it on the bench between her and the wall.

Sander's eyes widened at the sight of her. "Aren't you head of security at the casino?"

She nodded. "I'm also a neighbor of the Winters."

The man nodded. "I hear you are also the leading suspect in Paul's death." His lips tipped up in a smirk.

"I didn't kill him, but I've been wondering if your friend there," she motioned to the large man who had cleared out the booth next to them, "might not have killed him while looking for the money."

Sander continued to grin, though it wasn't genuine. His steely gray eyes peered at her. "Neither I, nor my associates, killed Paul. He was an asset to my business when he wasn't raging about his wife taking away his boy."

"Can you think of anyone who might have wanted him dead?" Dela asked, her fingers digging into the pack.

"Besides you?"

"I have never wished him dead and I didn't kill him. Since you say it wasn't you, who else had problems with the man?" Dela stopped as a waitress arrived.

"I'll have a beer," Marty said.

"Water for me," Dela said.

Sander ordered another of what he had and patted the woman on the backside as she walked away. Dela cringed at his blatant disregard for the woman's feelings.

"Whose feathers had Paul ruffled lately?" Dela

asked.

"Besides his wife's and yours?" Sander wasn't making this easy.

She had wondered if he'd know who she was, and now he used that knowledge to yank her around.

"Besides the two people who I know didn't kill him." Dela leaned back as the waitress delivered their drinks. Sander gave the woman a fifty and told her to keep the change. Dela thought she'd be less irritated at a man who paid well to pat her butt, however, the last drunk that had touched her inappropriately had ended up with a bloody nose and in the stockade overnight.

Sander sipped his drink and studied her. "Why do you care?"

"Because as you said, I'm the number one suspect and the dumb Fed and Tribal Police aren't looking any farther." She picked up her ice water. "I didn't do it and I plan on finding out who did. If it's not you, then you better give me some names because I'll keep digging into you and your 'business' if you don't."

She felt Marty shift nervously, and Sander's eyes narrowed.

"Are you threatening me?" the drug dealer practically growled.

"It's not a threat when it's the truth. I will dig for the real killer because it wasn't me. Plain and simple." She drank her water and watched him sizing her up.

"Where's the money you said you were bringing? Or did you use that as a way to get me here?" He waved his hand and his big goon stepped over to their table, standing beside Marty.

"I brought your money. Well, all but about five hundred. Ina said she spent some on food and clothes." Dela put the pack on the table and slid it across the table.

Sander pulled it down onto the bench beside him and opened the zipper. He thumbed through the contents and studied her. "I'm still not sure why you are giving this back and threatening me."

"I am only delivering it to you because Ina asked me to. She took the money to flee from Paul. She is away from him for good now and has no need for it. And as I said, I'm not threatening you. I'm merely asking for your help. You know the people through your business association with Paul who might be mad at him."

"You could try that worthless piece of shit who follows him around like a puppy dog. Booth has been trying to sell to me, saying he learned everything from Paul. I told him Paul was my man. He might have killed to sell to me." Sander glanced around the bar.

"Are you buying from Booth now that Paul is dead?" Dela asked.

Sander only shrugged.

"Anyone else? Or anything else you can think of?" Dela asked, shoving her glass of water to the middle of the table.

Marty downed the last of his beer.

"Not really. I know where you are if I think of anything."

And she knew that was a threat. His eyes were hard and filled with defiance.

♠ ♣ ♥ ♦

On the drive home, Dela filled Heath in on the conversation, with Marty adding things he felt Dela was leaving out.

"I'll have a talk with Booth tomorrow, in uniform. See what he has to say," Heath said, this time sitting in the front passenger seat as Dela drove.

She dropped Marty off at Molly's and continued down Mission and past the market to take Heath to his mom's. It was after ten and she was tired. It had been a long day.

"Don't worry. We'll find out who did this and get your name cleared." Heath put a hand on her shoulder.

"I know. I'm just tired. This sleuthing is harder when it's your own life on the line." She glanced at him and turned in his mom's driveway. "Are you working tomorrow? You said you'd talk to Daniel Booth in uniform."

"Yeah, Jacob said I'm patrolling tomorrow. I'm not allowed to look at or do anything for the homicide and neither is he."

Dela parked and shut off the engine. "I'm sorry you and Jacob are being treated unfairly because of me."

"Not because of you, for you. We both know you didn't kill Winter. If I can find something to turn Quinn's attention away from you, he has more pull and can overturn anything Jones does, patrolling and looking for anyone other than you is worth it." Heath grasped her hand. "Remember, if you do any looking around, make sure you take someone with you. Don't go talking to people or spying on people alone."

"I'll make sure I have someone with me. I think I'll take mom with me to visit Mrs. Swan. She shouldn't feel threatened if two women show up on her porch."

"Be careful."

When Dela stared at him thinking why would she need to be careful of an old woman, Heath added, "I'm more worried about someone thinking you are tampering with a witness."

Now she understood. Don't get caught speaking to the woman by Quinn or Dick. She nodded her head. "If I see any law enforcement around her house, I'll keep on driving."

"Better yet, take your mom's car. It will be less likely to catch anyone's attention." Heath opened the car door, stepped out, and leaned back into the cab. "I can't wait to get your name cleared. But be careful."

She nodded and he closed the door. Dela backed out of the driveway wondering why she should be careful when jail could be her new home if she couldn't prove someone else had killed Paul Winter.

Chapter Fifteen

Saturday morning after feeding Mugshot and Jethro, Dela called her mom while eating a bowl of cereal.

"Hello, Dela. I heard from Grandfather Thunder that you aren't working."

"That's what I'm calling about." *Grandfather Thunder.* Dela had an idea. "Mom, why don't you and Grandfather Thunder come over for lunch today? You can meet Jethro and visit a neighbor with me."

"That sounds lovely. Anything you need me to bring?"

Dela thought, *everything,* but said instead, "No, with this time off, I've been to the store."

"We'll see you at noon?" her mom asked.

"Yes. Noon." Dela ended the call, placed her empty bowl and coffee mug in the sink, and hurried down the hall to get dressed and go to the store. If Mom came over and saw the poor state of her refrigerator, she would know her daughter had lied to her.

Driving to the grocery store, Dela liked her idea even more. Not only could she ask Grandfather Thunder about Mrs. Swan's family, but his presence when they visited would also put the woman at ease.

♠ ♣ ♥ ♦

Dela returned home, unloaded six bags of groceries, and was mixing up tuna salad when there was a knock on her door.

"Come in!" she called out and continued working in the kitchen. The sound of footsteps had her glancing at the opening to the kitchen and dining room. Her hand stopped stirring as she peered into Quinn's face. "What are you doing here?"

"You're looking domestic. Is this for Heath?" Quinn walked into the room.

She felt his jealousy like a cloud heavy with rain.

"My mom and Grandfather Thunder are coming for lunch. I'd ask you to stay but, I didn't make enough for four." She tasted the mixture and added a few more chopped pickles, ignoring the man watching her.

"I had a phone call from Ina Winter. She wanted to tell me that she had called and asked you to take the donkey and that she had told you that Paul wouldn't be there. She had been told he hadn't been around for weeks and had been worried about the donkey." His monotone telling of the conversation pulled Dela's gaze to his face.

"You didn't have to come over here to tell me this." She swallowed the lump that crept up her throat as he continued to stare at her.

"I asked her why she hadn't told me this when I'd met with her."

Dela hoped the woman hadn't mentioned the

money or the visit. "And what did she say?"

"That she'd heard we thought you killed her husband." He leaned against the doorframe. "It's funny, I did tell her you were a suspect when I was there two days ago. Why would she just now decide to call me?"

Shrugging, Dela put three plates on the table along with corresponding silverware. "How should I know?"

"Word is, you and Marty have been doing a lot together lately. He's on vacation and told people at the casino he was going skiing."

"Dela, we're here!" Her mom's voice filled the house.

Walking out of the kitchen and into the living room, Dela greeted her mother and Grandfather Thunder.

"Who's SUV is out front?" Mom asked.

"Mine, Mrs. Belden," Quinn said, from behind Dela.

Her mom's face lit up. "Are you joining us for lunch?"

Dela said, "No," as Quinn said, "Yes."

Her mom's gaze drifted back and forth between them.

"Splendid," Grandfather Thunder said, shuffling into the dining room. He winked at Dela as he passed.

She wondered what he had planned.

"It smells like you are baking something," her mom said, taking a seat at the table.

Grumbling, Dela added another place setting to the table. "I bought a frozen berry pie. It should be done baking by the time we finish eating."

The way people had sat at her small wood table, she ended up sitting directly across from Quinn. She poured iced tea into everyone's glasses, and they started passing around the bread, cheese, tuna salad, and celery sticks.

Once everyone had a sandwich made, Grandfather Thunder touched Quinn's arm. "Moses Arnett said he saw a strange light bobbing across the field next to his place last week and again last night. Are you Feds doing night maneuvers on our land?"

Dela grabbed her napkin and hid a smile behind the folded paper. She had a feeling Quinn was in for some interesting meal conversation.

Grandfather Thunder asked Quinn three more similar questions. When the Special Agent finished eating, he excused himself.

Dela, her mom, and Grandfather Thunder had a good laugh after the door closed behind the infuriating man.

"Thank you, for getting him to leave. He was never invited. He came over to question me about a conversation he'd had with Ina Winter." The timer went off and Dela rose to take the pie out of the oven.

"Oh, dear, Quinn didn't get any pie," Mom said, sounding sad for the man.

"He doesn't deserve any. He thinks I killed Paul Winter." Dela couldn't get over the betrayal she felt that the man believed she would kill a human being in any situation other than war.

She cut and plated the pie, setting a piece in front of the two people at the table. Dela sat at her place and asked Grandfather Thunder, "What do you know about Sadie Swan and her family?"

He put his fork down and studied her. "They are a troubled family. The children, Levi and Lora, came to live with their grandmother, Sadie, when their father died and their mother, Sadie's daughter, killed herself."

"Oh, how unfortunate for the family," Mom gasped.

"When was this?" Dela asked.

"Not quite twenty years ago, I think." Grandfather Thunder raised a bite of pie to his mouth and hummed as he chewed then swallowed. "You make good pie," he said.

Dela laughed and said, "All I did was bake it. You'll have to send a letter to Mrs. Callender."

The man nodded and scooped up another bite.

Studying her mom, she asked, "Did you teach Levi or Lora?"

Mom shook her head. "I think they went to school in Pendleton."

"Yes," Grandfather Thunder said. "Sadie drove them to town to school. I think to keep them from being asked about their parents by the students and parents. People here are interested in tribal families."

"Do you know what happened to the father? How he died?" Dela asked. It made sense that Levi was counseling families and couples.

"He died in a car crash. After he and his wife had an argument." Grandfather Thunder shoved his empty plate to the middle of the table and picked up his iced tea.

"Do you think the argument caused the crash?" Dela asked.

"Ruth said her sister believed she'd caused the accident because she'd argued with her husband. That youngest daughter had always been afraid of everything. How she produced the strong children she did has always interested me." Grandfather Thunder shook his head. "She didn't have strength. A month after her husband's death, she took pills to kill herself.

She couldn't see that her children needed her."

"Were either of them addicts?" Dela asked.

"Neither. That's why it was so hard for the family to understand her using pills." Tears glistened in Grandfather Thunder's eyes.

Dela wondered if he was remembering his own son who had killed himself with an overdose.

"Let me help you clean up and we'll get out of your hair," Mom said.

"About that," Dela glanced at the two people who had been a constant her whole life. "I'd like you to go with me to have a talk with Sadie Swan. She is the witness who says I killed Paul Winter. I just want to see how well she comprehends time. She had to have waited at least twenty minutes to a half-hour before she went over and checked on Paul after I left. She told it to the police as if she'd walked over as soon as I'd walked away."

"Do you think she'll talk to you? After all, she thinks you killed her neighbor." Mom put a hand on top of Dela's. "Why don't you let Grandfather Thunder and I go talk to her?"

As much as Dela loved both of them, she didn't want to get them in trouble and she doubted they would ask the right questions. "I think I should go. I know what to ask."

Grandfather Thunder cleared his throat. "You know what to ask to worry her. We can ask roundabout questions."

She could see the two weren't going to budge on this and she really wanted to know more about the woman. "Okay, but don't leave there until you've talked about what happened to see if she really stood at the window the whole time."

They both nodded.

"I'll just be here cleaning up lunch." Dela fell to the task as the two left. After the kitchen was cleaned up, she grabbed her coat and laptop and pulled a chair outside to sit in the sun and enjoy Mugshot's company. She'd put Jethro out in the pasture this morning. From what she could see over the bottom half of the Dutch gate, he was enjoying the grass.

She found the archives for the CUJ, Confederated Umatilla Journal, the Confederated Tribes's newspaper. She tried to look at online copies from twenty years ago but discovered the online copies only went back seven years. She'd have to go to the Governance building and work her way forward.

She put in the name Lora Murdoch. An obituary appeared. The young woman had died nearly a year ago. Nothing in the obituary told the manner of death. Dela decided after her mom and Grandfather Thunder returned and told her what they knew she'd ask Grandfather Thunder how she died and if he didn't know, she'd go find the aunt at the travel center.

Chapter Sixteen

Her mother and Grandfather Thunder were back in thirty minutes. Dela was still digging around on the internet when the front door opened and her mother called out.

Dela stood and carried her laptop into the kitchen as her mom started brewing a cup of coffee. "That was quick."

"She wasn't home," Mom said.

"That woman goes out a lot," Dela said, feeling as if she'd never get a chance to talk to Sadie Swan.

Grandfather Thunder shook his head, as he accepted the cup of coffee her mom handed him. "She is gone. When she wasn't home, I called Ray's wife. She is friends with Sadie. Ray's wife said Sadie called her Thursday night and asked her to keep an eye on her plants for a couple of weeks. She, Sadie, was going to visit relatives in Idaho."

Dela plunked her laptop down too hard and grimaced. "She's left? Why? Because she lied to the police?" This had to be more than a coincidence.

She sat down at the table. "What can you tell me about Lora Murdoch's death?"

Her mom placed a cup of coffee in front of Dela and took a seat.

"It's no secret. She died of an overdose. While Levi worked hard at his grades and got a job at Yellowhawk, his sister battled her addiction. No one knows why she couldn't or didn't want to get off the drugs. I think there must be something from her childhood that tormented her as her father's death tormented her mother." Grandfather Thunder sipped his coffee.

"How close were the brother and sister?" Dela asked, wondering exactly how the young woman came by the drugs she used to overdose.

"I'm not sure. You could ask their Aunt Ruth or Levi," Grandfather Thunder said.

"I don't think Levi would talk to me. He got angry the day before yesterday when Heath and I talked to him. But the aunt… she didn't mind talking to us." Dela sipped her coffee and remembered her mother had been sitting silently through her conversation with Grandfather Thunder. "What are you thinking about Mom?"

Her mother's blue gaze swept across Dela's face. "It is sad when the traits of a parent manifest in a child."

The sadness on her mom's face scared Dela. What was she thinking about? Any trait she received from her mom was a blessing. Then it hit her. She knew nothing about her father. Had he had demons that could have been passed down to her? "Did my father have traits you worry about in me?"

Her mom shot a glance at Grandfather Thunder and shook her head. "No, I was thinking about some kids I taught."

Studying Mom, Dela wasn't sure she believed that. There had been a deeper sadness in her than that of a teacher and student.

"We must go," Grandfather Thunder said, standing.

Mom laughed and said, "It's time for his soap opera."

Dela studied the elder. "Are you still watching that?" She remembered times when she was sick and stayed home from school her mom would take her over to Grandfather Thunder's. She had to be quiet for the half-hour the soap opera was playing.

The man shrugged and grinned. "Their lives are more messed up than anyone who lives at Nixyáawii."

Dela laughed as she saw her company out the front door. Her cell phone rang. She hurried to the kitchen to answer it. Heath.

"Hello?"

"Hey, it's me. I can't find Booth anywhere."

"I hope my bringing him up to Sander last night didn't get him killed." Her mind went to the conversation. What had the drug dealer said about Booth? He hadn't liked the man. And didn't deny or admit he was buying from him after Paul's death.

"I don't see why he would knock off the person who was supplying him with meth now that Paul is gone. Booth could just be hiding from us. Especially, if Sander tipped him off you were asking about his involvement in the homicide." Heath's tone had calmed down.

Double Down

"I'll go to the casino and ask Jacee where Booth might be hiding." She thought about all she'd learned this afternoon from Grandfather Thunder. "What time do you get off work?"

"I'm headed to the station now. Why?"

"You can either meet me at the casino to talk to Jacee or come here for dinner. I found out a lot from Grandfather Thunder today. And I did some digging online." She headed to the back door to let Mugshot in.

"How about I do both? I'll meet you at the casino and follow you home afterward."

"I'll see you in twenty." She ended the call, smiling. For the millionth time since seeing Heath step out of the hotel room when a "Save The Fish" presenter was killed, she was glad he'd moved back and they had resumed their friendship. She hadn't realized how lonely she'd been. Even with friends like Molly and Faith here.

She gathered up her purse and ushered Mugshot back out into the yard. She opened the gate to the pasture. "Now you two can visit." Mugshot hopped out into the pasture, sniffing the ground. He would be happy nosing around while she was gone.

Once she was settled in the car, she decided to stop at the travel center on her way to the casino. She wanted to know more about the Murdoch siblings and their aunt was the only person she knew besides the grandmother who'd left.

At the travel center, Dela stood inside and to the right of the door, scanning the areas she could see. When the woman wasn't visible, she began walking, peering down the short aisles of merchandise. Arriving at the other end of the store she hadn't found the woman. She didn't remember or hadn't been told

Ruth's last name.

Dela walked up to a woman behind the counter. "Is Ruth here today?"

The woman looked her up and down and shook her head. "She stocks during the week."

"Could you tell me where she lives?" Dela asked.

"We don't give out employees' addresses." The woman motioned for the person behind Dela to move forward.

She'd have to ask Heath if he knew where Ruth lived. In her car, she backed out and headed to the casino. She started to pull around behind the building to the employee parking. Her security badge was in her purse but she felt funny using it when she was on leave.

Dela circled the building and parked in front. Walking through the mechanical doors, her name was called. She glanced to her right and smiled.

Alfred, the night valet, was waving her over.

"Hi, Alfred." She stopped beside the elderly Umatilla man. His silver hair was always neatly braided and draped down the front of his western-cut shirt.

"I heard they put you on leave. What is wrong with Bernie? Sometimes I think he doesn't use the good sense the Creator gave him." The man shook his head as if he pitied the chairman of the casino board of trustees.

"I have to admit, it has been easier to dig up information not having to come in here to work."

He smiled. "I knew you wouldn't let anyone push you around. If I can be of help, you know where to find me."

Dela thought about that. "Do you know Sadie Swan and her grandchildren?"

He studied her. "She's a good woman. Took in

those two grandkids when their parents died and their aunt couldn't provide for them."

"I'm not saying she isn't a good woman. I'm just curious why she would say I killed Paul. If she watched the whole time from the window, she would know that he was still alive when I left. Heath saw him sitting up." Her brain realized what she'd said after the words came out.

"Then why hasn't he come forward to say so?" Alfred studied her.

"He's afraid Detective Dick will think he's just saying that to cover for me. Because when Heath saw Paul, he received a call. When he arrived at the address there wasn't anything happening. We think the real killer was in the house, saw Heath drive up, and called nine-one-one to get him out of there." She sighed. "But we haven't told this to anyone because—"

"You don't think they would believe you about any of it," Alfred said.

"Yes."

Heath walked into the casino. He saw them talking and strode over. "Hi, Alfred."

The older man nodded. "Heath. I understand you've been pushed out of the investigation by Detective Jones. I hope you find the person who did it before him."

"Me, too. The Chief of Police doesn't care who makes the arrest, but I'm pretty sure if I don't, I can kiss my chances of taking over Jones's spot when he retires." Heath's gaze scanned the casino floor. "Shall we talk to Jacee?"

"Yeah." Dela smiled at Alfred. "If you hear anything—"

"I'll contact you." The older man winked.

Dela pulled out her cell phone and called the phone in the head of surveillance office. Knowing Marty was on vacation she wanted to ask Farley to send Jacee down to the deli.

"Farley, here," the younger man answered.

"Hi Farley, it's Dela."

"Hey, are you back to work?" he asked with enthusiasm.

"I wish. But, no. I'd like to talk to Jacee Bing, is she there?"

"Yeah. She's on duty until eleven."

"Could you fill in for her for about twenty minutes? I'd like you to send her out to the deli. Don't tell her it's me who wants to talk to her." Dela knew she was asking a lot of Farley, but she feared Jacee would refuse to see her after the way she'd bolted out of the bar the other night. "Tell her Officer Seaver wants to talk to her."

"Your dinner date? Sure." He ended the call and she sighed. The young man had listened in on her conversation before with Heath and now Farley called Heath her dinner date.

"Come on, Farley is going to send Jacee to the deli to talk to you." Dela took the table to the back of the eating area, with her back to the entrance. Her hair was hanging down loose, making her look less like her usual self with braided hair or a ponytail.

Heath walked over, purchased drinks, and then sat across from her. "Do you think she's going to tell us anything?"

Dela shrugged. "She sure didn't want to talk to me at the bar the other night. Hopefully, we can make her see she needs to tell us or Quinn what she might know."

"Over here, Ms. Bing," Heath said, raising his

hand.

Dela didn't turn to see if the woman hesitated.

When Jacee sat, her gaze landed on Dela. The woman straightened to her feet.

"Sit down unless you want me to take you to the police station to question," Heath said, using his authoritative cop tone.

Jacee lowered onto the chair.

"Can I get you something to drink?" Dela offered.

The woman shook her head. "Why are you here?"

"I can't find your boyfriend, Daniel Booth," Heath said, pulling out a notebook.

"And I want to know if you knew that Paul and Daniel were cooking meth." Dela peered into the woman's face. The twisting of her features was a pretty good indication that she had known.

"I met Daniel a year ago at Paul and Ina's. He was fun and liked to spend money on me." She shrugged. "I didn't figure out that he was helping Paul until six months ago. When Daniel started looking for a rundown piece of property to do his own cooking."

"Do you use meth?" Dela didn't think so, the woman appeared to be in good health.

"No. I told Daniel I didn't like him making something that ruined so many lives. But he said it was the easiest way to make big bucks." Jacee stared at the table and mumbled, "We both like money and nice things."

"Did Daniel kill Paul to take over selling to Gus Sander?" Heath asked.

The woman's head snapped up and she stared at Heath. "No! He didn't kill Paul. He was happy Paul wasn't cooking anymore. He had no reason to want to kill him."

"Then why has he disappeared?" Heath asked.

"He called me last night and said the man you mentioned, Gus, told him to get out of town and not bring trouble to his door. Daniel was scared when he called. He said he'd stay away awhile until Gus simmered down."

Dela smiled. Her visit with the drug dealer had made him nervous. Was that because he had Paul killed and didn't want Dela sniffing around the people he couldn't control? "Tell me about people who may have wanted Paul hurt or killed?"

Jacee stared at her. "How would I know?"

"If you met Daniel at your cousin's house, I would think that means you spent a lot of time there." Dela sipped her drink, watching the young woman. When Jacee didn't say anything, she continued. "You told me you were glad I saved your cousin from her husband. Did Paul beat up other people?"

"When he drank too much or used that stuff he cooked, he would get mean. Real mean. No one wanted to be around him then. That's why Ina sent Micah away."

"Who has he beat up lately?" Heath asked.

"Besides my cousin and Dela?" Jacee asked.

Heath shot a glance at Dela. She understood. Jacee's comment wasn't something they wanted Detective Dick to hear.

"Yes," Heath said.

"There was a guy, Daniel said, who tried to buy direct from Paul. When Paul wouldn't sell to him because he didn't want to make Gus mad, the man flew into a rage and Paul knocked him out. He told Daniel to take the man home and dump him out."

"You have a name?" Heath asked.

"No. Daniel might know but he…"

"Left town. Anyone else?" Dela pressed.

"Daniel said Paul found a note on his door about four months ago accusing him of killing someone." Jacee was staring at her clasped hands on the table.

"A note? And Paul didn't report it?" Heath said.

Dela's heart leaped. Here was a lead on someone who wanted the man dead.

"No. If he was being accused of killing someone, it was from the meth he was cooking. He wasn't going to go to the tribals about that." Jacee peered at Heath as if he had asked a dumb question.

"Do you think Daniel would know who?" Dela asked.

"I don't know." Jacee returned her gaze to her hands.

Heath pulled out a card and wrote his cell phone number on the back. "If he contacts you, have him call me. I just want to talk to him. Ask him the same questions I've been asking you."

Jacee took the card. "Can I get back to work now?"

Dela glanced at Heath. He nodded. "Yes, and thank you for talking to us."

The woman stood. She studied Dela. "I don't think you killed Paul." She said the words hastily and left the deli.

"We now have another suspect," Heath said.

"And a scared drug dealer," Dela added.

Chapter Seventeen

While Heath rounded up Jethro and Mugshot from the pasture, Dela made baked salmon and a salad. There were still two pieces of pie left from earlier. That would work for dessert.

As they sat eating, Dela told Heath what Grandfather Thunder had said about Sadie Swan and her grandchildren and that she had gone on a vacation at a suspicious time.

"That is all interesting. Especially that Lora Murdoch died of an overdose." Heath held his fork in the air. "Was she living here?"

"The obituary didn't say much. Just who she was related to and she died an early death. I found out about the overdose from Grandfather Thunder." Dela slid her finished plate to the center of the table and leaned back sipping an iced tea.

"I think we need to tell Quinn about this latest discovery," Heath said.

Dela splashed her tea as she jolted upright in her chair and glared at him. "Why?"

"Because he can dig up the information on the woman's death and he can get background on both Levi and his grandmother." Heath shoved his finished plate to the center of the table.

Shaking her head, Dela said, "Not yet. There could have been someone else who left that threat. Think about how many people we've talked to who knew how Paul was making money. If a family member died of an overdose, they could have sent him the note maybe to scare him out of cooking so no one else gets hurt, or to warn him they planned to exact revenge." She tapped a finger against her glass. "I wonder if Sander received any threats? Wouldn't the person wanting revenge go after the dealer as well as the person who cooked it up?"

Heath studied her. "It would be easier to take out Paul than a man who has a bodyguard. And it would end the dealer's supply."

"But the supply hasn't ended because Daniel started supplying Sander." Dela put her glass down. "It might be a good idea he is hiding. If the person who took out Paul so easily learned he was now providing meth to Sander he could be the next target."

"I think it is time to pull in Quinn. He can put out an all points on Daniel and dig deeper into the Swan and Murdoch family backgrounds." Heath grabbed his empty plate and Dela's.

"I'd still like to talk to their Aunt Ruth. Where does she live?" Dela asked, moving to plate the last two pieces of pie.

"She has a place off Cayuse Road." Heath sat at the table. "You aren't planning to visit her tonight, are you?"

Dela picked up her fork. "I'd like to know the relationship between Levi and Lora. And if he knew who she was buying from."

Heath shook his head. "Do you really think someone who helps people learn to deal with anger would kill someone for revenge?"

Shrugging, Dela said, "I've seen what loss does to people. They can snap at the slightest thing." She had seen the best and worst in people while in the Army. Soldiers she thought she knew could change in the flash of a mortar or the explosion of a Humvee. A civilian could snap from a number of things. Like the death of a loved one in a heinous way.

"I still think we need to pull in Quinn. He has more resources than we do since we can't ask for help through tribal channels."

Dela sighed. "Fine. I'll call him and invite him to brunch tomorrow. Can you be here at ten?" She watched her friend's face light up.

"I can be here at ten. Are you making waffles by any chance?" Heath licked his lips and asked, "With strawberries and whipped cream?"

She groaned at his antics. "You're a grown man. Licking your lips is something a child would do."

"But I remember the waffles your mom made and I'm pretty sure she taught you how to make them."

Dela laughed. "She did. And they are the best thing I make. Not that I'm trying to impress anyone," she said quickly.

Heath's eyes narrowed. "You do have something for Quinn, don't you?"

"Only that he is always making me feel inferior. I want to show him I can cook and I can be something other than a soldier." She peered into Heath's eyes. "I'd be lying if I didn't add, that I did, at one time, have fantasies about him. But that was before he turned into a jackass." Dela stood, taking the two empty plates to the sink. "Now I just want to show him I can do my job and I didn't kill anyone."

The next morning, Dela rose at eight to give herself plenty of time to slice the strawberries, make the waffle batter, and whip the cream. Not to mention set the table for three and heat the waffle iron.

While she was nervous to tell Quinn all that she and Heath had dug up, she was more nervous that he wouldn't like the waffles. Which was absurd. She knew the two of them would never be more than colleagues, but his approval meant a lot to her. Maybe because he never seemed to see her as a woman, only a soldier or a buddy. Or because deep down, she still had fantasies of the two of them wrapped in each other's arms.

A knock on the door broke her from her reveries. She walked across the living room to open the front door. Heath was smiling while Quinn frowned. That was why she didn't see their relationship going any farther than colleagues. It was a beautiful morning and Quinn stood on her porch frowning.

"Good morning," she said, retreating into the kitchen to pull a waffle out of the iron.

"Smells good!" Heath said, making himself at home, opening a can of frozen orange juice, and pouring it into a pitcher.

Quinn stood inside the dining room watching.

"Take a load off," Dela said, pouring more batter onto the iron and closing the lid. Steam had moistened her face and heated her skin. She wiped at it with a towel and discovered Quinn staring at her.

"I thought this was a brunch for two," he said.

She smiled. "I thought I said Heath and I had some information for you."

"That's what you said, but I didn't think it was a meeting when you said brunch." His eyes continued to hold her.

Heath put a glass of orange juice at each place setting. "Anything else you need help with?"

"You can grab the strawberries and whipped cream from the fridge." Dela opened the waffle iron and took another crispy golden waffle out, placing it on the plate that already held six. She pulled the plug on the iron and left the lid up.

After placing the plate on the table, she sat. "Dig in."

The two men grabbed a waffle and began piling them with berries and cream. Dela waited until they'd each taken a bite before fixing her own. She wanted to be occupied in case the waffles didn't measure up to her mom's. Cooking had never come easy to her. She could make food to fill her but she never seemed to get the fantastic flavors that her mom did.

"This is delicious!" Quinn said.

She raised her gaze and took in the admiration shining on his smiling face. "Thank you."

"These are as good as your mom's."

She glanced at Heath. His eyes were closed as he savored the bite. Dela laughed at his feigned ecstasy while eating. "I'm glad you both like them."

After they had all eaten one waffle and the men were started on their second one, Dela drank her orange juice and then made cups of coffee for everyone. She sat back at the table and cleared her throat.

Heath glanced up as if to say, "Are you sure this is the time?"

Dela picked up her coffee cup and peered over the rim of it at Quinn. "We've been doing some inquiries and thought you should be informed of what we've learned."

Quinn set down his fork, took a sip of coffee, and pulled a notepad and pen out of his back pocket. "You know anything you tell me is unofficial since you are the prime suspect in this homicide."

She glanced at the pad. "Then why are you taking notes?"

"To make sure I remember what you say."

His grey eyes peered at her with such intensity she wondered if he was trying to put a notion in her head.

"This is what we have learned…" She went on to tell him about Mrs. Swan's surprise trip, the connection her granddaughter might have to the victim through her addiction, and that the man who took over cooking was missing.

Quinn had watched her in between jotting down what she said. "I take it you need me to find out where Mrs. Swan went and ask her if she was telling the truth?"

"I want you to determine that she didn't see me holding that knife after Paul was killed. It was after our fight that I put it in the shed. She had to have not watched the whole time to say that I killed him." She nodded to Heath. "Tell him what we've withheld from Detective Dick."

Quinn turned his attention to Heath. His gaze wasn't as inquisitive. He glared.

Heath cleared his throat. "Dela called me after her altercation with the victim. She was worried he was going to call the police and claim she was trespassing. I drove straight to the Winter residence. I saw the victim sitting up in the area where Dela said they had their fight. She and the donkey were nowhere in sight. Before I could get out of my car to talk to him, I received a call. When I arrived at the address, no one knew why I'd been called. When I got back in my car, I heard the call about finding Paul Winter dead."

Quinn's gaze flit back and forth between Heath and Dela, until she wanted to grab the man by his ears and stop his movement.

"You both withheld this information?" he said, slowly.

"Think about it. What do you think Dick would have said if Heath came forward telling him what he just told you?" Dela crossed her arms and leaned back in the chair.

"That the two of you made it all up." Quinn shoved his notepad up by his coffee cup and studied her.

"Right. Instead, we've been trying to find out who else could have reason to kill a man I had no reason to harm. Well, other than to protect myself." Dela didn't feel bad for what she'd done to keep the man from running that knife through her.

Quinn turned his attention to Heath. "They could have pulled up the bogus call and talked to the people you talked to."

"But that still wouldn't have put me at the victim's house before he was killed and after Dela left. I would like to know where the call came from that sent me on the goose chase." Heath picked up his coffee. "But I'm not allowed to do anything except patrol. When I get to the station, no one talks to me, but someone is always following me. They have even, thanks to you, been treating Jacob the same way. It's as if Detective Jones doesn't want anyone who might be open to someone other than Dela being the suspect to have anything to do with the case."

"Why does he hate you?" Quinn asked.

Dela shrugged. "Only because I have always made him be respectful to my security members and the casino employees. There is no reason for him to come in and treat us like we are criminals when he is questioning us."

"I've noticed he has a bias towards anyone connected to the casino." Quinn picked up his coffee. "I'll see what I can do about the things you want me to look into." He sipped his drink and said, "What are you planning to do?"

She glanced at Heath and let out a breath, hoping Quinn didn't say she should stay out of it. "I'm going to have a talk with Levi and Lora's Aunt Ruth."

Chapter Eighteen

After Quinn left and they'd cleaned up the kitchen, Dela climbed into Heath's truck and they headed over Interstate 84 and deeper into the reservation. Heath said Ruth lived in the Cayuse area. The Cayuse name was given to the people of this area and the horses they rode. It wasn't the name they called themselves. *Wáylatpu* is the true name for the Cayuse people. At one time there had been a village in the area where Heath said Ruth lived. Later the village became a town with a post office and store. The town no longer existed but the area remained known by the name Cayuse.

They pulled up to a small house with two barking dogs and three children running after a chicken.

"Are those her children?" Dela asked, thinking the woman was too old to have such young children.

"Her grandchildren." Heath opened his door but didn't step out. "This family has lost many to addictions. Her son killed his wife and himself two years ago while high. Ruth is all the children have."

Dela's chest squeezed. Her heart ached thinking of what these three must have gone through. "Were they there when it happened?"

"No. They were here. Ruth discovered the bodies when she drove over to see why the parents hadn't come to pick up the kids." Heath watched the scurrying boy and two girls. "We have to keep drugs off the reservation. All lives are sacred but especially the children."

Dela nodded and they both stepped out of the vehicle as Ruth appeared around the side of the house.

The woman raised a hand to shield her eyes as she stared at them.

"Do you think she'll tell us anything?" Dela whispered as they walked across the scraggly winter-killed lawn.

Heath didn't answer, he said, "Ruth, we'd like to visit with you if you have a few minutes."

"Is this official?" she asked.

He motioned to his civilian clothes. "No. We just have some questions."

"Barry, quit chasing that chicken or she won't lay an egg for your breakfast," the woman raised her voice enough to carry to the children and nodded to the house. "We'll go inside."

Dela followed the woman, and Heath followed behind, into a house half the size of hers. She wondered where the children slept. Sadness overtook her not seeing any toys or even a television. No wonder the children were chasing the poor chicken.

Ruth led them into a small kitchen with a round table and four chairs. "Have a seat. I have some coffee on."

They sat and Dela's gaze traveled around the tidy kitchen. The stove was old. It looked like one that her mom had replaced when Dela lived at home. The sink was enamel with chips and scratches. The refrigerator was newer, but still at least twenty years old. The linoleum on the floor was worn. The dull grain of wood peeked through in several places.

Ruth set the cups in front of them and took a seat. "Are you still trying to find Levi?"

"No, we found him. I'm surprised he didn't tell you to not talk to us," Heath said, picking up the mug to take a sip.

"You must have asked him about Lora. He's been very sensitive about her death. He feels he should have known she was so far gone. But he'd been away at school and hadn't known how she could fool people. I thought sure she'd gotten clean, then I saw her at my Sonny's and she was on a high. That was before..." Ruth's face scrunched up and tears welled in her eyes. "I should have had them all locked up when I seen them. Maybe they'd all be alive now."

Dela put a hand over the woman's resting on the table. "If a person doesn't want help, it's damn hard to get them to listen to you." She knew this from one of her friends in the army. Dela had tried repeatedly to help her friend who'd become an alcoholic, but she liked the booze better than anything else. She'd ended up getting kicked out of the army and Dela had lost touch.

"That's what Levi says, but he still tried to get Lora to stop. Even though she'd just laugh at him and tell him he should join her and see how much better the world was while on drugs." Ruth shut her eyes, shook her head, and then stared at Dela. "Is this what you came to talk about? Lora's drug habit?"

Dela nodded. "Did you or Levi know where she got the drugs that she overdosed on?"

The woman's eyes narrowed. "That man they say you killed. Don't worry, I'm not afraid of you. You did a good thing killing him."

"I didn't kill him. But I think Lora's death may have something to do with it."

"Who do you think killed him?" Ruth glanced from Dela to Heath.

"We don't know, but the victim had been threatened before he was killed. And there are many who knew what he was doing and who paid him to make meth." Heath took over.

Dela was glad. She didn't want to be the one who suggested this woman's mother or her nephew may have been involved with the murder.

Ruth looked down at her hands. "There have been times when I'd pray that the police would raid him or he'd blow himself up. People like that shouldn't be allowed to do what they do. They prey on the weak. It's not right."

A shiver slithered up Dela's spine. Had this woman thrust the knife into Paul? She sounded like she could have for the sake of others.

"We let the community down by not stopping him legally," Heath said.

Dela's gaze shot to Heath's face. Guilt had replaced the compassion and determination that had been there before. Was that guilt over not knowing about the meth lab when the rest of the community had known or was it because he'd… No, Heath wouldn't have stabbed the man and left her hanging as the suspect for the death.

Ruth raised her face and studied Heath. "No, we let the tribals down by not telling you what we all knew. But…" She glanced at Dela and back at Heath. "Five years ago, after Tyler Brown died from an overdose, his father talked to Detective Jones about Paul Winter and the man he worked for."

Heath's eyes snapped with anger. "Detective Jones knew about what Winter was doing for that long and didn't shut him down?"

The woman nodded. "Derick Brown, Tyler's father, broke his arm and leg in a car accident shortly afterward and hasn't said another word." Suspicion bubbled in the woman's dark brown eyes, surrounded by worry lines. "I am all these children have. I can't go around pointing fingers."

"The people of Nixyáawii shouldn't be afraid to go to the police," Heath said firmly. "You tell everyone to come to me with information about drug pushers and manufacturers. I'll work to clean this community up." He stood. "Come on. We have someone else to see."

Dela stood, said her goodbyes, and followed Heath out to this pickup. "Who are we going to see?"

"The Chief of Police. He has to know that Detective Jones didn't follow up on what he was told about a meth lab in our community, and we need to see if Derick Brown's accident was an accident or if someone caused it on purpose." Heath cranked over the engine and backed out of the driveway.

"You need to cool down a bit before you go barging in on your boss and a man who may have been forced to keep his mouth shut." Dela hadn't seen this side of Heath before. He was pissed and he was determined.

The vehicle slowed down. He drew in a deep

breath. "Sorry. This was the kind of shit that I dealt with at Pine Ridge. It churns my guts to know people who are supposed to protect on reservations are some of the same ones who let predators like Sander deal to the community. As if we hadn't been screwed enough by others over the centuries, we screw our brothers and sisters to make money."

"If you want to make a change, you can't just attack straight on. Going to the Chief is a good way to start. Let him hear what we learned about Detective Dick." Dela took a minute to think. "It might be a good idea to talk to Derick Brown first. Get his side of things so you have more ammunition against Dick when you go to the Chief of Police."

"Call Jacob and find out where Derick lives." Heath pulled over to the side of the road, while Dela made the call.

♠ ♣ ♥ ♦

Dela directed Heath to the Brown residence. Jacob had wanted to know why they needed the address. Heath had nodded his head, and she told him about Detective Jones's disregard of a meth lab and drug dealer on the rez. He was fuming by the time she ended the call.

The Brown home was a small acreage toward Athena. Dela could see where the man would be worried about being laid up due to the accident or whatever harm came to him.

Heath parked next to a battered pickup and newer flatbed. Two dogs, one large and one small, stood on the porch barking.

"I bet that little one is the biter," Dela said. The larger dog's tail was wagging while the small dog had its ears back and teeth showing.

157

Before they had to find out, a man limped out of the shed to the right of the house. "Boomer, Blaster, quiet," he said in a gruff tone.

The big dog sat down and the little dog snarled.

"Blaster, knock it off." The man pointed at the small dog. Blaster tucked its thin tail and walked over to crouch by the front door.

"What do you want?" the man asked. He was dressed in a denim shirt and jeans. His dusty, leather boots were worn on the outside of his pant legs.

"Mr. Brown?" Heath asked, holding out a hand.

The man nodded but didn't shake.

"I'm Heath Seaver, I work for the tribal police." He pointed to Dela. "This is Dela Alvaro, she's head of security for the casino."

Derick Brown studied them and asked, "What do you want with me?"

"I'm investigating the death of Paul Winter. During my inquiries, I learned that Detective Jones didn't follow up on your information about the man, and now he, Jones, is trying to pin Winter's murder on Dela." Heath motioned to the house. "Can we go inside and talk?"

The man glanced at the house then turned on one heel and walked toward the shed. "My wife still hasn't recovered from the loss of our son. Best to talk about this outside."

Inside the shed, he handed a folding chair to Dela and Heath before sitting on one himself. "It was five years ago come July we lost Tyler. I was so mad when we learned what had happened to our boy. It was all I could do to drive to the tribal police station. I stomped in and poked my finger in Detective Jones's chest and told him to get out there and arrest Paul. That the drug he cooked up killed my son. He said they'd investigate, but they never did. Then I shot my mouth off at a gathering about how I was going to go to the Chief of Police since the detective wasn't doing anything. On my way home, I was run off the road by a tribal police vehicle. I didn't see who was driving but I'm pretty sure it was Jones. Who else would have wanted me to not tell the Chief he'd done nothing about a meth lab?"

Heath pulled out his notepad. "I plan on telling the chief what I've learned. But it would help if you could come in and give a statement."

When Derick looked apprehensive, Heath said, "Don't worry I'll make sure Detective Jones is nowhere near the station while you give your statement."

"What about afterward? He'll know I was there."

Dela had always despised the detective for the way he treated people, but knowing he had let a meth lab continue on the rez had her blood boiling. She hoped the man got more than a firing. He deserved to never work as a policeman again.

"I'll make certain he doesn't retaliate. Even if it means a tribal officer watches your farm."

Dela glanced at Heath, could he make such a grand gesture when he was a patrol officer?

"We'll keep you and your family safe. I promise." Heath held out his hand.

They shook and Derick said he'd come to the station at nine in the morning.

"I'll be there and make sure that Detective Jones isn't." Heath stood.

Dela followed him back to the vehicle and climbed in. When they were headed down the road, she asked, "Can you make sure they have a guard?"

He glanced at her. "When the chief learns of this

and gives Jones the boot, he won't be out for Derick's hide, he'll be after mine."

Chapter Nineteen

Dela stood on her porch watching Heath drive off. He'd thought it best if he didn't show up to talk to the chief with her in tow. After all, as far as the police were concerned, she was still a suspect.

Heath was certain the chief would believe him about Detective Dick. Especially after Derick Brown gave his statement. To make sure the detective didn't know about his talk with the chief, Heath was meeting Chief Steele at his home, today, Sunday, rather than at the police station.

Feeling as if she still didn't know enough about Lora Murdoch and her cousin who also died due to drugs, Dela checked in with her animals and then slid into her car. She'd go see if Grandfather Thunder had any more insights into the family or someone she could talk to.

Out of curiosity, she drove by the Winter residence, studying the house and grounds. She knew

Forensics had found the victim's blood in the house, but what else did they find? She pulled over in Mrs. Swan's driveway and scrolled through her contacts looking for Quinn's number.

"I'm still alive from your cooking if that's what you're calling about," Quinn answered.

She heard country music playing in the background. "Sorry to disappoint you. I know my cooking won't kill you. Did you have a forensic team go through the whole house after the murder?"

The music quieted and a heavy sigh came from the other end of the call. "What do you think? It was a crime scene."

"But the crime happened outside." She pointed out.

"However, the contents of the inside were destroyed, making it appear to also be part of the crime scene. Yes, evidence was gathered from the whole house. Why?" He sounded less confrontational and more curious.

That he had asked her about her thoughts was a step in the right direction. "My gut tells me that whoever killed Paul was in the house while he and I were having our confrontation. They had to have seen me put the knife in the shed, to have used it as the murder weapon. Otherwise, it was out of sight of anyone just coming along." She paused and then plunged on, "Did you find any fingerprints inside the house that shouldn't have been there? Or any other evidence he wasn't alone?"

"You're a suspect, I can't tell you."

"Dammit, Quinn! I didn't kill him." Then she went on to tell him what she and Heath had learned from Ruth and Derick Brown. "Heath is talking to the Tribal Chief of Police right now, and he asked Brown to come in tomorrow and give a statement about what had happened when he confronted Detective Dick about his son's death."

"It sounds like Heath is taking the correct steps. Dela, I'm sorry I have to treat you like a suspect, but with Mrs. Swan's statement, I have no other choice."

Was he weakening? Did he now believe she didn't do it? "Does this mean you think I'm innocent?"

A deep sigh echoed on the other end of the call. "I now believe you didn't kill the victim, but you can't keep butting into the investigation. We, Heath and I, can't cover up for you. It's our jobs on the line."

"But it's my life on the line if I get railroaded for a murder I didn't commit. I fought back from an IED attack, I'm sure as hell not going to sit around and not fight when someone is trying to frame me for something I didn't do." Indignation burned in her chest and heated her cheeks. He of all people should know she would fight twice as hard to save her own life as she had to save that young woman who'd been raped by his informant.

"As long as you are always with someone when you are asking questions you will have someone to vouch for your behavior. But I didn't say that. Because you shouldn't be digging into your own alleged crime."

She understood he wasn't telling her to back off, but giving her warning that things could go bad if she talked with people on her own. "I'll keep that in mind." She ended the call, glanced at Mrs. Swan's house, and started to pull away. Her foot moved to the brake as the thought, no one is home. I could find a way in and look around, came to her.

A car slowly drove past, and she pulled out onto the road, heading toward Grandfather Thunder's. She didn't need word getting back to the tribals that she was seen hanging around the crime scene.

At Grandfather Thunder's small house, that needed another coat of paint and soon a new roof, she parked and walked up to the front door. She knocked and waited. Not a sound came from inside. Sunday? Where would he be? Not at her mother's, she went to lunch with a group of retired teachers who met after church.

Dela decided to see if Sherry Dale, who lived in the mobile home behind his house, knew anything. Sherry's car wasn't parked beside the trailer. That meant she wasn't home either. She could have taken Grandfather Thunder to the casino. Though Dela had heard the woman didn't go to the Spotted Pony anymore after having been singled out there to be kidnapped by a human trafficking group. They'd been lucky Mrs. Shumack had brought in her son who worked with the State Police or Sherry might not have been found before she was shipped to another country as a sex slave.

Not finding the old man was an unfortunate turn of events. She'd planned to ask Grandfather Thunder questions. She walked into his house through the back door. She'd leave him a note to call her. The old man didn't have a cell phone and refused to have an answering machine. He felt if someone called him when he was home, the phone was to be answered by him. If he didn't answer they would know he wasn't home and to call later.

As a child, she'd spent as much time in this house as she had her own. Grandfather Thunder had been her babysitter. When she was young, this was where she came after school to do her homework and watch cartoons with the old man until her mother came home.

Her mom had never dated so she only came here on the occasional overnighter when Mom attended a teaching conference or classes.

Thinking back, her mom had never had a male or female friend that she'd leave her daughter with. Only Grandfather Thunder.

She dug around in the junk drawer and found a pen and small notepad. Dela wrote out
"Call me, Dela" and put it on the refrigerator under a magnetic photo frame of her in fourth grade.

As she returned the pen and notepad to the drawer, she spotted a wallet in the back of the drawer. If Grandfather Thunder's wallet was in the drawer, where was he?

She pulled the wallet out and opened it. The photo on the driver's license drew her attention. It was a man in his early twenties, with long dark hair, and a chin that resembled hers as well as eyes the same shape as hers. Only his eyes were brown while hers were blue, the color of her mother's. Slowly, she pulled her gaze from the photo to read the name. It had been scratched out along with the address. Her hands shook and she dropped the wallet onto the floor.

Bending, to pick it up, her gaze sought out the photo. There was a very strong resemblance between her and this young man. Why did Grandfather Thunder have this wallet and license in his kitchen drawer? Could she bring it up and ask? Was it his youngest son who'd died in a car crash? What had been his name? Grandfather Thunder rarely mentioned him. He had only told her about the car crash when someone who had been visiting mentioned a name Dela had never heard before.

She sat in the kitchen chair, closed her eyes, and

willed herself to go back to that day. Who had been here? A woman. What was her name? What name had she said?

The front door opened. "Dela? Are you here?" Grandfather Thunder's gravelly voice called.

"Kitchen," she called back and listened to the old man's shuffling gait coming toward the room. She remained in the chair staring at the open wallet.

"Why did you come to see me," he asked, stepping into the room. His rheumy gaze slid from her face to her hands.

"Who is this?" she asked, holding up the wallet with the license facing him.

"Someone I knew a long, long time ago." Grandpa Thunder sat in the chair across from her. "How did you come by that?"

"I came to ask you questions. When you weren't here, I went to the drawer and found a pen and paper." She pointed to the note on the refrigerator. "While I was putting the pen and paper back, I spotted the wallet and thought you might be in trouble if you went off without it." She shrugged. "It's not your wallet. But the man in the photo looks like me." She studied the old man she had known her whole life. Had Heath been correct in saying this man had known about both their fathers and never said a word?

"What questions did you come to ask me." He deftly ignored the wallet, watching her.

"Heath and I found out about three people who died due to taking meth that Paul Winter made. What can you tell me about Tyler Brown, Lora Murdoch, and her cousin who killed his wife while high?"

Grandfather Thunder closed his eyes. They remained closed for so long that she wondered if he'd dozed off. Just as she started to say something, he opened his eyes. Sadness welled in the depths of the brown orbs.

"First we were given alcohol to help us kill ourselves and now it is drugs made by our own." He stared at her. "Why do you think nothing is done about this?"

"I know that Detective D-Jones has turned a blind eye to the cooking of meth and the selling. He didn't turn in the full report Derick Brown gave about his son's death. He left out the part about the meth being cooked on the rez and the dealer having free reign to sell here." She couldn't hold contempt from her voice. There was nothing lower than a person in law enforcement who looked the other way to pad his retirement.

The elder narrowed his eyes. "I have thought that might be so for a while now, but no one was brave enough to say."

Dela took her phone out of her pocket and snapped a photo of the driver's license.

"What are you doing that for?" Grandfather Thunder asked, making a grab for the wallet. He snagged it with one of his long bony fingers and pulled it over, flopping it closed.

"I want to show it to a friend." She knew Heath would help her figure out if this man was related to the man sitting across from her and if he might be related to her.

"Don't go flashing that picture around." Grandfather Thunder stared at her cell phone.

"Why not? What don't you want me to find out? Who he is? That he might be my father?"

His shoulders sagged a bit at her last comment.

Shaking his head, he said, "There are some things that are better left a mystery."

"Are you talking about my father?" She studied the old man's face. Since he'd stepped through the kitchen door, it seemed as if he had visibly aged ten years. His faded eyes were sunken, the creases on his face dug deep into his flesh, and the usual turned-up corners of his lips were pointed downward. He was the epitome of sorrow.

"There are some people who pass through your life that take a piece of you with them. Each time they are brought up, a bit more crumbles until if you think about them too much you are gone." Grandfather Thunder stood and tossed the wallet in the drawer, closing it. "Take my word, you do not want to find out who this man is. If you love your mother, do not show her the photo or ask her any questions."

With him saying not to show this to her mother, Dela's gut said, this could be her father. But why would it harm her mother to see the photo? "I can't promise I won't, but I will keep this to myself until I am exonerated of killing Paul Winter."

"Just think about how one man, Paul, has hurt so many lives by cooking meth." He pointed to her camera. "This man, too, ruined many lives. Don't let him ruin more."

Dela shoved her cell phone into her coat pocket and stood. "I need to go." She walked over and gave the man a hug, to show she did care about what he told her, but she had a need to find out who the man was and if he was her father.

Dela was sitting at her kitchen table staring at the photo when Heath walked in the front door an hour later. She closed the gallery and glanced up. "How did your meeting with the chief go?"

"He has had his suspicions about Jones for some time. Chief Steele plans to have Quinn and crew do the investigation. In the meantime, he's pulling Jones from your case. He feels there is a conflict of interest." Heath grabbed a glass and filled it with milk. He pulled a box of cookies from the cupboard and sat across from her.

"If Jones is off my case, who is the lead investigator?" Dela was happy to know the man who had been a pain in her ass since she'd started working at the casino, wouldn't be able to fake evidence against her.

"It would have been me, if we weren't friends. Then it would have been Jacob, but ditto." He grinned.

"It can't be Quinn if the chief wants him to dig up dirt on Dick." She racked her brain to remember who else on the tribal police force would have enough experience.

"Chief Steele is leading the case as of thirty minutes ago." Heath bit into a cookie, chewed, and chased it down with a gulp of milk. He wiped his lips with the sleeve of his shirt. "He wants you to come to the station tomorrow afternoon and talk to him."

She studied Heath. "What am I to talk to him about?"

"He wants to hear your story, from you. It turns out when Jones had you in the interview room, he didn't tape the discussion." Hawke raised an eyebrow. "It was as if he knew your statement would clear you."

A grin slowly tipped the corners of her mouth and made her cheeks hurt. That jackass had known she wasn't guilty but had pursued the case as if she were. Now, things would change. Maybe Bernie would tell her she could go back to work, with the chief thinking she wasn't guilty.

Chapter Twenty

Dela started the day like all the others since Paul Winter was killed. She woke, thinking about what she needed to do at work, only to remember, she wasn't allowed to be there. However, she no longer felt trod upon. She knew Detective Dick wouldn't be on this homicide after this morning. She looked forward to this afternoon. It was her chance to prove to the Tribal Chief of Police she hadn't killed anyone since returning to Nixyáawii.

After feeding Mugshot and Jethro, she lifted weights in her workout room and took a shower. Walking down the hall after dressing, she heard someone talking in the living room. Stepping quietly into the weight room, she picked up a three-pound barbell and crept along the hall to the living room.

Just before she stepped out of the hall, she recognized the voice.

Milo Shaffer sat in her recliner, scratching

Mugshot under the chin. He glanced up. "When no one answered the front door, I went around back and this fella jumped on the gate, popping it open. I didn't want him running off, so I coaxed him to the back door and saw it wasn't locked. We let ourselves in when I heard the pump running and figured you were taking a shower."

Dela stared at him. These were the most words she'd ever heard him say at one time. But then, he was always with Quinn who liked center stage. "I'm not sure if I should thank you for thinking of my dog, or call the tribals because you came in uninvited." She crossed her arms and remembered she held the barbell. Setting it on the floor inside the living room, she walked over to one of the side chairs she'd purchased and sat.

"Quinn's been asked to look into a dirty cop on the reservation, and I'm taking over the Winter homicide." He pulled out a notepad and pen.

"I've told the tribal police and the FBI everything about that day. Do I have to go over it again?" she asked.

Shaffer shook his head. "Tell me what you and Seaver have dug up so far." When she didn't say anything, he added, "Quinn told me you two have been digging around talking to people who won't talk to us."

"Do you want coffee or iced tea?" she asked, rising and heading to the kitchen.

"Coffee, please."

She smiled while making a cup of coffee for the Fed and pouring a glass of iced tea for herself. It was a breakthrough that the Feds were coming to her and Heath for help. One would have assumed the tribal police would have been able to talk to people, but it was clear no one trusted Detective Dick. Dela carried the drinks back into the living room, handed the mug to Shaffer, and returned to her seat. After a long drink of tea, she began telling the FBI agent everything she and Heath knew to this point.

"You two have been busy," Shaffer said, studying her. "What do you need help with that I can do? It's obvious no one on the reservation will talk to me. But I can do digging on the computer to fill in blanks."

"If you could get the reports on Lora Murdoch's death and her cousin's," she rattled off the name, "and also see what you can find out about Levi Murdoch." She stared into her iced tea.

"Someone else? Maybe Sander?" Shaffer asked.

"As much as I would love to have this be something Sander did, I don't think he did. The one I have on the list is Daniel Booth. He learned how to cook meth from Winter and was ready to take over. He's missing. Whether of his own accord or Sander made him vanish, we don't know." Dela thought of someone else. "Jacee Bing. She works in surveillance at the casino, is Ina Winter's cousin, and is Booth's girlfriend. She didn't like the victim and according to her she doesn't like drugs, but she likes the things drug money can buy. She might have wanted her boyfriend to be making more money and took care of someone she hated." Dela shrugged. "Those are all the people who we have come up with in our questioning."

"It's a good list. I'll let you know what I find and you keep me in the loop of who you talk to and what you learn." He closed the notepad and stared at her. "Don't talk to anyone alone. Once word gets out you aren't the suspect, the real suspect is going to get nervous. If you talk to the wrong person—"

"The suspect," Dela said.

Shaffer nodded. "Alone, he, or she, may decide you are a threat."

"Heath and I have been talking to people together." She glanced at her watch. "Not to rush you off, but I need to grab lunch and go meet with Chief Steele. He wanted me to repeat what I said in my interview with Detective Jones."

Shaffer stood. "I heard you were being re-interviewed by the tribal police. Something about the whole interview you did with Jones was erased."

"Jones probably did it the minute the interview was over. Otherwise, he wouldn't have been able to keep saying I was the only suspect."

She moved to the door and opened it. "I'm glad to be dropped down on the suspect list."

Shaffer stopped and stared at her. "What do you mean dropped down? You're still at the top because of Mrs. Swan's statement. But we're following other lines of inquiry as well."

"If I were you, I'd do the same. But don't put too much in the old woman's words. Because you're going to find, I didn't kill him." She closed the door and leaned against it. When was this mess going to be over?

"Come on, let's grab some grub," she said to Mugshot and they walked into the kitchen.

Dela sat in the same interview room as before. This time the fifty-something Chief of Police sat across from her. His plump pale face glistened with perspiration while his doughy body stressed the buttons on his uniform. The man smiled at her when she entered the room. His thick lips drew back, revealing small stained teeth. The man clearly ate badly and drank too much coffee. She'd had few dealings with the chief and hoped he was as pleasant as Heath had made him out to be.

"Ms. Alvaro, have a seat." He pointed to the chair across the table from him. Once she was seated, he continued, "Would you please state your name and occupation for the recording?" His voice was surprisingly high-pitched for such an ample body.

She offered the information and leaned back in the chair, trying not to look nervous or uninterested. She wanted the man to believe her when she told him the truth.

"The reason for re-interviewing this suspect is due to the fact…" He went on to say the original interview had been wiped from the system and he had taken it upon himself to redo the interview.

Dela waited for him to say something about Detective Jones being taken off the case, but he didn't mention that. Instead, he said, "Tell me what happened the day Paul Winter was killed."

Feeling as if she'd recited this a thousand times, she started with the phone call from Ina, and this time she mentioned calling Heath and telling him that Winter would probably be calling them about the donkey being stolen.

Chief Steele held up a hand and circled his finger in the air. "Wind back up. You say you called Officer Seaver and told him you'd been in a fight with the victim and he'd be calling us to complain?"

She feared Heath still hadn't said anything to his boss and here she'd dropped the news. But it was out and she couldn't take it back. "Yes. He said he had to go to the casino first and then would stop by and talk to Paul. I called him when I was walking the donkey to my house."

The man's small, round, green eyes studied her as his thick bottom lip moved in and out. The air grew hotter and stifling. She held his gaze, feeling like she sat in the principal's office.

He finally asked, "Why haven't I heard this before?"

She sighed. "I didn't mention it before because I didn't want to get Heath in trouble. And I was afraid if you knew we were friends, you wouldn't let him work on the case."

The man poked a thick, stubby finger down on the tabletop. "I've known you two were friends since I interviewed him for the job here. I would have taken in anything he said and made my decisions from facts, not friendships. Now I wonder at you keeping this to yourself." His green eyes felt as if they were poking at her as his finger had the table.

"Ask Heath about his whereabouts. He said, instead of going to the casino he went straight to the Winter residence. And he saw Paul sitting up. Before he could get out and talk to him, Heath received a call about a disturbance, only when he arrived there wasn't anything happening and no one said they called the police." She leaned forward. "Which makes me think someone was in the house, watching my fight with Paul, and saw where I put the knife. When they were ready to go out and kill him, Heath arrived. They made a nine-one-one call which lured Heath away and then took the knife I had put in the shed and killed Paul." Dela stared into the chief's eyes. "It's the only thing that makes sense."

The man shook his head, jiggling the white jowls under his dimpled chin. "We have an eyewitness that says you killed Winter."

"An eye witness who has conveniently gone on a vacation." Dela leaned back and crossed her arms. "I concede she may have seen the fight, but if she had watched us fighting, she would have seen me put the knife in the shed, grab the halter for the donkey, and lead him away. And if she was watching so closely, she would have seen Paul sit up, Heath's arrival, and the killer stab Paul if she went over and found him dead after I'd been there."

"How do you know Mrs. Swan is on vacation?" Chief Steele asked.

"Grandfather Thunder told me. He is friends with the husband of one of Mrs. Swan's friends."

Steele studied her some more. "Anything else you care to tell me about that day?"

"There's nothing to tell. I gave you all the information I know." She returned his gaze, not flinching, wondering what was spinning in his mind.

"This interview ended at…" He recited the time and stared at the video camera in the corner of the room. The light blinked off, and he shifted his attention to her. "I understand you and Officer Seaver spent his days off interviewing people."

If he knew, there was no sense denying it. "Yes, we talked to people who might have a reason or know someone who had reason to want Paul dead."

"It is not regulation for an officer to take a suspect along on interviews." He continued to study her.

"I'm not going to sit around while my reputation, my job, and possibly my life, are in danger. I was trained to take action. I won't go with Heath when he questions people, but I won't stand by and wait for the slow process of a murder investigation to clear my name." She stood. "If I can't work, I need something to do. And that something is talking to people. Everything I learn I give to Heath or Special Agent Shaffer. I'm not withholding anything from them or you. I want my life back."

Her hand was on the door when the chief said, "If you interfere, we will have to put you in jail."

Dela glanced over her shoulder. "I'm not interfering; I'm collecting evidence to find the real killer." She opened the door, swung to the left to exit the back door of the building, and ran into Jacob Red Bear.

"Hey." He held her by her upper arms. "What's up?"

"I just re-interviewed with Chief Steele." She tipped her head to the room and stepped back out of his grasp.

"I see. Can I buy you a soda?"

She could tell by his tone he wanted to have a conversation with her outside of the police station. "Sure. Mission Market?"

"Yeah. Give me twenty minutes."

She nodded and walked out to her car. The Public Safety building had never made her anxious before, but she couldn't shake the feeling the Chief of Police didn't seem any more friendly toward her than Detective Dick. She backed out of the parking slot and headed to the market. It would be good to talk to a friend after the afternoon she'd had.

Chapter Twenty-one

Dela sat at a table in the little sandwich shop area of the market. She'd already ordered a soda and a bag of chips. She sat peering out the large glass window watching the locals come and go. The owner of the market called out to each person as they came through the door. The community and friendliness were why Dela had returned after being medically discharged from the army. She knew after the initial questions about the circumstance of her return, that she would be welcomed into the community once again.

"Dela, do you need a refill?" Jessie, a teenager related to Jacob, asked.

"No, thank you. I'm sipping slow." She'd told the teen she was waiting for Officer Red Bear. That's when the girl had told Dela she was related to him.

"Sometimes, he's late. Let me know if you need more."

"Thanks, I will." Dela shifted her gaze to the short

aisles of snacks and necessities and spotted the one person she didn't want to see today, or ever. Detective Dick. She started a mantra, "Don't look this way. Don't look this way." Her hand sought the issue of the CUJ that had been sitting on the table when she sat down. She held that up in front of her as if she were reading.

She wasn't in the mood to deal with him. He would blame her for getting pulled from the homicide and ratted out about helping Sander. Dela studied the photo in the newspaper of young children wearing regalia and dancing. She should have asked the chief what had been done about Detective Dick.

A glance out the window and she spotted Jacob parking next to her car. She let a breath out and peeked over the newspaper. Dick wasn't anywhere in sight from where she sat. She lowered the paper and folded it back up.

Loud voices jerked her attention back outside. Detective Dick was stabbing Jacob in the chest with a finger as he shouted and flung his other arm around wildly.

Jacob shoved the older man back, said something quiet enough Dela couldn't even hear the timbre of his voice, and walked by the detective.

A shiver slithered up her spine. Pulling her gaze from Jacob, she found Detective Dick staring daggers at her.

"Sorry, I'm late," Jacob said, before turning to the counter to order.

Dela nodded her head but her gaze remained locked on Dick. He grinned maliciously and pivoted, striding to his car. She watched the vehicle until she could no longer see it.

Jacob slid into the small booth seat across from

her. "Don't let him get to you. He's an asshole. Everyone knows it."

She knew he was talking about Dick. "I don't want to talk about him," she said, even though she really did want to know what had transpired that morning between the detective, his boss, and Quinn.

"Good. Let's talk about you." Jacob stared into her eyes. "How are you doing?"

Put some eyeliner and earrings on him and she would have thought she was staring into her friend, Robin's face. While Jacob was decidedly male in his appearance, he had the same qualities as his sister. Dela had found herself forgetting that Robin was dead, more times than not when she and Jacob visited.

"As well as I can considering I'm a suspect in a murder, I've been suspended from my job, and I keep being told to let the police handle finding the real killer." She leaned down and sipped her drink, watching Jacob.

His lips spread into a large grin. "So you're doing well."

She laughed and snorted pop out her nose. Grabbing a napkin, she closed her eyes to stop the tears from coming as the carbonation in the drink stung her nose.

Jacob laughed and said, "It's never a bad day if you can laugh and snort pop out your nose."

Dela tossed the napkin at him. "Says, you! What did you want to talk to me about? It couldn't have been just to make me laugh."

The man she'd known since they were both in grade school sobered. "You need to be careful. I've heard you are the one who pointed the finger at Jones being on the side of the drug dealers. Not only is he pissed, but so are the people he's been helping."

Wiping the last of the snot from her nose, Dela stared into her friend's eyes. "I'm sure there will be more people who step forward once the word gets around. He'll have more than me to worry about."

"But you're the one he has had the biggest grudge against for a long time. You're the one that will be retaliated against." Jacob studied her. "I know you've been through a lot while in the army, but this is different. Drug dealers and their minions aren't something to take lightly. They don't play by the rules and come up with new shit all the time. Be careful."

When she didn't say anything, he added, "Please. I don't want to lose you, too."

His words struck her in the heart. She knew he was talking about the death of his sister. Her childhood friend, whom Dela spent every day wishing she'd not been so nonchalant leaving her friend behind when she'd driven off to go to basketball practice.

"I'm not going anywhere. And no one is going to make me go away. Mentally or physically. I promise." She reached across the table and grasped his hand. They had been there for each other over the years having bonded over Robin's brutal murder.

"Make sure you don't meet anyone involved in this case alone. Always tell Heath or me where you are and who you are talking with." His dark brown eyes searched her face.

"I will let you, Heath, or Marty know where I am if I'm not at home. Chief Steele pretty much told me not to involve Heath in my investigations, so I'll be working with Marty from here on out, but I'll keep you all informed." She released his hand and leaned back. "And I have Special Agent Shaffer on speed dial. Since

Quinn is investigating Detective Jones, Shaffer came to see me this morning to find out what I've learned. He gave me the green light to keep talking to people and promised to get me information Heath was unable to dig up." She smiled. "That means I also have the Feds helping me. No one is going to harm me. Too many people know I didn't kill Paul and I'm a bulldog when it comes to justice."

Jacob slurped up the last of his drink and said, "Don't get too full of yourself. That's how most people end up in a box." He stood, walked over to the garbage can, and tossed the cup in. "Remember, call someone before you go anywhere."

She nodded and he walked out of the market, waving before he drove off in his tribal vehicle.

Dela dropped her cup and empty chip bag in the trash as she walked out of the building. It was four in the afternoon. She called Marty.

"Yo, Dela, what's up?" he answered.

"Can you come over to my place this evening? I have some good and some bad news and we need to plan a strategy for our moves the next few days."

"Can I bring Molly? We were going to go out to dinner."

"Yes. But go to dinner before you come over. I don't want her saying I ruined her evening." She was glad her two friends were becoming a couple. Molly deserved someone as fun and nice as Marty.

"See you around seven-thirty." He ended the call.

♠ ♣ ♥ ♦

Dela sat at her kitchen table, poking a fork at the salad she'd made for dinner. The list she'd made of people she wanted to check up on lay on the table beside her plate. Her gaze kept drifting to the page, reading through the names and the things she wanted to know.

Her phone rang, making her jump. Slowing her racing heart, she answered the restricted number. "Hello?" She had expected Milo Shaffer's voice.

"You think you're something special. Well, let me tell you, when this is all over, no one will remember you as the disabled war veteran. You'll be the sad, lonely woman, who couldn't keep her nose out of other people's business."

The line went dead and her hand shook as she set the phone down. She replayed the voice and words over in her mind. Was it Detective Dick? She wasn't certain. But who else would have gone to such a stupid means of scaring her?

She dialed Quinn. His phone rang several times and went to voicemail. "Quinn, it's Dela. I received a threatening call from a restricted number. Is there a way to find out who it belongs to? Call me back, please."

Then she wrote down the time and the call word for word the best she could remember it.

"Why?" she said out loud, staring at the kitchen window. It was stupid for Dick to call and harass her. He would know she would report the call. It didn't make sense.

She tossed the rest of her dinner into the trash, cleaned up the dishes, and went out into the backyard to pet Jethro and Mugshot, hoping to ease the frustration that had surfaced and made her antsy.

Her phone rang.

Heath.

"Hi, I know you aren't supposed to get involved in what I'm doing but can you come over?" she asked before he had time to greet her.

"What's wrong?" he asked, concern deepening his tone.

She told him about the call and that she'd notified Quinn and asked if he could trace it.

"I can be there in twenty minutes." The line went dead as a car engine died in her driveway. A glance at her phone and she knew it was Marty and Molly.

Dela entered the house and walked to the front door. She opened the door before anyone knocked.

Molly stood flushed-faced on Dela's front step. She could tell by the twinkle in her friend's eyes that something good had happened.

"Come on in. I'm sorry to pull Marty away from your date," Dela said, standing back to allow her guests to step in.

Molly walked into the house and held her left hand out to Dela. A modest shiny diamond ring sparkled on her friend's ring finger. "Marty and I are engaged," Molly said.

Dela drew her friend into a hug and said, "Congratulations. I can't think of a pair of people who deserve each other more."

Marty's face brightened as a smile spread across his face. "I thought it was foolish to not grab her up. I haven't enjoyed another woman's company as much as I do Molly's."

Dela released Molly and hugged her other friend. "Thank you for making her so happy," she whispered in his ear.

They were sitting in the living room with Molly telling Dela how Marty had proposed when the front door opened.

Heath strode through the door, his gaze moving around the room. He latched onto Dela and stopped in front of her. "Tell me what he said, again. Word for word."

Dela glanced at the happy couple. "Not now."

"What happened?" Molly and Marty asked at the same time.

"Someone threatened Dela," Heath said, pulling a chair over beside where Dela sat.

"Oh! Tell him and us," Molly said, sliding to the front of the couch and reaching toward Dela.

"I didn't want to ruin your special night." Dela studied her friend.

"It's more important you are around to be my maid of honor." Molly waved toward Marty. "We want you at our wedding."

Marty nodded. "We are in this to keep you safe and out of jail."

Dela sighed and repeated the phone call. "I couldn't tell if it was Detective Dick or not, but who else would threaten me? He saw me talking with Jacob at the market this afternoon. That was after he and Jacob had a discussion in the parking lot."

Heath leaned back in the chair he'd dragged over. "Jones was suspended until further notice this morning. His badge and gun were taken away from him." He ran a hand along the back of his neck under his long hair. "Jones only had six months left until he retired." Heath glanced at Dela. "He's not going to be happy if he leaves here in disgrace."

"I won't live in fear of him," Dela said, already moving into fight mode. She wasn't scared of the nasty man. But she was scared of Gus Sander and the possibility he wouldn't be happy his mole in the tribal police had been found. "We won't know for sure if he made the call until it's been checked out."

Her phone rang. Picking it up, she said, "It's Quinn." She swiped her finger across the screen and said, "Hello."

"You sounded upset. What happened?"

Dela retold the information to the Special Agent.

"I need the time the call came in," Quinn said, all business without a hint that the call had been anything other than ordinary.

She had to admit, that his ability to detach himself from anyone linked to a case was one of the things she admired about him. However, since it was her case, she would have liked him to have shown some hint of worry or care.

"I'll see what I can do. Are you alone?" Now there was a touch of emotion in his voice.

"Heath, Molly, and Marty are here. I'll be fine. Just find out who called, please." She kept her tone level and didn't give away how rattled the call had made her.

"I'll get on it. Don't go anywhere alone."

She glanced at the screen and saw he'd ended the call. Dela released a deep breath and studied her friends. "Quinn is going to see if he can find out who made the call. He told me not to go anywhere alone." Forcing her lips into a smile, she peered at Marty. "Looks like you are going everywhere I go the next few days."

"Not a problem," he said, his voice deeper than usual and more forceful.

She'd heard that tone before. Many times, as a matter of fact, when new recruits headed out on their first patrol. It was as if by affirming in a low forceful way that they were ready, they wouldn't be scared.

"I'll spend the night," Heath said.

Dela swung her gaze to him. "It would be stupid of

whoever called to come over tonight and try to harm me."

He shrugged. "I'm not leaving until Marty arrives back here in the morning." Heath exchanged glances with Marty.

Dela sighed and rose. "Who wants ice cream to celebrate Molly and Marty's engagement?"

"I thought we came over here so you and I can figure out the next move?" Marty said.

"That was before Molly walked in here showing off her ring." Dela smiled at her friend. "Now we have to celebrate. We'll talk about our plans tomorrow when you get here."

Even though she smiled and laughed with her friends, deep down, fear and anxiety started eating at her gut. How was she supposed to clear her name if someone out there was going to keep smearing it with mud?

Chapter Twenty-two

Tuesday morning arrived along with a cup of coffee in bed. Dela shoved her body up to lean against the headboard after Heath knocked on her door and walked in carrying what smelled like coffee in a mug.

"You're spoiling me," she said, blowing on the steam swirling up from the brown brew.

"Marty texted he'd be here in twenty minutes. You might want to get a shower and get dressed before he arrives." Heath studied her, then sat on the side of her bed. "Did you sleep last night?"

"Some." She wasn't going to admit that every sound she'd heard had her listening for someone's approach. It wasn't until she'd heard Heath moving around at five am that she'd truly fallen asleep. A glance at the clock told her that had been four hours ago.

"I'm not leaving until Marty gets here. I called in that I'd be late for work." His gaze rested on her phone sitting on the bedside table. "Hear anything from Quinn?"

She shook her head. "It was a restricted number. I'm sure they are harder to figure out." Drinking half the cup of coffee, she placed it on the table beside her phone and waved at Heath to stand.

He rose but didn't move away from the bed. His watchful stare had her slipping her legs over the edge of the bed and sitting in front of him.

"What's wrong?" She peered up at him.

He ran the fingers of one hand into her hair, cupping her head as he knelt in front of her. "I came back to Umatilla to see if we were still good for one another."

A knot lodged in her throat. She couldn't say anything, remembering how he'd always been gentle and kind. Finally, the word, "And?" croaked out of her mouth.

"I still think we would be good as a couple." His gaze searched her face. "What do you think?"

It had been years since a man had touched her with such tenderness. Her body trembled. "I think, once I am cleared of Paul Winter's death and I discover more about my father, we should re-evaluate your moving in as a roommate." Even though her body and heart told her this man would never hurt or abandon her, she couldn't throw herself in his arms and say she was ready to make a lifelong commitment.

His fingers, which had been massaging her scalp, stilled. His eyes narrowed. "Does that mean I can kiss you or are you going to keep me at arm's length until I move out of roommate status?" He raised one eyebrow.

She licked her lips, but said, "Why did you need to bring this up this morning?"

He released her and stood. That blank expression he was so good at had replaced the tenderness that he'd worn when he'd entered the room.

"Don't go stone-faced on me. You're the one who came in here pushing for us to be intimate. I'm not against the idea, I just want to know why this morning. Is it because of the threat I received last night? Or the fact that I might end up in jail for a murder I didn't commit? Do you think I won't be around long enough for a lifetime together so you want to make me happy while I still have time?" She grabbed the crutches leaned up against her bedside table and stood.

Heath faced her. "I've wanted to kiss you since I set eyes on you at the casino. But you had the look of someone who didn't want a commitment. And if we start up, that's what I want. Commitment."

Dela glanced down at the floor where her right foot should be. "I don't want someone committing to me without seeing all my flaws." She wiggled her stub. "This will not grow back. I will never be able to get out of bed and walk without my crutches. I'll need a prosthesis the rest of my life." Her gaze rose to his face. Compassion softened the blankness that had been there. "And I don't want pity."

Heath snorted. "Pity? How could anyone pity someone as bullheaded as you."

She walked over to Heath and raised her face to his. "Kiss me and then I need to take a shower."

His eyes flashed in surprise but he didn't hesitate.

The kiss was all she remembered from their teenage first kiss to the last kiss he gave her when she broke up with him. All the elation and sorrow from that time filled her before he pulled her tighter and kissed her like the man he'd become.

♠ ♣ ♥ ♦

Dela walked into the kitchen surprised and relieved to find Marty sitting at the table, drinking a cup of coffee.

"Heath said to tell you he'll be here around seven for dinner and to spend the night." Marty studied her over his cup of coffee. "Anything going on between you two that I need to relay to Molly?"

"Nope. He's a friend who is looking out for me." She was glad her back was to the man as her cheeks heated. The kiss Heath had left her with before her shower had kept her blood sizzling even as she'd dried off and dressed.

"I read the list you had sitting on the table. Where do you want to start?" Marty asked.

"I need to see if Special Agent Shaffer learned anything about the people I asked him to check on and see if he'll let us peek at the crime scene photos. Maybe I can see something that wasn't there when I retrieved Jethro." As if speaking his name had made it to his big fuzzy ears, Jethro let out a loud hee-haw-eee-haw.

"I'll go give him his grain and feed Mugshot." She opened the French door and glanced over her shoulder. "Do you know where Detective Jones lives?"

Marty's chin dropped, leaving his mouth open for several seconds. He snapped it shut and asked, "Why?"

"I'd just like to see where he lives and check out his neighbors."

"What does that have to do with clearing your name?" Marty studied her with the same scrutiny she was sure he would give a faulty computer motherboard.

"I like to know the habitat of my enemies. It's kind of like reconnaissance in the army. Know your enemies, their routines, their bases, their friends. Then you are prepared for whatever they might do." She walked out into the backyard and a thought struck her. Would her animals be safe from retaliation by whoever made the call?

♠ ♣ ♥ ♦

They sat in Marty's car a block away from Detective Richard Jones's house in Pendleton, deciding how to go about asking the neighbors about Jones. It didn't surprise Dela that the detective lived off the reservation. She had often wondered why he had applied for a job with the tribal police when he couldn't hide his disapproval of Native Americans.

Her phone buzzed. It was Shaffer.

"Hi," Dela answered.

"I have some of the information you wanted. You're not at your house but your car is here." The Special Agent's tone didn't hold the censure she was sure Quinn would have used at not finding her at home.

"Marty and I were checking out something. We can meet at the Mission Market in twenty minutes." She glanced at Marty. He nodded.

"I'll be there."

Dela studied the neighborhood as Marty pulled away from the curb and headed east. "We need to come up with a plan to talk to people. Since neither one of us are law enforcement, we'll have to come up with something else."

"I could get a couple of clipboards and check-off sheets. We can canvas the neighborhood as poll takers." Marty said.

"How do we get around to asking about Detective Dick?" she asked.

"It could be about police services. We can bring up we know there is someone in law enforcement on their street and see where it goes."

She glanced over at Marty. He had a grin on his face. "I think that's a great idea. We just have to make sure Dick doesn't see us."

"Maybe we can get him called away for some reason?" Marty turned onto Mission Road and they drove past the veterinary clinic.

"When you and Molly marry, are you going to move in with her?" Dela thought it made sense since she would continue with her veterinary practice.

"Until we build a house. Molly has some land that was left to her by her grandfather. It's along the river. We'll build there, and Travis will continue to live behind the clinic. That way there is someone onsite for emergencies." Marty glanced over at her. "I know her first husband was a scumbag. She said you know everything about it."

Dela nodded. "I was the one who talked her into leaving him."

"I'm glad you did from the little bit she and Travis have told me. Don't worry, I would never hurt her."

Smiling, Dela put a hand on his arm. "I know that. I'm happy you two are going to marry. Molly will have the life she should have had the first time around."

Marty parked in front of the market and Dela spotted Shaffer sitting in one of the small booths on the deli side of the building.

"At least he is willing to work with us," she said, stepping out of Marty's vehicle.

They entered the building, nodded at the store owner, and turned to the right. Shaffer looked up as they walked over to his booth. The man, while being short, was broad. He nearly filled his seat.

Dela knew they'd be knocking knees if they all sat

in the booth. She nodded toward the window. "Let's go sit at one of the tables outside."

Shaffer glanced out the window and shook his head. "That wind today is cold. It will be snug, but I'd rather we stay inside."

She motioned for Marty to slide into the empty bench seat. Dela slid in behind him, keeping her feet out from under the table. "What did you find?"

"Lora Murdoch died from an overdose of methamphetamine. Because of her past usage, it was written up as an accidental death. That drug is unstable because of how it is manufactured." Shaffer studied Dela. "Were you thinking it was murder?"

"No. But I think her death, and possibly her cousin's, could have caused the murder of Paul Winter." Dela could see someone close to Lora, like her brother Levi, wanting to rid the reservation of the man who caused so many deaths from what he cooked.

"What did you find out about Levi Murdoch?" she asked.

He rattled off all the same things she'd heard before. "When did he move back to the reservation?" Dela asked.

Shaffer shuffled papers. "Six months before his sister died."

"That is plenty of time to discover she was using and who she bought from." Dela didn't like the idea of Levi ruining his life by getting back at the man who stole his sister's. But revenge killings did happen. "I wonder if he confronted Gus Sander? And how would he have found out about Paul?"

"I'd stay away from Sander. He hasn't been brought in on any charges but people who work for him go missing," Shaffer said.

"Like Daniel Booth," Dela muttered.

"Booth? He's still alive. He used his credit card in Wyoming yesterday. I have an agent looking for him back there." Shaffer slid a paper across the table.

Dela recognized Booth from a photo taken at an ATM machine. "We know he's still alive. But why did he leave? Was it because Sander was mad at him or because he killed Paul to take over his cooking business?"

"The other woman, Jacee Bing," Shaffer said. "I'm surprised she was able to get a job at the casino in surveillance. She has prior felonies for criminal mischief."

"What did she do?" Dela couldn't think of anything the timid woman would do that could get charges of criminal mischief.

"She set fire to a neighbor's house and was caught running away from another place that was set on fire." Shaffer looked up from the page he was reading. "She is an arsonist in the making."

Dela shook her head and peered at Marty. He appeared as surprised by this knowledge as she was.

"Jacee Bing? She's quiet and goes about her own business. Did the houses have any connection to her?" Dela asked.

"The first one blew up like a meth house. She swore she didn't set it on fire, but the person who owned the house said he saw her throw a lighted jar in the window." Shaffer studied the paper in front of him. "She was given the lesser charge because it was the man's word against hers and since the house was affirmed to have been a meth house, the man was also charged for manufacturing meth."

"And the other fire?" Dela asked, thinking that

arson and stabbing someone were two completely different levels of confidence. One you didn't have to face whoever you were hurting, the other you had to be up close and personal. That didn't sound like something Jacee could do.

"The one where she was seen running away. Again, she said she didn't start the fire. She'd been waiting outside the house for a friend when the house exploded and she ran." Shaffer glanced up from the papers. "I think it's a bit of a coincidence that she was at the scene of two meth house fires. Want me to talk to her?"

Dela glanced at Marty, the woman's supervisor. "What do you think? Will Jacee respond better to us or the Feds?"

"I think she would say more to us. She is a loner and doesn't say much. But I have noticed she avoids the security guards. I think anyone in uniform makes her uncomfortable."

Shaffer waved his hands up and down, motioning to his suit. "I'm not in uniform."

"No, but your initials and Special Agent are going to make her press her lips together tight." Marty shrugged. "Sorry, but that's how I see it."

The Special Agent nodded. "You know her better than I do. I'll leave her to the two of you. Since the eyewitness, Mrs. Swan, is in another state, I'll go see if I can locate her at her relatives in Idaho. We believe she is on the Lapwai Reservation. She has a niece and a sister living there."

Dela leaned forward. That was good news. "I believe she would respond better to you than to us. Since she told the police I killed Paul Winter, I doubt she would let me get near enough to ask questions. But

I have some I would like you to ask her." Dela stated how she wanted him to see if she really stood by the window for, she figured, a good thirty to forty-five minutes from the time Paul launched at her to when Heath drove away. "She had to have seen Heath drive up and Paul sit up if she remained at the window. If she went over and checked on Paul and found him dead, she had to have been watching everything and knows who really stabbed him."

"I'll touch on all the things you want to know," Shaffer said. "What about Sander? Do you want me to have a talk with him?"

Dela shook her head. "No. I think we'll get farther with him if we leave the Feds out of it." She motioned to Marty and herself. "We can't arrest him. He might open up to us better."

Shaffer chuckled. "Why would he open up to the two of you?"

"Let's just say he owes us a finder's fee." She hoped the man would consider them as allies since they returned his money when they could have given it over to the police.

Shaffer studied her. "You're not going to tell him where Booth is, are you?"

"No. We want Booth alive to ask him questions. We did Sander a favor, and I'm hoping he will reciprocate, that's all." She stood.

Marty didn't slide to the end. "Did Quinn tell you that Dela received a threat last night?"

She put her hands on her hips. "Why did you have to say anything? I wanted to keep it low-key so whoever did it won't think I'm scared by telling everyone around me."

Marty ignored her. "Well, did he?"

"Yes, I've been apprised of the threat to Dela. Quinn is working on that as well as investigating Detective Jones. He feels the threat came from the detective." Shaffer slid to the end of the booth and stood. "That's all I can tell you. Keep me informed of what you learn. I'll do the same."

"Thank you. We will." Dela said, leading the way out of the market.

At Marty's vehicle, she stopped with her hand on the passenger door handle. "Call Farley and see if Jacee is at work. I'd like to visit with her."

Chapter Twenty-three

Dela walked up to the door of a small single-wide mobile home in the area where Mugshot had been hit by a teenage driver. She was glad she'd been there for the dog and even happier she'd purchased the house in Tutuilla. The crowded mobile homes were depressing to her. She liked having space between her and her neighbor. Even her mom and Grandfather Thunder had a row of bushes between their properties for privacy.

The bark of a large dog sounded on the other side of the door before Dela knocked. She glanced over her shoulder at Marty. He shrugged and she rapped on the door.

The dog's bark became deeper and more threatening. Dela stepped off the small porch and stood on the ground beside Marty. She hoped the dog didn't come barreling out when the door opened.

"Quiet, Angel!" a woman's voice shouted above the barking. It sounded like Jacee but Dela wasn't certain.

The barking stopped.

"Who's there?" Jacee asked.

Dela motioned for Marty to speak up.

"It's me, Marty. I wanted to talk to you about work," he said.

The lock on the door clicked and Jacee peeked out. Her brows met above the bridge of her nose at the sight of Dela. "What is she doing here?"

Marty stepped forward. "We need to talk to you. Some information has turned up about you and it could be harmful to your job at the casino."

Jacee's eyes widened and she pulled the door open. "What are you talking about? What information?" She backed up, allowing them to enter.

A large black and red dog, that Dela recognized as a Rottweiler, stood in the hallway. The animal's bowling ball sized head came to her waist. The dog eyed them but didn't make a sound or attempt to move from the hallway.

Jacee sat on the couch and made kissing sounds. The dog trotted across the room and lay down sprawling the length of the furniture with its head in the woman's lap.

Dela took the rocking chair, and Marty sat on an overstuffed chair that looked about fifty years old.

"What could possibly interfere with my job?" Jacee asked.

The fact the woman seemed completely oblivious to her being surveillance at the casino and having a felony record made Dela wonder if, perhaps, she had been at the wrong place at the wrong time in both instances.

Marty cleared his throat. "Because of Paul's death,

the Feds have been looking into everyone close to him. They came across your felony misdemeanors of lighting two houses on fire."

Jacee's eyes widened. "But I thought those were taken off my record. They both happened before I was eighteen." She glanced at Dela and back to Marty.

"You were a minor when they happened?" Dela asked, wondering why Shaffer hadn't mentioned that when he brought it up.

"Yes. I hung out with the wrong crowd in high school. I didn't set those houses on fire. I was there when both happened, but I didn't do it. However, when I was brought in, I protested I didn't do it, but I wouldn't point any fingers." She hiccupped. "Not if I wanted to stay safe and my family to stay safe." The dog started growling as Jacee became noticeably more and more agitated.

"Calm down. We need to know all you know about Paul's cooking meth and why Daniel took off," Dela said, hoping by changing the subject the woman would become less upset and the dog would be lulled into complacency.

Jacee sniffed, wiped the tears from her cheeks on the top of the dog's head, and said, "I told you all of it before."

"No, you didn't." Dela stared at the woman. "Do you use meth?"

"No! It's nasty stuff."

"Then why is your boyfriend making it?" Dela asked.

Jacee hung her head. "Daniel said he'd learn how to cook it from Paul, then go out on his own until we had enough money to start over somewhere else. He knows that even though he isn't using, just being around the fumes is harmful, not to mention the whole thing could blow up." She shuddered. "I told him I would rather we just took off and figured out how to live when we landed somewhere. But by then he'd already talked to Mr. Sander and couldn't get out."

Dela narrowed her eyes. "I think it was more like Daniel didn't want out. Because right now he's in Wyoming not worrying about making money by cooking."

The woman's eyes bore into Dela. "He's hiding from Mr. Sander because you told him lies."

"I only told Sander the truth. The one telling lies is your boyfriend." Dela leaned forward. "Do you think Daniel killed Paul to take over the business of selling to Sander?"

The pause told Dela the woman hadn't ruled out her boyfriend had killed her cousin's husband.

Jacee shook her head slowly. "He told me he didn't do it. But it was good for us."

"Were you with Daniel the morning Paul was killed?" Dela asked.

"No. He'd said he had to go to town. I didn't go to work until the night shift, so I stayed home to get some laundry done." The woman patted the dog's head in her lap.

"Then you can't say that Daniel didn't go to Paul's that morning," Marty said.

"No." Jacee slid her gaze over to her boss.

"What kind of vehicle does Daniel drive?" Dela asked. She hadn't seen any vehicles at the Winter residence, nor parked out on the road. She would have noticed since she wanted to be sure no one was there when she retrieved Jethro.

"He has a green Ford truck." Jacee played with the

dog's ears as she talked. "I'm sure he would have told me if he'd killed Paul. He knew how much I hated Ina's husband. Lately, Daniel has been doing things to make me happy because he knows how much I hate what he does to make money."

"He would have bragged about killing a man you despised?" Marty asked.

She nodded.

Dela stood. "Thank you for talking with us." She started for the door and had a thought. "Has Daniel ever had conversations with Detective Jones of the Tribal Police?"

Jacee moved the dog off her lap and stood. "That's funny you asked. I'm pretty sure that's who was talking to Daniel the night before he left. I didn't get a good look at him. It was when I was getting ready to go to work. I looked out the door to see where Angel was and saw Daniel and a man standing next to a tribal vehicle. My first thought was he got caught cooking meth. But when I went out to go to work, the vehicle was gone and so was Daniel and his truck."

"You may have a visit from FBI Special Agent Quinn Pierce. He is trying to get information on Detective Jones and his involvement with the drugs on the rez." Dela walked to the door and opened it.

Once she and Marty were seated in his vehicle, Dela pulled out her phone and texted Quinn.

Jacee Bing has information about Det. Dick and his involvement with Daniel Booth.

"Now where to?" Marty asked.

"Let's go have a visit with Mr. Sander." Dela punched in the phone number she'd saved for the Sander residence and listened to the dial tone and ringing.

"Hello?" the same female voice from the other night answered.

"Mrs. Sander, I'm trying to schedule a meeting with your husband. Where could I do that?" Dela asked.

A hiss came over the line. "He has an office number for that." She rattled off the number and hung up.

"I'm not scoring any points with Mrs. Sander," Dela said as she dialed the number the woman had given her.

"Sander Construction, this is Genie, how may I help you?" asked a young female voice.

"I'd like to talk with Mr. Sander about a job I'd like to hire his company for, can I get in to see him today?" Dela asked.

The woman said there was an opening at four-thirty. "What name shall I put down?"

"Marty Casper." Dela ended the call and glanced at Marty.

The man was staring at her. "I don't need my name in that man's schedule when the Feds bring him down on drug charges."

"I couldn't give him mine, he would make sure he wasn't in the office when we arrived. I'll let Quinn know we used your name to talk to him." She then googled Sander Construction to find out where the office was in Pendleton. "Let's grab a late lunch," she said as Marty drove back to Pendleton on Mission.

"We could stop in at the clinic and get a sandwich there," he said.

Knowing she had ruined his vacation by having him play bodyguard, Dela agreed that was a good solution.

Dela and Marty sat in the reception area waiting for the clock to tick 4:30 and the receptionist to usher them into Mr. Sander's office.

They couldn't talk about what they were going to say. The woman glanced up at them every minute as if to see if they were still seated.

The phone buzzed, the woman answered, and said, "Yes, your four-thirty is here. I'll bring them right in." She replaced the phone and stood. "Follow me."

Dela and Marty walked behind the woman down a hall to a large wooden door.

She knocked and held the door open, motioning for them to enter.

Dela walked in first.

Sander's face reddened and his cheeks puffed out as he stood. "What are you doing here?"

The man who seemed to be the drug dealer's shadow appeared to Dela's right.

"We have some questions to ask you." Dela continued into the room with Marty behind her. She took one of the chairs in front of Sander's desk.

"I don't have to answer any questions you ask. You aren't the police," Sander said, motioning for the bodyguard to move them out.

"You're right, we aren't the police, and I don't plan on saying anything about your other profession to any cops. I want to find out if you called last night and threatened me." Dela wasn't going to let this man shove her out the door without some answers.

Sander stared at her. "Why would I do that?"

"To keep me from finding out you killed Paul Winter."

The CEO slapped a hand on the desk.

Marty flinched.

She didn't. Dela had seen Sander's theatrics before. She wouldn't have expected anything less than his outburst.

"I didn't kill Paul. He made me money."

"Except when his wife ran off with the front money." Dela kept her gaze on Sander.

It was as if someone punched a hole in the dealer's body and he slowly deflated down into the chair behind his desk. "You brought that money back to me. I had no reason to kill Paul."

"Ahh, but the money was given to you after he was dead." Dela wasn't going to let Sander think she could be deterred from the reason she was here.

"I did not kill Paul." He glared at her.

She hooked a thumb toward the bodyguard. "Did you ask him to kill Paul?"

"No. I didn't want Paul dead. He made me money. Lots of money. Why would I kill the person making me rich?"

"Fair enough. What about Detective Richard Jones? I understand he has been keeping your business on the reservation under wraps for you."

Chapter Twenty-four

"Where the hell did you hear that?" Gus Sander roared as he once again pushed up to his feet. He gave the impression of a bear with his lips rolled back away from his teeth and his shoulders hunched as he leaned with his fists on the top of the desk.

"It seems to be known by nearly everyone on the reservation except for the other tribal police members and those of us who would have turned Detective Jones in if we'd have known." She smiled. Having this knowledge against the tribal officer who had thrown roadblocks in her way every time she'd tried to work with the tribal police, was a heady feeling. She had been justified in her instinct that the man was rotten.

Sander eased back down in his chair as Dela spoke. Now he leaned back, studying her. "If you know this, what are you doing about it?"

"First, I'm going to clear my name, then I'll be doing all I can to clean up the reservation." She peered straight into his eyes. "If I were you, I'd start clearing up any business you have there."

"You didn't come here to warn me about cleaning up the reservation."

"No, I asked you about the threat to me, and I'd like to know if you received any threats. Paul had received one before he died. I'm thinking that someone close to a person who died due to an overdose is out for revenge. They killed Paul and may be coming after you next." She hid the triumphant smile that wanted to spread across her lips at the sight of fear that flashed in the man's eyes.

The bodyguard moved closer to Sander. The man behind the desk waved him away and opened a drawer. He pulled out a piece of paper. "I received this in the mail a month ago." He slid the paper across the desk top toward Dela.

She and Marty leaned forward reading without touching.

You caused the death of someone I loved. An eye for an eye.

Dela glanced up at the drug dealer. "Where did you find this?"

"It was taped to the windshield of my car when I came out of Harry's Bar one night. I figured it was someone just trying to scare me." He puffed up. "If someone is chicken shit enough to leave a note on my car window, they haven't got the balls to really do anything."

"Are you sure?" Dela asked. "Whoever it is did kill Paul. Stabbing is a personal way to kill someone." She studied the man whose face had paled.

"I have my bodyguards. They'll keep me alive."

"For your wife's sake, I hope they can." Dela rose

and walked to the door. Marty followed.

"What are you going to do?" Sander asked.

Dela stopped at the door. "About what?"

"The note and Jones."

She shrugged. "I can't tell the police any of it if you don't want me to bring up your dealing."

The man scowled, and she walked out of the office.

"What do you think he's going to do?" Marty asked as they walked down the hall and out of the building.

"He's going to call in Jones and ask him questions and probably tell him to get lost." She had a feeling Quinn needed to move quickly to get the goods on the tribal police detective.

"What about the note?" Marty beeped his vehicle to unlock and they slid in.

Dela stared at the building. "Sander is probably safe with that bodyguard. I think the opportunity of the fight I had with Paul had weakened him enough that the real killer felt confident they could take his life." She glanced at her friend. "Unless I get convicted and the killer feels he or she can't be touched, I don't see them trying to kill Sander."

"How can you be sure?" Marty backed out of the parking slot.

"I'm not. But the phrase *an eye for an eye* means this is a revenge killing, and the only people who would want revenge are family members of people who have overdosed. We need to find out about all the overdose deaths on the reservation in the last two years."

"Where to?" Marty asked.

"Home. I want to ask Heath to look up all the overdoses, and we need to write down what we learned today."

♠ ♣ ♥ ♦

Back at her house, Dela sent Marty off. There wasn't any need for him to hang around when she was just going to call Heath and go through the details she'd discovered so far.

Mugshot lay beside the recliner where Dela sat with a notebook on her lap, a pen in one hand, and phone in the other. She'd already talked to Heath about gathering names of the families of overdose victims. Now she was on the phone trying to contact Quinn. She wanted to know where he was on finding enough evidence to detain Detective Dick before Sander told him to, or made him, disappear.

"You've reached the number of FBI Special Agent Quinn Pierce, leave a message and I'll return your call." The beep irritated Dela.

"Quinn, it's Dela. We need to talk ASAP about Detective Dick. Sander is going to make him disappear. You need to work faster." She ended the message and set her phone down.

A knock at the door caused her to jump. A glance at the time and she figured it must be Heath. She hadn't taken off her prosthesis yet, making answering the door quicker.

Pulling the door open, she was surprised to see Quinn standing on the porch holding a pizza box that gave off a wonderful aroma. She'd only downed a peanut butter sandwich at Molly's because she wanted to get on to Sander's office. "What a surprise. Did you get my message?"

"Just as I pulled up." He stepped into the house and crossed the living room to place the pizza box on the dining room table. "How do you know Sander is going to make Jones disappear?"

Dela set plates, forks, and napkins on the table for three, causing Quinn to frown, and then asked him what he wanted to drink.

"Iced tea or water." He motioned to the third plate. "You expecting someone?"

"Heath should be showing up any time." She poured a glass of iced tea and set it in front of the chair where Quinn stood.

"He seems to be spending a lot of time here lately." Quinn waited for her to sit and then he sat across from her.

"Get used to it. When I'm cleared of this murder, he's moving in as a roommate." She felt her cheeks heat.

"Roommate as in renting a room or sharing your bed?" Quinn's gray eyes bore into hers.

What was he trying to see? "Renting a room. We'll see where it goes from there." She dropped her gaze to the pizza box and opened it. She hid the astonishment that he had brought her favorite. Chicken, olives, artichoke, and white garlic sauce.

"How did you know this was my favorite?" She ran through as many of their meals together as she could remember and none of them had been pizza.

He grinned. "I have my ways."

The door opened and Heath strode across the room. "Why wasn't that door locked?"

She stared up into his stormy brown eyes and frowned. "Because Quinn is here and I knew you would be coming any moment." If he was going to be this paranoid, he wouldn't be spending the night as he'd offered. She wasn't scared of whoever wrote the note. Not now that she was pretty sure the killer wasn't some lunatic. Just a grieving relative.

"You have to take any threats you receive seriously." Heath took a seat to the side of Dela and glanced at Quinn. "Hey." And nodded his head.

Quinn did a head bob and they both pulled a piece of pizza out of the box.

Dela stared at them. She no longer had an appetite. The two men seemed to speak volumes without saying much of anything. They were both going to make sure the little woman didn't come to any harm.

She put two pieces of pizza on a plate and stood. The two looked up at her. "I feel like eating outside away from all of this testosterone." She walked to the French doors, opened them, and joined Mugshot and Jethro in the yard. She sat on the step and ate her pizza, enjoying the snuffling, drooling, and bird songs.

The door opened when she'd finished eating and continued sitting outside.

"Dela, I don't know what we did, but could you come in while we discuss what we all learned today?" Heath asked, offering her a hand.

She grasped his hand and he pulled her to her feet.

"I'm sorry," he said.

Peering into his eyes she asked, "Do you know what for?"

"Not entirely, but you can explain it to me when Quinn leaves." He smiled as his gaze lingered on her face.

She released his hand and put her plate in the sink before returning to her seat at the table.

"How many families lost a loved one to an overdose?" she asked Heath.

"Besides the Brown and Murdoch families, there were three others in the last two years. The other three were closer to two years ago. I think for someone to be avenging now, they would have lost a loved one in the last year." Heath's gaze held hers. "I don't think revenge would smolder over two years."

"I agree." Dela glanced at Quinn. "What did you find out about Detective Dick?"

He pulled out his small notepad and flipped through the pages. "He lives alone, his neighbors don't care for him. They say he leaves his garbage can out all week, and fills it while it sits alongside the street."

Dela laughed. "That sounds about right."

"I talked with Derick Brown. He is now willing to say that Jones told him to keep quiet about where the drugs came from that killed his son after Jones ran him off the road. That was enough evidence to get Jones pulled in and a search warrant for his house. We conducted the search this afternoon and found what looked like a file he was keeping for blackmail." Quinn glanced at the two of them. "You were both on his list of 'disposable people.' I'm not sure what that meant but all the names on it were people who were in his way."

Dela studied Heath. She understood why Jones was threatened by Heath. He had been hired to take Jones's place. But why her?

"Does this mean you have him in custody?" Heath asked.

"Yes. Pending further investigation to pile up as many charges against him as we can." Quinn put a hand on Dela's arm. "You won't have to worry about him anymore."

She nodded. "Do you think he was the one who called and threatened me?"

"We're still working our way through the phone records to see."

Heath cleared his throat, and Quinn lifted his hand

off her arm.

"It's good to know that Jones is in custody but we need to discover who killed Paul." She asked Heath, "Does Chief Steele still have me at the top of the suspect list?"

"He's wavering but with Mrs. Swan's eyewitness account, he can't take you off the list." He grasped her hand, entwining their fingers.

"Shaffer was going to travel to Lapwai and talk to Mrs. Swan." She released her hand and shifted her attention to Quinn. "Have you heard anything from him?"

"No. But if he traveled to Lapwai today, I won't hear anything until tomorrow when he returns with his report." Quinn pushed his empty glass to the center of the table. "If there isn't anything else we need to discuss, I'm heading home. I have a kitchen that needs readied for new cabinets to be installed."

Dela thought about the day he'd taken her to the old Victorian house he was remodeling. "How is your remodel coming along? I'd love to see what you've done to it."

Quinn smiled. "You could come by on Sunday afternoon."

"We'll do that," Heath said.

Dela stared at Heath and then smiled at Quinn. "See you Sunday."

She walked Quinn to the door. "Thanks for the pizza, I didn't feel like making anything tonight."

"You're welcome. And how I knew about your favorite pizza…that day we ate at the Italian restaurant in Boise, you mentioned what kind of pizza you liked." He winked and walked out to his vehicle.

Dela shut the door and stood staring at it. She

couldn't believe he remembered such a mundane thing.

The clanking of dishes in the kitchen yanked her from her ruminating and she entered the kitchen to find Heath cleaning up.

"About earlier," Dela started.

Heath spun from the sink and leaned his butt against it with his hands holding a plate he was drying. "Yes?"

"You two were like a couple of bull elk battering your horns together to impress me. I don't like it. Never have. If I wanted a man who thought he had to prove to me he was a man, I would have dated Randy Samuels in high school."

"The quarterback? He asked you out?" Heath put the glass and towel down.

"Yes, he did ask me out. But I knew he'd try to mold me into the kind of girlfriend he wanted. I am not malleable."

Heath laughed. "That you are not."

She walked over to Heath. "Don't try to prove to me you are better than Quinn. I know who you are and I like who you are. You don't need to puff up your chest and pound on it to get me to notice you."

"Are you calling me a gorilla?" He pulled her into his arms.

"I call it as I see it." She smiled up at him.

Chapter Twenty-five

Dela toyed with calling Bernie Moon and asking if she could go back to work since the police hadn't arrested her. It was Wednesday and the day they could use all the help they could get at the casino. There was a conference starting today and Wednesday was the weekly Bingo event.

Heath had left for work, and she sat in the kitchen rereading all the notes she'd made on everyone they'd talked to and what they'd learned.

Her phone rang. Shaffer.

"Hello, what did you find out?" she answered.

"That I went all that way for nothing. Mrs. Swan's sister said she hasn't seen or heard from her sister in several weeks. She thought Sadie must have been staying with her daughter Ruth because there wasn't any cell phone reception out there." Shaffer sounded frustrated. "I asked if there were any other relatives Sadie might be staying with and she couldn't think of anyone."

Dela stood up. "I'm going to talk to Ruth and Levi. They have to know where she is or else they would have contacted the police."

"Don't go alone," Shaffer warned.

"I won't. Thank you for trying to find her."

"I haven't stopped. I'm back in Pendleton and will start digging into the family. In fact, I could go with you to talk to the grandson and daughter."

"Thanks, but I'll get more out of them if I take a tribal member with me." She wasn't going to tell Shaffer that person was in his eighties and wouldn't be much help should someone become physical.

"Report back to me with what you learn."

She agreed and then called Grandfather Thunder. The phone rang six times. She started to hang up and heard an out-of-breath, "Hello?"

"It's Dela. I need to talk to Mrs. Swan's daughter, Ruth, and Levi Murdoch. We can't find Sadie. She's not at her sister's in Lapwai. Would you come with me?"

The man's breathing had returned to normal. "If you can run me to the store afterwards."

She grinned. "I can do that. I'll be by to pick you up in fifteen minutes."

"I'll be ready."

Dela made sure Jethro and Mugshot had plenty of water and walked back through the house gathering her purse and phone.

She locked the front door and walked over to her car. Her phone rang. It was Heath.

"Hello?"

"I just had a visit with Chief Steele. Jones has been tossing names around right and left to the Feds. One of those names is yours."

Dela let loose with a curse more vulgar than her usual double frickin' shit. "What is he saying about me?"

"That you knew all about Paul's meth operation and wanted in on the take. That's what both your fights with him were about."

"Oooo, if he wasn't in custody, I'd kick the shit out of him." She slowed her breathing and asked, "Does Chief Steele believe him?"

"I don't think so. Jones also accused the chief of taking bribes. Which I'm pretty sure he hasn't done. Steele is to by the book to bribe anyone."

"I'm headed to pick up Grandfather Thunder. He wants to go to the store. And since I have nothing better to do…" She left it unsaid she was bored. Dela also didn't tell him she was taking an old man to talk to a hostile young man and a woman who didn't care for her much either about their missing relative.

"Have fun shopping with Grandfather Thunder." Heath rang off.

Dela slid into her car, fuming over the lies dickhead, as she was now going to call him, was spouting trying to give evidence to lessen his convictions, no doubt.

Driving by the Travel Center, Dela thought she should go in and talk to Ruth without Grandfather Thunder. She was here and there wasn't any sense in backtracking. He wouldn't mind if she was a few minutes late to pick him up.

She parked not far from the main entrance and walked into the warm interior. This time of year there weren't as many travelers on the road. The shelves were well stocked with souvenirs and food.

Dela stopped ten feet inside the door and scanned the heads she could see above the short aisles. She didn't see Ruth. Walking up to the counter, she was happy to see it wasn't the woman who had brushed her off the last time she came in here looking for Ruth.

"May I help you?" the woman in her twenties asked.

"Is Ruth here today?" Dela smiled.

"She's on break. You can't go into the breakroom." The woman looked at her watch. "She'll be out in fifteen minutes."

"I have to pick someone up. Can you go back and get her for me?" Dela continued to smile. There were only two other customers in the place and they were still looking at the souvenirs.

"I'm the only cashier until Deanne comes back out. I can't leave the till." The woman shrugged.

"Okay, I'll come back." Dela decided to go get Grandfather Thunder and return.

"What's your name so I can tell her you'll be back?"

"Just say a friend." Dela exited the building and slid into her car.

♠ ♣ ♥ ♦

"What took you so long?" Grandfather Thunder asked when she walked up to his front door.

"I stopped to talk to Ruth, but she was on break. We're going back to the Travel Center." She motioned for the elder to step out of his house.

"I thought *we* were going to talk to her?" The old man shuffled across his winter-worn lawn to her car. Her mom kept his lawn watered and mowed these days. While it was too soon to mow a lawn, it was cropped short from the last cutting her mom gave it in the fall.

In past years, when her mom was working, Grandfather Thunder had mowed their lawn. Her mom had taken over his lawn when she'd retired.

"I thought since I was passing the Travel Center on my way to get you, I'd talk to her rather than backtrack." Dela slid behind the steering wheel of her car and watched Grandfather Thunder buckle his seat belt. His hands shook but the click of the fastener registered he'd accomplished the task.

"I called my friend while waiting for you," Grandfather Thunder said as she backed out of his driveway.

"Which friend?" she asked, maneuvering the car onto the road.

"Ray. It was his wife who said Sadie was going to Idaho to see relatives. His wife still stands with that is what Sadie said."

Dela glanced over at Grandfather Thunder. "Either Mrs. Swan never made it to her sister's or she only said that because she wanted to hide from the police because she'd lied about seeing me."

"Don't jump to conclusions. Maybe she changed her mind. It's been almost a week since she left. Ruth should know where she is." Grandfather Thunder closed his eyes.

Dela knew he was taking a nap to keep his faculties sharp when they talked to Ruth.

As she drove toward the Travel Center, she passed Yellowhawk Health Center. Levi Murdoch should be at work. They'd go see him after they spoke to Ruth.

She pulled into the Travel Center and something tapped her arm. She looked down at a handicapped hanger.

"I brought this along so I don't have to walk too

far." Grandfather Thunder grinned as she pulled into a handicapped spot close to the entrance and hung the sign from her rearview mirror.

"Let's go talk to Ruth." Dela exited the car and hurried around to the passenger side to hold the door while the elder pulled himself out of the seat, using the door, and stood.

Dela kept her pace to match the man beside her. They entered the store which had several employees moving around and six to eight customers. Three of which appeared to be truckers. She stopped Grandfather Thunder as she scanned the visible heads. "Over there by the cold drinks."

She walked up to Ruth who was cleaning the soft drink dispenser. "Hi, Ruth."

The woman glanced at her and frowned. "What do you want now?"

Grandfather Thunder stopped beside them. "Níi łqwí, Ruth." He smiled at the woman and she smiled back.

"Níi łqwí, Grandfather Thunder. Why are you with this woman?" Ruth asked.

"We are concerned about your mother," the elder said, his smile fading.

"My mother? Why? She is visiting my aunt." A frown rippled across the woman's broad forehead.

Dela shook her head. "Special Agent Shaffer went to your aunt's yesterday to talk with your mom and she hasn't seen or heard from your mom in weeks." She took a step toward the woman. "That's why we are concerned. Whoever killed Paul could have hidden your mom to keep her from telling the truth."

Ruth glared at Dela. "Wouldn't that be you?"

Holding out her hands in supplication, Dela shook

her head. "I didn't kill Paul. He was alive and breathing when I led Jethro down the road. Someone else killed him. That someone may have paid or threatened your mom to say it was me. We won't know until we can talk to her. And right now…no one knows where she is." Dela stepped forward as the women's knees buckled.

Dela held Ruth up as best she could, leading the woman toward the back of the store where there were cases of water stacked. She eased Ruth down onto the cases and then grabbed a bottle of water from the refrigerated case nearby.

Grandfather Thunder held Ruth's hand. "This is a shock. Can you think of anyone else your mom might visit in order to stay away from whoever might have threatened her?"

Ruth sipped the water and shook her head. "I can't think of anywhere she might be. Have you talked to Levi? Maybe he sent her to one of his friends."

"That's where we were going to go next." Dela felt for the woman. If her mom wasn't where she thought she was and knew that she had witnessed a murder, Dela wouldn't be sitting on a case of water fretting. She'd be calling everyone her mom had ever come in contact with.

"She told Mary Shepherd that she was staying with relatives in Idaho," Grandfather Thunder said gently. "Is your aunt the only relative she has in Idaho?"

Ruth nodded. "Mother's family was small and many didn't survive before the seventies due to poor health facilities and lack of nutritious food."

"Thank you for talking to us. I'm sorry to have alarmed you, but I want you to know that the FBI is looking for your mom." Dela motioned to Grandfather

Thunder they were leaving.

The woman made an irreverent sound. "Like that will help my mother. The Feds aren't known for finding Indians, alive or dead."

Once they were in the car, Grandfather Thunder said, "She has a point."

Dela put a hand on his arm. "You both are jaded by the past. The Feds and all other law enforcement entities are trying harder to work with the reservations to find missing people. And I trust that Special Agent Shaffer will do his best to find Mrs. Swan."

The elder crossed his arms. "You only say that because you need her to prove you're innocent."

"No, I mean that because it is true. Heath told me about how local law enforcement—tribal, county, and state—are working with the Feds to move quicker when someone is reported missing. It's called Savanna's Act. You can ask anyone or look it up yourself." Dela drove the short distance to the Yellowhawk Health Center.

They entered the building and followed the green signs to the mental health department. Dela walked up to the receptionist that had thought she and Heath were a couple there for counseling and asked to see Levi Murdoch.

"He isn't available for any meetings other than his appointments for the day. He was put behind by an emergency this morning."

"It's still morning." Dela glanced at her watch. "Barely. Could we catch him on his lunch?"

"He's not taking lunch today to make sure he can see everyone." The woman stared at her, then flicked her gaze to the hallway as if saying, leave.

Dela sighed. "Come on, we'll go get lunch and your groceries." She followed Grandfather Thunder's shuffling gait out of the building and to her car.

When they were seated in the car she said, to no one in particular, "Do you think he really had a patient emergency that put him behind?"

"What does he drive?" Grandfather Thunder asked.

"I don't know." Dela texted Heath. *What is the make, model, and license plate for Levi Murdoch's vehicle?*

Why?

To see if he's at work or not.

She drove around to the back of the large building with five different wings. On the way to the back of the building, a blue sedan and a green Jeep left the parking lot. She waited five more minutes before her phone dinged.

According to DMV Levi drives a 2005 Jeep Wrangler. License 539 ZDU

Color? Dela had a sinking feeling the Jeep that left was his.

Green

He's avoiding me. I saw that vehicle drive out of Yellowhawk employee parking.

I thought you weren't investigating today? Was Heath's reply.

She shoved the phone into her purse and asked Grandfather Thunder, "Where did you need to shop?"

Chapter Twenty-six

The whole time she took Grandfather Thunder to Pendleton and back, Dela kept a lookout for a green Jeep with Levi's license plate number. Luck wasn't with her. She didn't see it again.

After dropping off Grandfather Thunder, Dela swung through the parking lot at Yellowhawk but didn't see a green Jeep. She decided to check out what was happening at the casino. The itch to get back to work was gnawing at her. Anything was better than sitting around waiting to hear from Shaffer, Quinn, and Heath about the progress of Paul Winter's murder.

Entering the Spotted Pony from the main entrance, Dela wandered over to Alfred, the valet, sitting on a stool and keeping tabs on everyone.

"Dela, good to see you. Have you come back to work?" Alfred asked.

"I haven't heard from Bernie if I can." She pulled over a slot machine chair and sat. "But I couldn't keep away. How are things going without me?"

"There was a problem with security for the conference. One of the speakers is a politician who thinks someone is after him." The man chuckled.

"Was Kenny able to take care of the problem?" Dela was ready to head to the security office and radio up.

"Bernie came in and talked to the politician. They managed to calm him down, he put in his appearance and left." Alfred pointed to a group around a carousel of slot machines. "That's part of the conference crowd. They seem to think they have special privileges. The old people here for Bingo have been crowded out." He sighed. "No one knows how to share anymore."

"I agree." She had an idea. "Do you happen to know who Levi Murdoch is?"

"Sure. He's the new therapist at Yellowhawk. They say he could have taken a job in any city and made more money, but he came here to give back." Alfred nodded, brushing his long gray braids up and down over the pockets of his western shirt.

"Does he ever come in here?" Dela asked.

"He's been in a time or two. Why?"

"Just curious. Do you happen to know his grandmother, Sadie Swan? Or his Aunt Ruth?"

"Sadie and I went to school together. She was smart and married into the Swan family. Good family. They were good to her and the kids when her husband died. But once Jack was gone, she seemed to have trouble upon trouble. Her son died in a car crash, her daughter-in-law couldn't handle his death and took her life. Then Sadie ended up with the grandchildren."

"Why didn't Ruth take her niece and nephew?" Dela asked the question that had been plaguing her from the start.

"Because she married a drunk and didn't want to bring those two into the house. She had enough trouble keeping her daughter off the bottle." Alfred swept his gaze to the outside and jumped up. "Car to park."

Dela slid off the chair and put it back where she'd found it. She wandered around the casino floor talking to the security personnel. They all asked if she was back. She wished she could have told them yes. Finally feeling like she was missed and needing a caffeine jolt, Dela wandered into the deli.

Rosie stood behind the counter smiling. "Dela, good to see you. You have been missed."

"Thanks, Rosie. I've been running in circles trying to figure out who killed Paul Winter." She pointed to the paper cups. "I'll have a large iced tea and can you join me?"

"Take a seat, I'll bring it out."

As Dela turned to walk to a table, Rosie called back to the kitchen she was on break. Dela sat and watched Rosie fill a large cup with iced tea and fill another one with soda. She carried both to the table, setting one cup in front of Dela.

"Thanks. You don't happen to know of any relatives Mrs. Swan would have in Idaho, other than her sister, do you?" Dela raised the cup to take a drink.

"No. But her family was originally from Warm Springs." Rosie sucked on her straw.

"Warm Springs? The reservation along the Deschutes River kind of north and central in the state?" Dela had never been to that reservation but had heard of it from people who had moved to Umatilla from there.

"That's the one. I have a couple of distant relatives from there." Rosie waved at someone.

"Do you have a way of asking if Sadie Swan is there visiting?" Dela wanted to know if the woman was safe or if they should be looking for a body.

"I can have my mom ask her cousin." Rosie set down her cup and pulled a cell phone out of her dress pocket. She typed away and then put the phone back down. "I've heard you and Heath are living together." The woman's eyes glittered with excitement.

Dela shook her head. "We aren't living together. He has been staying over at night since I received a phone threat."

The merriment slipped from Rosie's face. "Oh no! Who is threatening you?"

"We don't know for sure. I think it is Dickhead Jones but Heath thinks it might be the real killer. He refuses to let me spend the night alone." She shrugged. And then admitted to her friend. "It has been nice having him there. He makes breakfast every morning. And there is someone other than Mugshot to talk to in the evenings."

Rosie studied her before saying. "You can't tell me there isn't anything else going on. I can tell by the light in your eyes."

"We might have kissed and I liked it. But that's all. I told him we can't let it go any farther until I'm exonerated. I won't be the one to ruin his career." She would never forgive herself if he was demoted or fired from the tribal police because he was consorting with someone they'd arrested for murder.

The gleam returned to Rosie's eyes. "Don't worry, everyone is working hard to make sure you are cleared. The hunky Special Agent has been in here asking questions about Detective Jones and looking at surveillance tape. I don't know what he's looking for, but he left here yesterday with a smile on his face." She looked at her painted nails. "Of course, that could have been because I visited with him a bit."

Dela laughed. "And what did you and Quinn talk about?"

"This, that, what he was doing this weekend." Rosie winked. "I invited him to my sister's birthday party."

"Did he accept your invitation?" Dela wondered how Quinn would act surrounded by Rosie's family.

"He said if nothing came up, he'd be there." Rosie's cheeks deepened in color. "Do you think he likes me?"

"I think no one has the ability to tell you no." Dela smiled. "I hope he shows up."

"Me, too." Rosie's phone dinged. She glanced at it. "It's Mom." She scrolled and read through the message. "She says that there is someone staying with Myrtle Woods by the name of Sadie."

Dela stood and hugged her friend. "Thank you. This could be the information we've needed." She picked up her drink and headed out to her car.

Once in her vehicle, Dela called Shaffer and told him what she'd learned.

"I'll head down there right away and see if it is Sadie Swan and talk to her." Shaffer ended the call before Dela could say any more.

Still wanting to talk to Levi, she headed to Yellowhawk again. Maybe this time she'd get lucky and find him at work.

Dela ended up back home after one more canvas of the Yellowhawk parking lots. She'd thought about marching into the receptionist and demanding to know why Levi wasn't at work when she'd said he had a tight schedule. But not wanting to make others curious, she'd driven home.

Mugshot and Jethro were happy to see her. They wandered around her as she sat in a lawn chair, staring at the Blue Mountains. She had the notepad with her notes on her lap. Something wasn't right about all of this.

Who had been watching her fight with Paul? Was it someone in the house? Mrs. Swan had said she saw the fight and checked on Paul when Dela had left. Had someone else been in the house with her? Had that person, Levi, used her fight to do something he'd been wanting to do for a while?

No one had been looking at Levi as a suspect. He had a very good motive. His sister's death. And he could have persuaded his grandmother to lie so he wouldn't go to jail. Then when she couldn't keep lying, she disappeared.

"Dela?" Heath called from inside the house.

"Out here!"

Heath appeared carrying a duffel bag.

"Moving in?" she asked.

He grinned. "Not completely. But since I've been staying here, it saves time if I don't have to run home to change after work and before work."

She stood, dropping her notebook on the ground.

Heath was down the steps and by her side before she had time to bend to retrieve the book.

This wasn't going to work. "You have to let me do things on my own. I won't use all my muscles and learn to be self-sufficient if you keep doing things for me." She glared at him. "And that's why I wanted out of Mom's house. She kept running to do things for me."

"Sorry. It's in me to help." He handed her the notebook. "How was your shopping trip with Grandfather Thunder?"

She waved him inside. "Go change out of your uniform, and I'll find something for dinner. We'll talk while we eat."

While Heath changed, Dela started frying hamburgers. She was putting together a salad when Heath returned to the kitchen. He poured them each iced tea and sat at the table, watching.

"I'd offer to help but you said you wanted to do things on your own."

She glanced over her shoulder to see if he was being sarcastic. He appeared to be. "You can help me cook, after all, you will be eating most of it."

He grinned and picked up the server, turning the burgers in the pan.

Once they were seated at the table with their plates filled, Dela told Heath about her day.

When she'd finished, he said, "I can't believe you took an elderly man as your backup."

Dela studied him. "I'm pretty sure Ruth hasn't killed anyone. She's had too much loss of her own to want to put that on anyone else. Now, Levi…I can see him rationalizing killing Paul to stop more overdoses. He could have talked his grandmother into lying for him. But I'm pretty sure it wasn't his voice that threatened me on the phone." A thought struck her. "Quinn never did say if he discovered where the restricted call came from." She started to stand to get her phone.

Heath put a hand on her arm. "Sit. It can wait until we finish eating."

She relaxed back onto the chair but studied him.

The serious line of his lips and concern in his eyes had her asking, "What aren't you telling me?"

Heath grasped her hand in his. "Jones has a good lawyer. He's out on bail. His charges aren't serious enough to keep him in jail. I want you to go nowhere without someone with you. If he is the person threatening you, he has even more reason now that he's lost his job."

Her body sagged in the chair before her spine straightened and she peered into his eyes. "I'm not afraid of him. In fact, I hope he comes after me. It will only prove his vendetta against me."

"Dela, you need to be afraid of him. He has been working with a drug dealer and letting the people of Nixyáawii die. Or threatening them so they keep quiet and he can continue as a tribal officer and keep the drug problem here quiet. He is not a man you want to go against alone."

She studied him. "That's why you brought clothes. You aren't going to leave me alone."

"I asked for a leave of absence as soon as I learned of Jones's bail. I told Chief Steele you needed protection and I was going to provide it." Heath touched her cheek. "He agreed with me. Think about that. Chief Steele believes your life is in danger by one of his former officers."

Dela wouldn't admit to anyone, even Heath, that she was scared. She'd been the recipient of dickhead's hate-filled stares ever since her first meeting with the detective. Back then she'd wondered why he hated her without knowing her. As the years went by, she just decided he hated anyone on the rez.

"I promise to be careful and have someone with me at all times." She squeezed his hand and peered into his eyes as she crossed her ankles under the table. There was no way she would put Heath or anyone else she cared about in danger.

Chapter Twenty-seven

The next morning Dela woke to two messages on her phone. She used her crutches to get to the kitchen, following the smell of bacon and coffee. "You're spoiling me," she said to Heath.

He handed her a cup of coffee and kissed her on the cheek. "I like to cook; you like to eat. It's a good match."

"I have messages from Quinn and Shaffer this morning." She put the phone on the table and tapped the message from Shaffer and the speaker icon.

"Dela, this is Special Agent Shaffer. As far as I can confirm, it is Sadie Swan here at the Warm Springs Reservation. But she's refusing to speak to me. I'm going to instruct Quinn to bring her grandson down here to see if we can't get her to open up with him present."

Heath stood beside the table. "It sounds like your theory that she has been lying, for whatever reason, is correct."

Dela nodded and opened the message from Quinn.

"Dela, Shaffer asked me to bring Levi Murdoch to the Warm Springs Reservation to see if he can get his grandmother to talk to us. Only I can't find him. Do you have any suggestions of where to look or any connections? Give me a call back."

She shoved to her feet. "We need to talk to Ruth. She must have called Levi after Grandfather Thunder and I talked to her. That must have been why he left and never went back to work."

Heath gently urged her back onto her chair. "We'll eat, you can call Quinn, and then we'll go see what we can find out."

He was thinking clearer than she was. "Right. But I'll call Quinn back now."

Heath nodded.

She hit the call button and Quinn picked up on the first ring.

"Hey, did you get my message?" he asked.

"Yes. Grandfather Thunder and I talked to Ruth, Levi's aunt, yesterday." She continued telling him about the conversation and then seeing Levi leave Yellowhawk and his not returning.

"Any ideas where he might be?" Quinn asked.

"His house, his grandmother's house, his aunt's? I'm not sure who his friends are. But Heath and I will see what we can dig up." Dela glanced at Heath who sat across from her staring into the cup of coffee he had in his hands.

"We checked his place and his aunt's. She hasn't seen him but did say she talked to him yesterday about his missing grandmother. Do you think he went looking for her?"

Dela could see him doing that. "It could be. You might have someone look in Lapwai to see if he went there. I wonder if he knew about the relatives at Warm Springs? We'll ask Ruth when we talk to her."

"Keep in touch. I'll put out an all-points on Levi's vehicle. And be careful. Jones has a real hard-on about you for some reason." He said the last in a softer tone before hanging up.

She stared at her phone.

"What did he have to say?" Heath asked.

"He's putting an all-points out on Levi. He suggested it was okay for us to go talk to Ruth." She shoved her eggs around on her plate and smiled. "As if we needed his permission to do anything."

"That's all he had to say?" Heath pressed.

"He said to be careful. Jones didn't like me." She settled her gaze on Heath's face. "We already know that. And we'll be careful. Nothing like looking for a murderer with a pissed-off ex-cop out to take revenge."

♠ ♣ ♥ ♦

Once Dela was dressed and the kitchen was cleaned up, she and Heath put the animals in the back pasture.

"Let's take my vehicle," Heath said as she locked the house.

Dela walked to the passenger side of his pickup and climbed in. When Heath was backing out of the driveway, she asked, "Why your vehicle? Don't you trust my driving?"

"Because if your car is here, Jones might think to visit you." He pointed to a battered and rusted car sitting down the street about 50 yards. "It's Jacob's day off. He'll be sitting here watching."

Dela grinned. "You really think Dickhead is dumb

enough to do something during the day?"

"When he's angry he doesn't think straight. I gathered that information from the tribal officers who have been working with him for years." Heath drove slowly past the rusted car.

Jacob waved and pulled a ball cap down low over his face.

"I just hope Jacob gets to the house before Dickhead does anything to Mugshot or Jethro." Dela worried about her pets. While they both had strengths, they would be no match for someone with a gun.

"Jacob won't let anything happen to them. He has orders to move in as soon as he sees Jones approaching the house. He has a body camera on to video everything." Heath glanced at her. "We're not taking any chances of him talking his way out of anything."

At the Travel Center, they learned that Ruth didn't go to work. She'd said one of the grandkids was sick.

"Do you think a child is sick or she is frantically calling everyone she knows trying to find her mom?" Dela asked.

"She hasn't called the police as of last night," Heath said as they drove by Yellowhawk.

Dela stared at the building. "Let's see what we can find out from Levi's receptionist when we finish with Ruth."

"I'd thought of that as well. Do you have any idea who Levi might have friended since moving back here?" Heath continued past the market.

"No one has said anything about him having friends. I wonder if Quinn thought to get a list of phone calls he's made lately? That might give him some names of people to ask about Levi." She pulled out her phone and texted the special agent.

Double Down

Can you pull Levi's phone records to find out who he talks to?

Already did. Interestingly, he's called Jacee Bing three times since Daniel took off. He also called a Trace Talent and Daisy Tapas.

Dela read the text and smiled. *Daisy is Rosie's sister. I'm sure she will know who Trace is as well.*

I can talk to them.

Heath and I will talk to Rosie when we get back from Ruth's. You talk to Jacee. She doesn't like me.

Quinn sent her a laughing emoji. She made a face at her phone.

"What is that about?" Heath asked.

Dela read the texts to him.

He nodded. "Better to let Quinn deal with Jacee. She doesn't seem to respond to either of us. Maybe talking to a Fed will make her tell the truth."

"Hopefully. I've had the feeling she hasn't told us everything and she may have been more involved in the whole meth thing than she's let on." Dela stared at the small house of Levi's Aunt Ruth. "We'll talk to Rosie when we finish here."

Heath parked and they both exited the vehicle. The sun was shining, giving the impression spring might be around the corner. Dela knew better than to think that since it was the middle of March. Spring didn't really arrive for at least another month.

They walked up to the door and knocked. The sound of cartoons on the television could be heard from inside.

Heath rapped harder.

"Turn the television down," Ruth said right before the door opened. Her eyes widened but she stepped back to let them in.

"Have you heard from your mom?" Dela asked as the woman led them through the children lounging on the living room floor, staring at the television.

They stopped in the kitchen. An address book and telephone book were open on the table.

"No. I've been calling everyone I can think of trying to find her." Ruth sat down, her hand shook as she shoved the hair off of her weathered face.

Dela glanced at Heath, he nodded, and she said, "We think she might be at Warm Springs."

Ruth stared at her. "Warm Springs?" She rustled through the pages of the address book. "There is a distant cousin who lives there."

"An FBI agent is there now. We really need to talk with her. She could be in danger."

"Why?" Ruth scanned both their faces. Her eyes were runny with puffy bags under them and the lines on her face had deepened since their last conversation. She was a woman who hadn't slept well for a long time.

Heath took over the conversation. "We believe she was threatened by whoever did kill Paul Winter to say it was Dela. We think they may have also told her that once she talked to the police to hide or they would hurt her."

Ruth's hand rose to her mouth. "You think my mother lied to stay alive? And that's why she's hiding?"

"Yes. But we don't have enough evidence against the killer. That's why we are trying to contact her and let her know if she tells us the truth, we will protect her and her family until the person is arrested." Heath leaned back in his chair. "As soon as the FBI agent makes contact with your mom, we'll let you know."

Ruth glanced at the door to the living room. "The

grandchildren? What about them?"

"We'll watch over everyone. You, the grandkids, Levi, and your mom." Heath pulled out a notepad. "Do you have the address of the relative in Warm Springs?"

"I think so. I didn't think Mother kept in contact with him. I only have his information for when Mother passes. She wanted to make sure that side of the family knew." She hiccuped. "I hope I don't have to call this number for that reason."

She read the name, address, and phone number off for Heath.

"I'll send this to Special Agent Shaffer," he said, typing on his phone.

Dela watched the woman. "Did you call Levi after Grandfather Thunder and I talked to you yesterday?"

"Yes. I asked him if he knew where Mother was. He said he thought she was in Lapwai. That was where he had taken her."

This was interesting. "He took her to her sister's in Lapwai? Then why didn't she see them?"

"That's what he said, but when I talked to my auntie she said she hadn't seen Sadie in months." Ruth put her hands on the table and stared at Dela. "Do you think he had something to do with Paul Winter's death?"

"We've been wondering. Just how close were he and his sister?" Dela might finally get some straight answers out of the woman.

"They were only twelve months apart. You would have thought they were twins they were so close." Ruth stood, walked over to a drawer in a small desk, and pulled out a photo album. "They were close but as different as the moon and the sun. Levi was always inquisitive, ready to work and please. Lora was sulky, lazy, and pulling Levi into trouble every chance she got."

She opened the album. The first half a dozen pages were photos of the two as babies, then toddlers with a handsome man and smiling woman. The family appeared to have a happy home. As the children grew older the differences started to emerge. Levi smiled in the photos; Lora pouted.

"That's the last photo taken of the whole family. It was before their father died and their mother began drinking."

Dela studied the adults and then the children. The father had a weary look to him. The mother's smile wasn't genuine. Her eyes were dull. Levi was smiling but not as bright. Lora had a scowl. The children looked to be around eleven and twelve.

"I don't have any more photos. Mother thought because I saw them often, I didn't need photos." She closed the book. "From the time their mother died until Lora overdosed, that girl caused my mother nothing but pain. When she wasn't using, she was drinking or sleeping around. Not that I wanted to lose my niece in the way we did, but her death eased my mother's burdens."

"How did Levi feel about his sister doing all those things?" Dela asked.

"He was always trying to talk to her, but she would just sneer and say she wasn't going to regret anything when she died." Ruth stared at the corner of the kitchen. "I don't know what she meant by that."

"Do you think Levi would take revenge on the person who caused his sister's overdose?" Dela didn't see him as lashing out, but each person had their breaking point.

"Before I talked to him yesterday, I would have said he couldn't have killed a man."

Heath's attention shifted from his phone to the woman.

Dela asked, "What happened yesterday?"

"When I called him about Mother, he started swearing and said, he'd told her the truth but she wouldn't listen." Ruth glanced up from the album. "That's when I wondered if he killed Paul and asked his grandmother to lie for him."

Dela and Heath's gazes collided. In the back of her mind, she'd wondered if the man had anything to do with it. This was a pretty good indication that he had.

"Thank you for your help. We'll keep you informed about your mother and Levi." Heath rose and Dela followed him out of the house and into his vehicle.

He faced her before starting the vehicle. "I think we need to call Quinn about this."

Dela nodded. She opened her phone and dialed the special agent.

Chapter Twenty-eight

Back in Mission, they pulled into Yellowhawk and entered the building, following the green signs.

The receptionist glanced up as they approached. "He isn't in," she said and went back to typing.

"We know he isn't in. He's on the run." Dela said, standing so close to the desk her thighs were touching the metal trim.

The woman's hands stopped typing and she looked up. "On the run? What are you talking about?"

"Can you tell us who Levi's friends are?" Heath asked.

"He is my boss, not my buddy," the woman said tersely.

Ahhh. Dela leaned down, putting her palms on the top of the desk. "Did you try to make friends with him and he turned you down?"

The woman's face flushed. "I might have thought we'd make a good couple but he was clear he wasn't interested.”

"Did anyone call him that wasn't a patient?" Heath asked.

"His grandmother and Aunt Ruth." She placed her hands on the keyboard, then glanced up. "Oh, and Jacee Bing called a lot when he first arrived. But she hasn't called much since."

Heath grasped Dela's arm. "Thank you." He drew her out into the hallway. "Who keeps popping up?" he said, staring into Dela's eyes.

"Jacee. She hated Paul. And why would she be in contact with Levi when he first arrived?" Dela pulled her phone out of her purse.

"You can text that information to Quinn as we drive to talk to Rosie."

Dela already had the message typed and sent by the time they left the Yellowhawk parking lot.

Quinn replied. *Good to know. I have her in for questioning. I'll let you know what I find out.*

"Quinn liked the information. I hope Rosie can explain her sister's involvement with Levi and who Trace Talent is." Dela tried to lean back in the seat and relax, but for some reason, she felt as if there was a ticking bomb and they had to pull the right wire to stop more destruction.

At the Casino, Heath kept his gait even with Dela's. He walked close enough she could feel his nervous energy. "We're getting close," she said, as they both stepped into the designated deli area.

"I feel it, too," he said, walking up to the counter.

A young Umatilla woman stood behind the counter. "May I help you?"

"Is Rosie working today?" Dela asked.

"No, she had to help her sister. I can give you her

phone number." The young woman reached into her pocket and pulled out a phone.

"I know her number, thank you. Which sister is she helping? Is it Willow?" Rosie lived with her oldest sister, brother-in-law, and their children.

"No. I think she is helping Daisy move."

"Thank you!" Dela led Heath back to the entrance as she called her friend.

"Hey, Dela," Rosie answered.

"Hi, Rosie. Heath and I were at the casino looking for you. Can we come chat with you and Daisy?" Dela walked through the doors and into the parking lot.

Heath touched her elbow, directing her around objects as she focused on the call.

"Sure. I'm helping Daisy move out of her trailer and into her boyfriend's place. We're headed there with a load." Rosie rattled off how to get to where they were headed. "We should be there in about twenty minutes."

"We'll meet you there." Dela climbed up into the passenger seat of Heath's Chevy. "They are moving Daisy in with her boyfriend. He has a house in Minthorn."

The drive took them less than ten minutes. Dela pointed out the small house that had a fresh coat of paint, but the porch looked dubious.

Heath parked on the road in front of the house and they waited for Rosie and her sister to arrive.

"Do you know who the boyfriend is?" Heath asked.

"No. Rosie didn't say a name." Dela studied the small house. It wasn't in as bad a condition as hers when she'd bought it. The change Travis had made in the shell she'd bought and what she lived in today was a miracle. And as a newbie carpenter, Travis had been half the cost of a regular contractor.

A yellow VW bug drove up the road toward them followed by a slow-moving truck with furniture piled in the bed. Dela recognized Daisy driving the truck. Rosie parked her Volkswagon behind Heath and the truck drove up onto the lawn in front of the porch.

Dela and Heath exited his truck and walked behind Rosie up to the truck.

"What did you need to see me about?" Rosie asked when Daisy stood beside her.

The sisters were close in age. Daisy looked a lot like Rosie in the face. They shared the same welcoming smile. That is where the similarities stopped. Rosie was stout and round, while Daisy was long and lean.

"We actually wanted to talk to Daisy. We had asked for you at the casino to ask how to contact her," Heath said.

"Oh! Why do you want to talk to her?" Rosie took one step in front of her sister as though protecting her.

Dela smiled. "We just want to know how well she knows Levi Murdoch. His phone records show they talked frequently on his private phone, not at work."

Daisy stepped around her sister. "Lora and I went to school together. When Levi first came back, he called all her old friends. He was worried about her and wanted to know if we still hung out together and how she was doing." Daisy shrugged. "I couldn't tell him much. Lora was always into using substances to forget about the real world. We went our separate ways after high school."

Heath nodded. "Thank you. We're trying to locate Levi. Did he and Lora have any place they liked to go together?"

"I'm not sure. I can't remember anywhere in particular. You could ask Trace Talent. He and Lora were seeing each other in high school and later. He would know more about Levi and Lora's actions since he was also one of Levi's friends." Daisy shook her head. "When I heard about Lora I wasn't surprised, but at the same time, she was careful about who she bought her stuff from and having someone around when she used. I never thought she'd die all alone like she did."

Dela glanced at Heath. Did Levi know this about his sister? "Thank you, Daisy. Did you happen to know if Lora bought her drugs from Paul Winter?"

"You'll have to ask Trace that."

"Thanks," Heath said, capturing Dela's elbow and leading her away.

"Aren't you going to stay and lend some muscle to help unload this truck?" Rosie called after them.

"Not today. We have more people to talk to." Heath faced the house and Rosie. "Where's the boyfriend? He should be helping."

Rosie walked closer to them. "He's in the military. He sent her money to buy a house for them. Daisy and Dave have been working on this every spare minute because Eddie is coming home in a couple of weeks and she wanted the house ready when he arrives."

"If you still need some muscle later today, give me a call," Heath said.

When they were settled in the truck, Dela said, "Softy. You're going to help them get moved in, aren't you?"

Heath shrugged. "Sounds like a good way to help Rosie for all the information she and her sister have given us. Find out how we can talk to Trace."

"If you had your work vehicle you could look him up on your computer," she said, dialing Quinn.

"Special Agent Pierce," he answered.

"It's Dela. We found out that Daisy was a high school friend of Lora Murdoch's, Levi's sister. Levi had contacted her asking questions about his sister." She went on to tell him all they learned and asked if he had an address for Trace Talent.

He rattled off the man's work and home addresses.

Bells rang in Dela's head. "Trace works for Sander Construction?"

"That's the last known place of employment," Pierce said. "We had a sighting of Levi's Jeep. He was in Idaho, but when they staked out his Jeep he never came back to it."

"Double frickin' shit," Dela muttered. "From what we heard from Daisy, he could be out to kill everyone who might have sold or left his sister alone during her last high."

"Shaffer is still sitting at Warm Springs trying to get someone to help him talk to Mrs. Swan. He won't leave until she's talked to him. There's a reason other agents call him Bulldog. He's as tenacious as a bulldog when it comes to waiting out and getting information from someone."

"We'll go talk to Trace, now. I'll let you know what we learn." Dela ended the call.

"Trace works for Sander?" Heath asked, pulling away from the curb and turning the vehicle toward Pendleton.

"That's what Quinn said." Dela drew in a deep breath and let it out. The tension that had built on the way over to talk to Daisy felt like a vise squeezing her head and shooting phantom pains down her missing leg. She breathed in deeply again. They told her stress could bring on the pains in her non-existent leg. The kicker was how did she exorcise pain from a body part that didn't exist. Her brain was using her anxiety to transmit false pain out the end of her stub. She massaged her thigh and continued to even out her breathing.

"What's wrong?" Heath asked, slowing the truck as they entered the Pendleton city limits.

"Phantom pain." She grimaced as a pain shot from her knee to the invisible big toe.

He pulled into the first parking lot and faced her. "What can I do?"

"Nothing. That's the problem. There is nothing that anyone but me can do. I have to relax and try to think of other things."

Heath unbuckled and twisted in his seat. "Unbuckle, turn, and lay your head in my lap."

She wasn't sure what good that would do, but it would take her mind off her leg for a few minutes. Once she was situated with her head in his lap, Heath began messaging her temples, her ears, and down to her neck and shoulders.

"Breath slow and easy," he said quietly, his strong but gentle fingers sending the tension away. They remained like this for what seemed like only a few seconds, but when Dela sat back up and looked at the clock on the dash, he'd spent fifteen minutes soothing her nerves.

The pain in her leg was gone. "Thank you. I might just keep you around."

Heath grinned. "I'm going to remember you said that." He put the vehicle in gear and headed to the Sander Construction office.

Parked in front of the building, Dela said, "We only have to ask where to find Trace. We don't have to talk to Sander himself."

Heath nodded. "We'll ask the receptionist and see

if we can find out how long he's been working for Sander."

Dela walked up to the receptionist, smiled, and asked, "Could you tell me where we could find Trace Talent?"

"He's in the office with Mr. Sander," the receptionist replied.

"Do you know when he'll be coming out?" Dela asked.

The woman frowned. "He'll be in there until Mr. Sander leaves."

Seconds ticked and Dela gasped, facing Heath. "He's the bodyguard."

They both stared at the receptionist.

"Yes. Trace was hired when Mr. Sander received death threats." The receptionist studied them as if they had a problem putting two and two together.

"When was that?" Heath asked.

"Not quite a year ago." She picked up the phone. "Would you like me to buzz the office and tell them you want to talk to Trace?"

Dela's heart raced. How would they get him away from Sander? Did he ever leave Sander? "Does Mr. Sander only have the one bodyguard?"

"No, he has a different one every twelve hours. They change at noon and midnight."

It was shortly after noon, which meant Trace must have just come on duty. Dela walked away from the desk and Heath followed.

"What do we do?" Dela asked. She wanted to talk to Trace but didn't want to encounter Sander's wrath any more than they already had. "If Sander or Trace had something to do with Lora and Paul's deaths, they aren't going to want to talk to us and will know we are getting close to the truth if we start asking questions."

"I agree, but on the other hand, we could ask to talk to Trace alone and if Sander agrees, he either has nothing to hide or knows Trace is loyal." Heath put a hand on her arm. "We're this close, we need to talk to Trace."

She nodded and gave herself a firm reprimand for letting someone like Sander scare her while Heath told the receptionist they'd like to talk to Trace. Would she please ask her boss if he'd allow it?

The woman relayed their request. Her eyebrows rose at something said on the other end of the line and she replaced the phone. "I'll show you back."

They followed her quick steps down the hall. She knocked, opened the door, and stepped aside for them to enter.

Dela walked in ahead of Heath. It was her way of telling herself she wasn't scared to go into the lion's den.

Sander stood up behind his desk. "Why do you want to talk to my bodyguard?"

"We wanted to talk to him about a friend he grew up with. Levi Murdoch," Heath said.

"Levi? What do you want to know about him?" Trace asked, stepping up beside the desk, ignoring his boss.

"We can't find him. We need him to help us talk to his grandmother. We're talking to all his friends to see if they might know a place he would go to hide." Heath pulled out his notepad.

Trace narrowed his eyes. "What makes you think I'd tell on a friend?"

"You are only helping us make sure he is safe," Dela chimed in. "His grandmother is scared. We think

Levi is running scared, too. If we could get them together it would be easier to help them."

"I don't understand." Trace said, moving closer to them.

Dela glanced at Sander. He was listening intently. "Is there a chance we can go somewhere and talk with you?" she asked.

"He's paid to be by my side at all times," Sander said.

"Even when you go to the john?" Heath asked.

"Don't be absurd." Sander glared at Heath.

"What does he do when you go to the john?"

"I go in first, check to make sure there isn't anyone else in there and make sure there isn't another way in, then I stand at the outside door," Trace offered.

"You've been in this room and there isn't anyone else in here, correct?" Heath asked.

The bodyguard nodded.

"Then you could stand outside the door and answer our questions." Heath walked to the door.

Dela followed, opening the door.

Trace glanced at Sander. "Sir, I'll be right outside the door."

Sander nodded and sat behind his desk.

Chapter Twenty-nine

Standing in the hall with Trace's back to the office door, Dela began discussing what she hadn't wanted to say in front of Sander. "We know you were Lora Murdoch's boyfriend. Did you also do drugs with her?"

The man dropped his crossed arms to his side and stared at her. "What the hell is this about?"

"We believe Lora's death has something to do with Paul Winter's death," Heath said.

"I thought you wanted to talk about Levi." Trace studied them both.

"We do. We think Levi discovered where Lora was getting her drugs and after her death decided to take revenge," Dela said.

"You think Levi killed Paul?" Trace shook his head and walked a few steps away, then back. "No way. Not the guy I knew in high school. He was the local evangelist. That's what everyone called him the way he preached about how drugs and alcohol would destroy us."

"Well, look where it got Lora." Dela shifted her weight onto her left foot.

Trace ran a hand over his short-cropped hair. "She was a wild child. There wasn't a drug in this corner of the state that she didn't try once." He made a derisive snort. "And she slept with anyone who was willing. That's why I left her. She didn't want to be with one person. She wanted to experience every Tom, Dick, and Jane. And not just people but different ways. It was like there was a demon in her that couldn't get enough of everything that would give her a high." He sighed. "She was sulky and enjoyed fighting when she was in between highs. Looking back, I don't know why I stayed with her as long as I did. I think I felt sorry for her, and Levi had hoped I could get her to like me and not the drugs and different partners."

"We were told Lora always had someone with her when she did drugs. Is that true?" Heath asked.

"Yeah, she was afraid of dying alone. She always said if this high was her last she didn't want to be by herself. She talked about how her dad was alone in the car when it crashed and her mom had been alone when she took her life. Lora didn't want to be like them. She wanted to die holding someone's hand."

Heath flipped back several pages in his notepad and said, "Yet, the police report said she was alone when she took the overdose that killed her. That she was found by her grandmother in her own bed."

"No. That can't be right. Lora never used in her grandmother's house. She'd do it at parties or at a friend's house. She never wanted her grandmother to see her high. If it took her a couple days to get herself back together, she'd stay away. Have her friend call and say she was staying longer."

"Did she shoot up across the street at Paul's?" Heath asked.

Trace shook his head. "No. He didn't sell or give the stuff away. He made it strictly to sell to Mr. Sander." A disgusted expression marred his face. "I know that a tribal officer raided where she was shooting up once and picked her up."

"She was never charged with anything," Heath said.

"That's because she had sex with him and he let her off. She commented once that he'd been rough but she'd do him again if it kept her out of jail." Sadness drooped the man's face.

"How did she pay for the drugs? As far as I can tell she didn't have a job." Dela hadn't heard anyone say anything about where she worked.

"She did odd jobs. Cleaning houses, waitressing, anything she could pick up. If she was needing a hit and didn't have the money, she worked out other ways of paying for it." Trace opened and closed his fists. "I wanted to help her, but she didn't want it. Levi and I got into fights about that. He was always trying to save her. But until she wanted to be saved, she wasn't about to leave that life behind."

"I find it ironic that you are working for one of the men who helped feed Lora's habit and many other addicts," Dela said.

"I started working for him as a carpenter. When he offered me this job with double the pay, I jumped on it. I figure a year and he'll realize the threat was a crank and I'll be demoted to carpenter again. In the meantime, that extra money will put me closer to getting a house built so I can get married."

"You don't have any idea who sent your boss and Paul the notes?" Heath asked.

"I never saw the notes, and Mr. Sander never talks about them, other than to say he received them and wanted protection."

"Do you think Levi could have sent them?" Dela asked.

Trace stared at her. "Why?"

"Because he knows where the meth came from that his sister overdosed on." Dela watched as Trace studied her and Heath.

"How would he know?"

She shrugged. "Process of elimination. Talking to people. He's been talking to you. Did you tell him who his sister had been buying from before her death?"

"We talked about the good times before Lora got so crazy about using. But I didn't have anything to tell him about lately. I'd separated myself from her five years ago. It hurt to watch her." The sadness washed across his features again.

He had loved the woman who was bent on destroying herself.

"Did she ever give you a clue to the tribal officer who had sex with her instead of filing charges?" Heath asked.

"Not really. Only that he came around another time with something for her to get her to have sex with him again."

"And did she?" Dela asked.

"Yeah. It was a free high. And double the excitement since it was with a cop while she was high." He threw his hand out as if giving up on the whole thing. "She lived for a high. Any kind and she didn't care who she hurt in getting it."

"If you hear from Levi, please give me a call. We only want to talk to him and take him to his grandmother." Heath handed the bodyguard his card.

As they walked down the hall, Dela shuddered. "I feel like I need a shower."

Heath nodded and was quiet all the way out to his truck.

"What did he say that has you thinking so hard?" Dela asked when they were seated in the truck and Heath turned the key in the ignition.

"There is only one tribal policeman I can think of who had access to all the meth he could want and who would stoop to having sex with an addict." He glanced over at her.

"Dickhead. Do you think he was with Lora when she died? He could have waited for the grandmother to leave and then put Lora in her bed." Dela thought about that. "And it's across the street from Paul. He could have seen Dickhead carrying Lora into the house and when he heard about her overdose, he could have blackmailed Dickhead."

"There could be any number of reasons Jones killed Paul. For all we know, he wanted to take over selling meth and push Sander out of business. He could have been working with Daniel Booth to start up their own production chain. With Paul gone and Booth hiding, for now, it puts Sander low in product." Heath drove back toward the reservation.

"We still haven't ruled out Levi. He could have killed Paul in revenge over his sister's death." Dela leaned back in her seat. They had learned a lot today, but none of it really put them any closer to presenting new evidence about the stabbing of Paul Winter.

Double Down

After feeding the animals and petting them, Dela made a salad. Heath had dropped her off to head over and help Rosie and Daisy. He figured with Jacob watching down the road, she'd be safe for a couple of hours. She smiled. He had such a soft heart and loyalty to everyone who lived here. It had surprised her when she'd learned he'd moved away from Nixyáawii. It was his home and his heart. But she also understood the need to find out more about a man that he hadn't known who carried half of his DNA.

Dela understood the need to know. As she ate her salad, she opened the photo on her phone and stared at the license she'd found in Grandfather Thunder's kitchen drawer. What was the mystery behind him? Why did she see herself when she looked into his face? Who was he and why did Grandfather Thunder have the wallet and license?

Mugshot stood at the door, wanting out. His large tail fanned a cool breeze across the room.

"Okay, you go play with Jethro while I take a long soak." Dela let the dog out, locked the door, and carried her dishes to the sink. When the dishes were cleaned and sitting in the drainer, she made sure the front door was locked and walked down the hall. In the master bath, she started the water running into the soaker tub that sat next to her walk-in shower and returned to the bedroom to retrieve a set of sweats. It was still early to be sitting around in her pajamas if someone came by. With all that had been going on lately, her house had become a magnet for friends and enemies.

Taking her prosthesis off, she thought about how Heath's touch had relaxed her earlier and eased the phantom pains away. She'd tell her doctor about it on her next trip to the VA to have her stump checked.

Using her crutches, she swung into the bathroom and holding onto the handicapped bars, lowered herself into the bubbles and hot water. She sighed and relaxed back against the tub, closing her eyes.

Mugshot's frantic barking, jerked her eyelids up. Her muscles tensed. He continued barking and Jethro's braying joined in. Something was wrong.

She grabbed the bar, pulled her body up, tucked her full leg underneath her, and stood on one foot. Sitting on the side of the tub, she pulled on the sweatshirt and pants. That's when she realized the animals weren't making noise any longer.

Her heart jumped into her throat, clogging her breathing. No! If someone hurt her animals, she'd kill them. The sound of glass breaking dropped her to the floor. She crawled on her hands and knees to the bedside table and took out her Beretta M-9. Easing the cartridge into the handle to minimize the click, she kept her gaze on the closed bedroom door. She hadn't locked the door, believing the outer doors were enough with Jacob outside watching.

Jacob! Would he show up to help or had whoever was walking down the hall hurt him?

Dela shifted, sitting with her back between the corner of the wall and the bedside table. She used the bed to cradle her hands clutching the weapon. All she had to do when the person opened the door was raise her hands enough to get a shot at his heart and pull the trigger. She'd killed before and always to save her or a fellow soldier.

The doorknob turned and the door slowly opened.

"You must be in here. I didn't find you in any other room."

Her stomach churned. It was Dickhead and he held

a weapon as well. She raised her hands.

"Ahh, I should have known you'd be waiting. But I didn't think you'd be cowering in the corner. You talk big, but I guess you're a coward at heart, just like your daddy."

The rush of blood from the adrenaline of staying alive almost drowned out his words. But she heard daddy. "What did you say?"

He grinned that slimy sneer she always wanted to slap off his face. "You don't know about your daddy?" He waved a hand. "Why don't you get on up from there and I'll tell you about him."

Her mind spun. Did she trust what this man said? Not really. And there was no way she was going to stand up and give him a bigger target to put a bullet in, not to mention she couldn't stand on one leg without aid.

"I'm not getting up. I suggest you leave before I put a bullet in you for trespassing." She used her best bossy voice.

He laughed. "If I leave here, I'll just go over and give your mother something she hasn't had in a long time." He thrust his hips three times.

Dela held the bile down by swallowing convulsively. "You go near my mom and I'll make sure you get to hang out with some lusty prisoners." Her arms were getting tired. It had been a while since she'd had to hold her weapon at the ready for so long.

He laughed. "All I have to do is pull this trigger and say that you called me over here to confess then turned your gun on me. I'll get my job back, you'll be gone, and I'll ruin Seaver. Not to mention, I get the satisfaction of knowing you died without learning the truth."

"The truth about what?" Was he talking about her father or the murder of Paul Winter?

Dickhead held up a hand and tossed a mugshot photo on her bed. "How do you think I found that?"

She didn't take her gaze off Dickhead.

He laughed. "You didn't know your old man was in jail? Someone didn't want you to know who he was." He cocked his head. "Your mother? Or was it Mr. Know-it-all Silas Thunder? Interesting. Why wouldn't they tell you about this man? The man who gave you life."

She glanced down at the photo on the bed. It was the same man as the photo on her phone.

A movement caused her years of training to kick in. She raised the weapon and pulled the trigger, putting three rounds into the chest of the man lunging at her.

Chapter Thirty

Dickhead landed face down on her bed. She shoved back against the wall as someone called out her name.

"Dela! Dela!" Jacob's frantic voice shook her to her senses. She grabbed the photo, shoving it into the bedside table as her friend's brother ran into the room.

"Oh my God! Are you okay?" He walked around the end of the bed toward her.

Her hands shook and she pressed into the corner.

Jacob took the Beretta from her hand and lay it on the corner of the bed. "Let me help you up." He reached down with one hand.

She grasped his hand and he pulled her to her foot.

"I can't stand."

He started to set her on the bed.

"No. I mean I can't stand on only one leg. I need my crutches in the bathroom."

Jacob stared down at the floppy right leg of her sweatpants as she moved the leg back and forth.

"I lost my lower leg in Iraq. That's why I was sent home." She put a hand on his shoulder. "Walk to the bathroom and I'll hop alongside."

He didn't say a word, just walked slowly to the bathroom.

Once she had her crutches and could move on her own, she nodded to the body bleeding on her bed. "Call it in. I'm going to check my animals and call Heath."

"Shit! He's going to kill me. I'm so sorry. I was watching the house and the bastard snuck up behind me. The next thing I knew I woke up and heard shots." Jacob pulled his cell phone out of his pocket as Dela swung her body down the hall.

In the kitchen, there was glass everywhere and the door stood open. She hadn't put on a slipper or shoe. Grabbing a towel, she folded and tossed it where she could place her foot and get out the door in one step. She used the crutches to swing her body, place her foot gingerly on the towel, easing the weight down to make sure she didn't get cut, and then placed the crutches outside the door and stepped out, scanning the backyard for her dog and donkey.

"Mugshot! Mugshot!" she called.

Whining came from the other side of the backyard gate. She hurried across the yard and swung the top of the gate open.

Mugshot jumped up, whining and trying to lick her. Jethro put his head over the bottom half curling his lip.

"Are you guys okay?" she asked, petting them both and trying to see if there was any blood on either of them. Mugshot dropped his front legs down and cried out. "That bastard!" she said and dialed Molly.

"Hey, I'm surprised to hear from you. Aren't you

and Heath—"

Dela cut her off. "I need you to come check out Mugshot. That dickhead Jones came here to get me and hurt him." Tears burned behind her eyes. She bent her head to rub them with her free hand.

"Are you alright?" Molly asked.

"Yes. No. I-I shot him." She started shaking. This had happened in the army, too. After the adrenaline wore off from trying to stay alive, you realized that you'd just killed someone to save your life and that of your comrades.

"Honey, we'll be right over. Where is Heath?" Molly asked.

"He went to help someone. I-I need to call him." She ended that call and found Heath's number. The phone rang several times.

"Do you miss me?" he asked and giggling in the background had to be Rosie.

"I just shot Dickhead." That was all she could get out.

"Are you okay? Where was Jacob?" He started asking questions and she could tell he was running.

"I'm…not hurt. He knocked Jacob out. I called Molly. He did something to Mugshot."

"I'll be there soon. Keep talking to me." An engine roared and tires squealed.

"Don't kill yourself getting here. I'm fine." But she wasn't. She'd killed the man who said things that made her think he had known her father. But how? Why had he kept it to himself all this time? Was that why Dickhead had hated her? Because of her father? Who the hell was he?

"Did you get him to confess to killing Paul?" Heath's voice invaded her thoughts.

"What? No. He talked about—"

"Dela, I need to take your statement," Jacob said from behind her.

"I have to go. Jacob needs my statement." She ended the call as Heath told her not to hang up.

Sirens screamed in the cold night air. Dela swung back into the kitchen, using the same towel.

Jacob picked it up when she was seated in the living room. "Can't have that there when they take photos."

She nodded, but her mind was on the conversation Dickhead taunted her with before she'd shot him.

Mugshot started howling as the sirens grew closer.

"Do you want me to bring him in here?" Jacob asked.

She shook her head. "I don't want him walking across that glass. Molly's coming. He acts like D- Jones hurt his front leg."

There was a knock and Chief Steele entered, along with a tribal and county officer. "Special Agent Quinn will be here shortly," the chief said. He studied Dela. "Did you shoot him?"

She nodded. "He broke the back glass door while I was in the bathtub. I had heard my dog and donkey making noise and was listening. That's when I heard him break the glass. I got out, went into the bedroom, and pulled my Beretta out of the bedside table. I could hear him coming down the hall. I didn't know it was him but had a suspicion. We told you someone had called and threatened me to back off and let the law arrest me for Paul Winter's death."

The chief nodded.

"I shoved my back into the corner of the room and rested my hands with my weapon on my bed. He came in and started talking trash. I told him to leave or I'd shoot. He lunged at me and I shot three rounds." She glanced up at the chief. "Training is hard to stop."

The county and tribal officers had already dispersed to take photos.

The front door slammed open. Heath stood in the doorway until his gaze landed on Dela. He crossed the room and pulled her into his arms. "Are you really okay?" he whispered against her hair.

She nodded, but her arms wrapped around him and she buried her face against his chest.

He picked her up and sat down on the couch, holding her. He didn't ask questions, didn't even murmur words of encouragement. He just let her take time to pull herself together.

♠ ♣ ♥ ♦

Dela didn't know how long she sat curled up on Heath's lap. Molly and Marty arrived. Heath told them to use the side gate to get to the animals. Quinn arrived. When she looked up at him, concern had softened his grey eyes but he talked only to Heath, who answered his questions.

Molly returned. She said it looked like Mugshot had sprained his front leg, but he'd be fine if he stayed confined to a small area. And Jethro was healthier than when she'd first checked him out.

"Why don't you come stay with Travis and me for a few days? It sounds like your bedroom is going to be a crime scene for a while." Molly sat on the couch beside Dela and Heath.

Dela glanced around to see who else was in the room. "I don't want anyone here to see I can't walk," she whispered.

Molly shook her head. "All you have to do is use

your crutches and walk out of this house and get into my car. No one is going to say anything." Molly moved her gaze to Heath. "Right?"

"Right." Heath wiggled underneath her. "You look more vulnerable by curling up on my lap than by swinging out of here with your crutches."

Dela sat up. She was feeling less shaky and their words were putting the fire back in her gut and her spine. "What about my prosthesis? I'll need it in the morning."

Heath sat her on the couch between him and Molly. "I can go back there and get everything you need. I've watched you take that thing off enough times I'm pretty sure I can pack the right things." He watched her closely. Dela could tell what she said next mattered to him.

She sighed. "There is a duffel bag on the floor of my closet. It should have clothes and toiletries in it. All you have to add is my prosthesis, liners, sock, and liner-liners." He stood. "And bring me the matching shoe to the one on the prosthesis, please."

He nodded and walked down the hall.

Molly put a hand on her arm. "Are you really feeling better?"

"Yes. I just needed to settle down." Dela straightened as Quinn walked into the room.

"Where are you going?" he asked.

"I invited her to stay with Travis and me," Molly said.

Quinn nodded. "That's a good idea. I'll be by in the morning to ask more questions. I want you to know this is going down as self-defense. It is obvious by what Officer Red Bear told me and evidence that Jones had a vendetta to settle with you and you won."

"Thank you. If my animals hadn't made such a racket when he came through the backyard, he would have caught me in the bathtub unarmed." She shivered thinking about it.

"I guess that big goofy dog is a watchdog after all," Quinn said, studying her.

"Yeah." She peered into his eyes. They were saying something but she couldn't quite decipher what.

Heath returned with her bag, handing her the shoe.

She pulled it on and tied it.

"Ready?" Heath asked.

"I am." She stood with her crutches and faced Quinn. "We're taking Mugshot with us. Please don't let them tear my house apart. Only the kitchen and my bedroom need to be searched for evidence."

"I'll see what I can do."

Heath put a hand on her back and they headed to the door Molly held open.

"Seaver, are you coming back to help?" Quinn asked.

"I'm staying with Dela. I'll be back to work tomorrow."

Dela didn't care if the two butt heads tomorrow or any time after that. Right now, she only wanted to get to Molly's and lock herself in a room and think about what the man she'd killed had known and would never be able to tell her now.

Chapter Thirty-one

Dela woke with a start. Sun was shining through a window in a room she didn't recognize. And someone snored quietly beside her. Moving her head to look without disturbing the bed, Heath came into her sight.

That's when the night before came back in vivid detail. The fear, the confusion, the man face down on her bed.

Would they ever know if he killed Paul Winter? Did that mean she would still be a suspect in that murder even though Quinn had said what happened last night was clearly self-defense?

Mugshot walked over to the side of the bed and whined. Dela reached out to pet him. He'd spent the night in the room with her. He hadn't wanted to leave her side.

The snoring stopped. Heath's eyes opened. He studied her gazing at him.

"How are you feeling this morning?" he asked, rolling to his side and draping an arm over her.

"Better. I know it was me or him. Like in Iraq. But he said things—" she stopped. Heath was a police officer. She wasn't sure she could count on him keeping the part about her mother and father to himself.

Heath studied her. "What did he say? You said he didn't confess to killing Paul."

"He didn't. He said things to taunt me. I'm thinking he wanted me to shoot him. But why? I don't understand."

"You said you shot him when he lunged at you." Heath's eyes darkened and hardened.

"He did lunge at me and that's when I shot. Before that, he—" She stopped. Touching his cheek with her hand, she said, "You know the thing that brought us together?"

"The need to learn more about our fathers?" he questioned.

"Dickhead, I mean Jones," she sighed. It would be hard to call him by his correct name, but it didn't feel right to use her nickname for him anymore. "He talked like he knew who my father was and he didn't care for him." She let her hand slip from his face and said, "I found something at Grandfather Thunder's the other day when I went over to talk to him. He refused to talk about it." She peered into his eyes. "You have to promise you won't tell anyone what I'm about to tell you."

"Is it illegal?"

She shook her head. Then shrugged. "I don't think so. But I won't tell you if you can't promise to keep this between us." Dela knew it was asking a lot of this man. He had integrity and believed in always doing what was right, no matter the consequences.

"It has to do with your father?" he asked, rubbing

the hand he had draped over her up and down her side.

"Yes. Or I think so." She let out a long breath. "I have no idea." She went on to tell him about finding the driver's license with the information scratched out and her thoughts on the photo.

"You think this person is your father?" Heath asked.

"It-it felt like I was looking at me. So yeah. Did you feel that way when you met your relatives?"

"Kind of. I did feel a connection of sorts. What does this have to do with Jones?"

She told him what the man had said and about the photo in her bedside table. "I didn't get a good look at the photo. I'm not positive it's the same person, but it looked like him." She rolled and grabbed her phone from the bedside table and scrolled through to find the photo she took. "See?"

Heath held the phone in his hand and studied the photo. "You're right. There are similarities in his eyes and your mouth." His gaze roamed over her face and then back to the photo. "What do you want to do?" He handed the phone back.

"I want to find out who he is. According to Grandfather Thunder it would hurt my mom to ask her questions. I don't understand, but she has never spoken about my father other than to say he was dead." She studied Heath. "And I believe Grandfather Thunder will go to his grave keeping this secret. I would bet that he has thrown the driver's license away so I can't see it again. He knows I took a photo of it."

A knock on the door stalled their conversation. "Breakfast is ready and Quinn is sitting out here waiting to talk to Dela," Molly said.

Mugshot walked over to the door and whined.

"We'll be right out," Heath replied. He kissed Dela on the lips. "Get dressed and I'll entertain Quinn." He rolled off the bed and walked to the door. He was still dressed in the clothes from the night before. At the door, he stopped and said, "I'll get that photo from your bedside table and we'll talk about this some more tonight."

She nodded, feeling better that she'd told Heath about the photo. Dela sat up, stretched, and moved to the chair where her duffel bag sat on the floor. She slipped out of her sweat pants, put on underwear, and began the process of putting her prosthesis on.

♠ ♣ ♥ ♦

Thirty minutes later she joined Molly, Marty, Travis, Heath, and Quinn in Molly's small dining room. They had all started eating. A plate filled with her favorites sat in front of the chair next to Heath. She smiled at him and sat.

"How are you feeling this morning?" Quinn asked.

She glared at him. "I wish people would quit asking me that. I'm fine. Or I will be if I could move on." She stared pointedly around the table.

Molly stared pointedly back at her. "We only ask because we care."

Dela sighed. "I know. I'm pretty sure if I wasn't okay, you would all notice."

Heads bobbed.

"I've made my point." She sipped her coffee and studied Quinn over the rim. Putting the cup down she asked. "What did you need to see me about this morning? I told Chief Steele everything last night."

Quinn glanced around the table and said, "We'll discuss it after breakfast."

She understood the code for, not for other people's

ears. Namely Molly, Marty, and Travis.

"Fine." She dug into her food, enjoying every bite.

When everyone leaned back, full and sipping coffee, Quinn shoved his chair back. "We need to talk." His gaze was on Dela.

She pushed her chair back and saw Heath doing the same.

"Just Dela," Quinn said.

She wasn't sure what he would want to talk to her about that Heath, as a policeman, couldn't hear, but she shrugged while holding Heath's gaze and stood, following the Special Agent into the living room.

Quinn motioned to the couch. Dela sat and was surprised when he took a seat not six inches from her.

"Is this a business talk or…" She was getting a weird vibe from him this morning.

He cleared his throat but kept his voice low. "I just wanted to say, I'm sorry I didn't believe you when you said you didn't kill Winter. I have seen your temper at full boil and know you are well trained."

She studied him. This was the most vulnerable and sincere she'd ever seen him. "Thank you. But what changed your mind? Did you find evidence at D-Jones's house that proved I didn't do it?"

"Not that you didn't do it, but that the man really had hate for you. There were photos of you jogging around the neighborhood, petting Jethro at the Winter residence, walking out of the casino, being cozy with Heath. He had to have been following you to get the photos he did. And he knew your movements. Knew you had a soft spot for that donkey. I'm now wondering if he didn't have Mrs. Swan call Ina and tell her she couldn't feed the animal and that her husband hadn't been home for weeks, just to get you over there."

Relief relaxed her body. She smiled. "I knew Ina wouldn't have sent me there knowing her husband was there."

"We still haven't found Levi, so I'm not ruling him out as the one who killed Winter, but there is the possibility that Jones set you up for it."

Dela hopped on an idea. "Shaffer needs to let Mrs. Swan know that Jones is dead. That might get her to talk or at the least come home and someone can maybe persuade her to talk once she gets home."

"What if she implicates Jones in the death to throw suspicion away from her grandson?"

Quinn is always the pessimist, Dela thought and said, "I'm sure if that is the truth you will discover it. I just want you and Chief Steele to tell Bernie Moon I am no longer a suspect so I can go back to work."

Heath walked into the room. He studied the two of them sitting close but not touching. "I'm headed home to change into my uniform." He walked over and kissed her cheek. "See you tonight?"

"I'll be here unless Bernie calls and says I can work." Dela folded her hands on her lap. She wanted to jump up and call Bernie herself but knew she'd only irritate the man. The news had to come from law enforcement.

"You aren't going to run around trying to find Levi, are you?" Heath knew her too well.

"If the FBI can't find him, he doesn't want to be found. But I don't understand, if he's innocent, why is he hiding?" She glanced from Heath to Quinn and back to Heath.

"We won't know until he surfaces," Quinn said, standing.

The two men left the house at the same time. Dela

was curious if they talked or just walked to their vehicles and drove off. She stood and walked over to the window. They stood by Heath's truck talking. Well, Quinn was doing the most talking and Heath looked upset. What were they talking about?

"Dela, do you want me to take you to your place so you can feed Jethro and get your car?" Travis asked, startling her.

"Yes, thank you. I should probably take Mugshot and let him hang out with Jethro. The two of them have bonded more than I'd realized they would." She started to grab her purse and realized it was at her house still.

"Mugshot, come on, we're going to go see Jethro!" Dela called and the dog trotted into the living room followed by Molly.

"You're coming right back here, right?" Molly asked.

Dela frowned. "I wasn't hurt last night. I'm not an invalid."

"You weren't physically hurt but you had a shock." Molly put her hands on her hips.

She hadn't told many people, including Molly about her army life. "It wasn't the first time I've killed someone." She tried to convey to her friend that while it wasn't easy to do, it had been necessary.

"I've figured that since you were an M.P. in a war zone. But that is different than someone coming into your home and threatening you." Molly's usually smiling face held concern.

"I'll admit, that was different. But I'm fine. Honest." Dela smiled and walked to the door. "Come on, Travis. I'm sure Jethro has awakened the whole neighborhood with his braying for breakfast."

Chapter Thirty-two

At her house, Dela and Mugshot entered the backyard through the gate on the side. Jethro's braying sounded hoarse as if he'd been calling for his friend all night.

"Hey, boy, we're both here." She opened the gate and the donkey pushed into the yard, sniffing Mugshot and then pushing his head against Dela for a scratch between the ears. "Sorry you were worried about us," she said, playing with his big furry ears.

Mugshot wandered out into the pasture and Jethro followed.

That's when Dela looked up and saw that the door with the broken glass had been covered with a piece of plywood. She wondered who had thought to put the wood on the door.

"I'll measure the door and get some glass ordered," Travis said, standing behind her.

She spun around. "You don't need to stay with me.

I'll just get the things I need and head back to your mom's."

"I can hang out until you're ready to leave. I'll get a tape measure." He disappeared out the side gate.

Dela took a step toward the door. She'd noticed crime scene tape on the front door when they'd driven up. But there was only the plywood on the back. She turned the knob and walked in. The glass had been cleaned up, but she could feel the house was different. More than the boarded-up door.

She grabbed her purse hanging on the coat rack by the front door and walked cautiously down the hall to her bedroom. The door stood open. She focused on the beautiful mural Toby had painted on the wall above her headboard. The dreamcatchers and feathers calmed her rapidly beating heart.

While it was true, she had killed people before; she had never come back to where it had happened. Most of the time, she'd never even seen the face of the person she'd shot. They had been the enemy. They had been out to kill her and her fellow soldiers. She'd seen Jones's face many times, quarreled with him, been disgusted by him, and she had been the one to end his life.

As these thoughts circled in her head, her gaze lowered to the bloody spot in the middle of her mattress. That was blood she'd spilled.

She spun around and peered at the mural on this wall. It was a beautiful sunset over the Blue Mountains. Again, it brought her a sense of peace and tranquility.

"Dela, do you need help?" Travis asked from the hallway.

"No. Stay there. I'll be right out." She didn't look at the bed again. She walked over, pulled the photo out of the bedside drawer, and put it in her purse. Then she went to her closet and grabbed two sets of work clothes, two more sets of everyday clothes, and a pair of pajamas. She had plenty of toiletries in her duffel to use before she could move back into the house.

She found another duffel and filled it with everything she'd grabbed.

At the end of the hall, Travis took the bag from her. "I'll put it in your car. Do you want me to grab the dog food bag, too?"

"Thank you, but I'll just get enough to last Mugshot a few days. I'm sure I'll be able to move back in by Monday." She went to the pantry with the large bag of dog food and scooped out enough into a paper bag to tide Mugshot over for several days.

Travis returned from putting her duffel in the car and grabbed the bag of food. "Anything else?" he asked.

"That's it." She followed him out the back door and closed it. Then she walked out into the pasture, watching Jethro eat and Mugshot laying on the ground beside him chewing on a stick.

"Come on, Mugshot. We'll come back this evening and check on Jethro." Dela walked back to the gate. Mugshot hopped through the gate. Jethro watched them but continued eating. "He must be satisfied we're okay," she said, patting the dog on the head. "Let's go see a couple of people before we go back to Molly's."

Travis had left already. Dela loaded Mugshot into her car and drove down the road to Mrs. Swan's house. There was a small building behind the house. She wondered if there might be something in it to shed light on what had happened next door. Dela parked in the driveway and walked over to the building. There weren't any windows to look in. She raised the board cradled in a U-shaped piece of metal on each door and set it to the side.

Opening one door, the sunlight flashed in a side mirror of an older car. She caught a glimpse of an Idaho plate before an arm wrapped around her neck.

Dela dropped her chin, spread her legs, bending at the knees, grasped the arm around her neck with both hands, and bent forward, flinging the person over her head.

Mugshot's barking nearly drowned out the sound of Levi as he lay on his back gasping for air. Dela grabbed him by one arm and rolled him over, sitting with one knee in his back as she pulled out her phone and called Heath.

"Hey, how's it going?"

"I'm in Mrs. Swan's driveway, sitting on Levi. Can you or someone else get here quickly?"

A siren rang out from the other side of the phone. "Ten away," he said and she heard him calling it in on his radio. "Hold on, we're on our way."

"Thanks. I need both hands. Just get here quick." She ended the call as Levi started to gain his breath and struggle to get up.

"Get off me. You are the one trespassing." Levi squirmed and she knew there was no way she'd be able to keep him restrained like this for ten minutes.

"If I let you up do you promise not to attack me?" she asked, easing up on the pressure of her knee in his back.

"Yeah. Why'd you call the police?" he asked as she rose to her feet and he rolled to his back.

"Because they have been looking for you."

His eyes darted from side to side in the sockets. He

appeared to be looking for an escape route.

She grabbed an arm, helping him to his feet, but instead of releasing him, she wrenched his arm behind his back and walked him over to her car where Mugshot was barking and frothing at the mouth. "If you take off, I'll open that door and let my dog bring you down."

Levi glanced at Mugshot and stood still.

It wasn't long and the sound of sirens filled the air. She could see the lights from the street a block away. She had so many questions but wanted to wait until Heath was here to record them.

To her surprise, Quinn's SUV parked behind her car. He stepped out and strode over to them, taking Levi's arm and cuffing his hands behind his back.

"Hey, what have I done to be treated like this?" Levi asked.

"You've been evading the authorities," Quinn said. Then he turned to Dela. "What made you think he'd be here?"

"I just noticed the shed behind the house and wondered if I'd find anything of use to find him." She shrugged. "I saw a car and a glimpse of an Idaho plate when someone attacked me from behind, I was pretty sure it would be Levi. Who else would be living in Mrs. Swan's house and hiding a vehicle from Idaho here."

Heath pulled up, followed by another tribal vehicle. He strode over, studying her. "Are you okay?"

"Fine." She faced Quinn. "Can I listen to his answers?"

"You caught him, you should get to ask him questions and hear his answers." Quinn nodded to his SUV. "I'm going to take him to the tribal station and we'll interview him there."

"Why are you asking me questions, why were you

even looking for me?" Levi asked.

Dela poked a finger in his chest. "Stop playing stupid. You knew we were looking for you or you wouldn't have dumped your Jeep in Idaho and hid this one with Idaho plates. Do you know where your grandmother is?"

He stared at the ground.

"Did you know all the police at my house last night was because I shot Detective Jones?"

Levi's gaze latched onto her. "Is he dead?"

She nodded.

A smile spread across his face. "I need to call grandmother."

"When we get to the tribal station." Quinn led Levi away, stopping halfway to his vehicle. "Are you coming?" he asked Dela.

She glanced at Heath then back at Quinn. "I'll bring my own car."

When the SUV pulled away, she told Heath and the other officer what had happened. Heath told the other man to take photos of the vehicle in the shed and then he walked Dela to her car. "What were you doing here?"

"Travis brought me to my house to check on Jethro and get more things and my car. As I was driving away, I spotted the shed and my curiosity took over." She smiled. "I think we'll get some answers now."

"Me, too. See you at the station."

Chapter Thirty-three

At the tribal police station, Dela sat in on the questioning with Heath and Quinn. It had taken Quinn telling Chief Steele she had information that would help get answers to get the Chief's approval.

The three of them sat across the table from Levi Murdoch after he'd been read his rights and waived them when Quinn suggested the crimes against Levi and his grandmother might be dropped if they cooperated with the investigation.

Levi had been given his phone to call his grandmother as they all sat in the interview room.

"Hello, Grandmother? Yes, it's me, Levi." He listened. "I have good news. Detective Jones is dead." He listened. "Yes. And the FBI I'm with says you need to talk to the FBI man who is there, at Warm Springs." He listened some more. "Grandmother, don't cry. Tell the man the truth. You don't have to hide or lie anymore." He nodded his head. "Yes. It is true. He is dead. He can't hurt us." He ended the call and placed the phone on the table. "My grandmother and I can tell the truth now."

Quinn started the recording machine and asked Levi to state his name. Then Quinn stated who was sitting in on the interview.

"Levi, tell me why you and your grandmother lied about who killed Paul Winter," Quinn started the interview.

Levi glanced at Dela, then down at his hands. "When I came back here to work at Yellowhawk, I started asking questions about Lora's death. After I sent threats to Mr. Sander and Paul Winter, Detective Jones came to my grandmother's house when I was there and told us if we didn't stop trying to make trouble for Mr. Sander, something bad would happen to Ruth's grandchildren." Levi fisted his hands. "But I was too mad to think straight. I went over to Paul's and told him to tell me what he knew about my sister's death. I told him I wouldn't turn him in to the cops if he'd just tell me what happened."

"Why didn't you come to us?" Heath asked.

"Because Detective Jones would have known that I wasn't keeping my mouth shut. I thought it would be better to talk to other criminals."

"You could have come to the FBI," Quinn said.

Levi shook his head. "My grandmother doesn't trust the Feds. She agreed I should try to discover the truth from Paul." Levi glanced at Dela. "Grandmother thought I should say something to you. She said you have been catching bad people on the reservation. But I didn't think a casino security guard could help with our problem." He shrugged and smiled sheepishly. "I was wrong."

Dela nodded. "There were so many different ways you could have helped your family besides going to the people who had caused your sister's death."

He nodded. "I see that now. I was at Grandmother's house that day when you took the donkey. Detective Jones had told my grandmother to call Ina and tell her the donkey needed better care and that Paul hadn't been to the house for weeks. He said if she did that, he would tell us what we wanted to know. Only after Grandmother made the call, Detective Jones said he wouldn't tell us until he saw if the plan worked." Levi ran a hand over his face. He kept his gaze to the table.

It was clear he was embarrassed at the trouble he and his grandmother had caused while trying to deal with the nasty piece of work Jones had been. Dela glanced at Heath, he was studying Levi. A glance at Quinn found him studying her.

"The next day when I arrived at my grandmother's to take her shopping, she said Detective Jones put his car in her shed and told her to stay inside. I asked where he was and she said he was over at Paul's. I opened the door and saw you walking up the road. I stepped back and stood by the window, watching. I couldn't believe the way Paul charged out of the house at you. And the knife! My god! I thought he was going to slice you up. But you managed to get the knife away. I saw you put it in the shed and take the donkey." He shook his head. "I should have come to your aid then and later, but…"

"Jones threatened your family," Heath said.

"Yeah. I saw a tribal car come down the road and stop. I thought, good, he's going to get caught in Paul's house. But then the car left."

"That was me. Dela called and told me about the

fight she had. I came to calm Paul down, but I received a call and left to take care of that."

"I finally discovered that call and the threat that was made to Dela, came from the same phone owned by Detective Jones," Quinn said.

"I thought it must have been someone watching who called me away," Heath said.

"When you left, Detective Jones walked over to the shed and came out with the knife. He walked up to Paul and stabbed him. Then he went into the house. He was in there about ten minutes before he walked over to Grandmother's house." Tears glistened in Levi's eyes. "This whole thing has been a nightmare. One I wanted to wake up from and know it wasn't real. But it was. Detective Jones was smiling and happy when he came in the house. He saw me and frowned. Then he said if we told anyone, he'd kill each one of Ruth's grandchildren and then Ruth and me, leaving my grandmother all alone with the guilt she'd killed her family." Levi peered at each one of them. "He was a nasty, sick man."

Dela agreed with him. She'd seen that in the detective from their first meeting.

"Then he told Grandmother to call the police and say she saw her neighbor, Dela, kill Paul. Grandmother doesn't believe in lying but to save her family, she did. Then we talked it over and I told her to hide so she didn't have to keep telling the lie. I was going to go to her but then I heard everyone was looking for me." He shrugged. "We are guilty of not telling the truth. But we didn't kill anyone." Levi stared into Dela's eyes. "I am sorry we didn't stand up to him. But I knew the way he killed Paul he would kill the children with a smile on his face. It was easier to live with a lie than that."

Dela nodded. "You did what you needed to keep you and your family safe. I'm glad we were able to find enough evidence to have a suspicion of Jones." She reached out across the table, putting her hand over his. "I also believe he killed your sister."

Levi's eyes widened. "How?"

She glanced at Heath. He gave a slight shake of his head. She understood. The dark side of Lora didn't need to come out. Levi's friend had kept it from him this long there was no need to bring it up. "Just through the leads we followed. I want you and your family to mourn her loss and then move on now that Jones can no longer cause anyone harm."

Quinn's phone rang, he glanced at the number and said, "This interview ended at…" He stated the time and turned off the recording. "It's Shaffer, I'll take it in another room."

After Quinn left, Heath stood. He motioned for Dela to stand as well. "Levi, you are free to go. You were under duress when you didn't tell the truth and evaded us. I don't see why we should punish you any more than I'm sure you have punished yourself."

"Thank you! I'll call my grandmother and see if she needs a ride home." Levi exited the room.

Heath faced her. "How does it feel to be exonerated?"

"Good and sad. So many people were hurt or frightened by one nasty cop. I hope you and Chief Steele do a better job of recruiting help than whoever gave Jones a job here." She peered up into Heath's face. The muscle along his cheek was twitching. "Something is bothering you."

"Yeah, that Jones did so much damage. It's going to take as long as he was a tribal policeman to undo all the distrust and fear he spread here."

Dela put a hand on his arm. "You, Jacob, and the rest of the tribal police can prove to the Umatilla you want to help, not hurt them." She smiled up at him.

The door opened and Quinn strode in. "Shaffer finally got Mrs. Swan's statement. She said all the same things that Levi told us. Dela didn't kill Paul and Detective Jones was threatening to kill her family if she didn't lie. When Jones doubled down and tried to ruin you and Mr. Sander's drug business, he underestimated you."

Dela's phone rang. It was Bernie Moon. She smiled. "Someone else underestimated me too." She walked to the door, answering her phone. "Hello, Bernie, did you hear who really killed Paul Winter?"

The man cleared his voice as Dela headed out of the public safety building. It was ironic that a building that sounded so inviting had housed such a mean malicious man.

"I heard from Chief Steele that they found the person responsible. Now Dela, I never thought for a minute that you would kill someone…" he continued talking and Dela's mind drifted to the blood stain on her bed. She was going to have to buy a new bed frame, mattress, blankets, and sheets.

"…Well, can you?"

She shook herself. "I'm sorry, can I what?"

There was a pause. "Is this your way of getting back at me?"

"No, I'm sorry, my mind drifted."

"Oh, then maybe you aren't ready to come back to work tonight." His voice trailed off.

"Tonight? I'll be there. I'm tired of twiddling my thumbs." She hung up and smiled as Heath jogged out of the building.

"Want to go to dinner tonight and celebrate?" he asked.

"I can't. Bernie wants me to come back to work tonight." She hugged Heath. "But I'd love it if the bed in my room right now was gone so you and I can go bed shopping tomorrow."

A grin spread across his face. "Does this mean we are shopping for one bed?"

"Maybe." She kissed his lips and slid into her car. Her future was looking brighter every day. She pulled out her phone to tell Molly she'd be by to drop Mugshot off and change into her security uniform, and the photo Jones tossed on her bed floated out.

She studied it. He looked like her. But what was he in jail for?

Heath rapped on her window.

She rolled it down.

His gaze landed on the mugshot. "That the photo you were talking about?" He plucked it from her fingers. "I'll keep it. I can look up the number in the case logs."

Dela's chest squeezed. Grandfather Thunder told her this would hurt her mom. She didn't want to do that, but at the same time, she wanted to know who this man was. "Thanks. But keep it just between us."

He smiled and held out his pinky. "I swear." They locked their pinky fingers just as they had over twenty years ago when they'd discovered they both wanted to learn about their fathers. They'd made a pact that they would help each other in their search.

Thank you for reading book three in the Spotted Pony Casino Mystery series. If you enjoyed the book, please leave a review where you purchased *Double Down*. Reviews are the best way to let an author know you enjoyed the story.

As I continue the series there will be surprises about Dela's heritage and more murders that she, Heath, and their friends will solve.

If you enjoyed this mystery series you might like my Shandra Higheagle Mysteries and my Gabriel Hawke Novels listed on the following pages.

Paty

Shandra Higheagle Mystery Series

Double Duplicity

Tarnished Remains

Deadly Aim

Murderous Secrets

Killer Descent

Reservation Revenge

Yuletide Slaying

Fatal Fall

Haunting Corpse

Artful Murder

Dangerous Dance

Homicide Hideaway

Toxic Trigger-point

Abstract Casualty

Capricious Demise

Vanishing Dream

Gabriel Hawke Mystery Series

Murder of Ravens

Mouse Trail Ends

Rattlesnake Brother

Chattering Blue Jay

Fox Goes Hunting

Turkey's Fiery Demise (continued)

Stolen Butterfly

Churlish Badger

Owl's Silent Strike

About the Author

Paty Jager grew up in Wallowa County in NE Oregon and has always been amazed by its beauty, history, and ruralness. She has always had an interest in the Indigenous people and their culture and enjoys learning more every time she writes a book.

Paty is an award-winning author of 51 novels of murder mystery and western romance. All her work has Western or Native American elements in them along with hints of humor and engaging characters. She and her husband raise alfalfa hay in rural eastern Oregon. Riding horses and battling rattlesnakes, she not only writes the western lifestyle, she lives it.

By following her at one of these places you will always know when the next book is releasing and if she is having any giveaways:

Website: http://www.patyjager.net

Blog: https://writingintothesunset.net/

FB Page: https://www.facebook.com/PatyJagerAuthor/

Pinterest: https://www.pinterest.com/patyjag/

Twitter: https://twitter.com/patyjag

Goodreads:http://www.goodreads.com/author/show/100 5334.Paty_Jager

Newsletter- Mystery: https://bit.ly/2IhmWcm

Bookbub - https://www.bookbub.com/authors/paty-jager

Thank you for purchasing this Windtree Press publication. For other books of the heart, please visit our website at www.windtreepress.com.

For questions or more information contact us at info@windtreepress.com.

Windtree Press
www.windtreepress.com